The
Crimson
Shard

Teresa Flavin

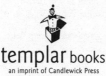

templar books
an imprint of Candlewick Press

Copyright © 2011 by Teresa Flavin

First U.S. paperback edition 2015

The Library of Congress has cataloged the hardcover edition as follows:
Flavin, Teresa.
The crimson shard / Teresa Flavin. —1st U.S. ed.
p.   cm.
Summary: During what seems like an ordinary museum visit, a tour guide lures Sunni and Blaise through a painted doorway—and they discover they've stepped into eighteenth-century London. When they realize their "tour guide" will do anything to get more information about what Sunni and Blaise know about magical paintings, they attempt to flee and encounter body snatchers, art thieves, and forgers.
ISBN 978-0-7636-6093-2 (hardcover)
[1. Painting—Fiction. 2. Space and time—Fiction.
3. Adventure and adventurers—Fiction. 4. Magic—Fiction.
5. Great Britain—History—18th century—Fiction.]   I. Title.
PZ7.F59861Cri 2012
[Fic]—dc23   2011048343

ISBN 978-0-7636-7172-3 (paperback)

14 15 16 17 18 19 BVG 10 9 8 7 6 5 4 3 2 1

Printed in Berryville, VA, U.S.A.

This book was typeset in Adobe Caslon.

TEMPLAR BOOKS

an imprint of
Candlewick Press
99 Dover Street
Somerville, Massachusetts 02144

www.candlewick.com

For Mr. Rapoza, artist and mentor

Prologue

Taking care not to wake anyone, the traveler crept back into the house, shielding his candle.

In the scullery, he rinsed the last traces of blood from his hands and dried them on a cloth. He felt for the leather sheath sewn into his tunic and slid out a flat shard of red flint, smoothed and sharpened to a point at one end and carved into an animal's head at the other.

He examined it closely. The crimson hue grew darker at its point. Every time the stone shard cut into flesh, the tip's red color became darker.

He picked up a piece of lye soap and a rough cloth and began to wipe clean the shard. As he worked, the face of the dead alchemist, Peregrin, edged into his mind. He scrubbed harder and cursed his associate for being so reckless with the lethal substances in his laboratory. If Peregrin had taken more care, he would still be alive and producing the miraculous elixir.

The traveler seethed, knowing he could no longer make unlimited use of the elixir's astonishing powers; with so little left, there would not be many more crossings into other centuries. He must make the most of the few opportunities he had left to obtain the information he needed to track down Fausto Corvo.

When he was satisfied that the dark stain had faded, he returned the shard to the hiding place in his waistcoat and, stealthy as a cat, climbed upstairs to his study. He ran his eyes over the bookshelves, then glanced at the door in the far wall, its frame crowned with two carved faces.

Content that nothing had been disturbed in his sanctuary, he settled himself at his desk, dipped a pen in black ink, and, on the first page of a notebook bound in red morocco leather, scrawled two names:

SUNNIVA FORREST
BLAISE DORAN

They were only children, and twenty-first-century ones at that, but they had the knowledge he needed. And destiny had just brought them to London.

Whatever it takes, *he thought, patting the shard through his waistcoat.* Whatever it takes.

Chapter 1

Sunni raised her face to catch the sun and wished she were lying on the grass in Hyde Park instead of hanging around in Phoenix Square while her friend Blaise tried to decipher a map scrawled on a paper napkin.

A distant siren wailed, and something clicked in Sunni's head.

"It's so quiet here," she said. "Like someone closed a window on the rest of the world."

"Mmm," Blaise mumbled, turning the napkin upside down. "Okay, I've got it now. It's that house over there with the blue plaque on it."

"So, you still want to see this place?" Sunni sighed as Blaise stuffed the napkin in his pocket.

"No, I've made us come all this way for nothing." He had that look of bright intent that he always got when his mind was set on something. "What's the matter—don't you want to see it?"

"I don't know. Just because some weird beardy bloke in a café says it's a cool place doesn't mean it is."

"It sounds cool to me," Blaise said. "I thought you'd want to check it out, too."

"It's just that it's bound to be full of sheeplike tourists, just like all the other museums in London," she said.

"That's what *we* are—tourists. And by the way, I am not sheeplike."

"No, you're more doglike, with a bone that you just won't give up," Sunni said. "I'm fed up with museums, Blaise. We've seen tons since we arrived. If I have to look at another china shepherdess or Roman mosaic, I will curl up and die." She stopped walking. "Let's hang out in a park for a change. We've only got a few hours till we meet your dad—and it's our last day in London!"

"If you don't want to come in, go sit in that park over there," he said, nodding at the fenced-in scrap of grass and elm trees in the middle of the square. "I'll meet you afterward."

A jolt of irritation coursed through Sunni. "No, I'll come along," she said. "Unless you *want* to go by yourself."

"Of course I want you to come! Why are you making such a big deal about this?"

"I'm not making a big deal."

"Yes, you are." Blaise gave a gentle tug on her ponytail. "Hey. You look like a celebrity with those sunglasses on. Trying to hide from all your fans?"

"Yeah, right. Can we get this over with? Which house is it?"

"This one." Blaise stopped in front of number 36. "And look, no lines of sheep trying to get in."

"Except us. Baa!" Sunni bleated like a sheep, and Blaise laughed.

"Look," he said. "We'll go wherever you want after this. I just want to check it out."

He stepped up to the red door, which had columns on

each side and an arch above it. In the middle of the door was a bronze head with a ring-shaped doorknocker in its mouth.

"Now we'll see if the guy in the café sent us on a wild-goose chase or not." Blaise rapped the doorknocker.

"Yeah," said Sunni. "I wouldn't put it past—"

She stopped in mid-sentence as an outlandish figure pulled the heavy door partway open. The man wore breeches and a red silk vest, topped with a long dark overcoat. His extravagant cravat was as white as his powdered wig.

"Good afternoon," said the man in a light but resonant voice with a slight foreign accent. He had languid, heavy-lidded eyes and a nose that had been broken at least once. But the uneven angles of his face did not diminish his handsomeness—they made him all the more striking.

"Is this Starling House?" asked Blaise.

"Yes. Have you an appointment?"

Blaise's shoulders slumped. "Appointment? No, we didn't know we needed one."

"One usually makes an appointment to see the house." The man consulted a leather-bound book on a side table. "But today it is not a problem. We will find the time for you."

"Okay . . . thanks."

The man swept the door fully open and ushered them into the hall.

They both stopped short, gaping. It was as if someone had peeled away the walls and ceilings to reveal an unspoiled landscape that had existed there before houses were ever built—a 360-degree panorama of rolling hills, trees, and pastures below a canopy of light blue sky.

"This is all painted, Blaise," Sunni said, inspecting the wall. "You can hardly tell it's not real."

The man looked at them with polite amusement, as if he had heard comments like this a hundred times before. "Yes. It takes a few moments to remember you are in a house, not in the countryside."

Even the staircase continued the illusion, decorated with painted sky, clouds, and flocks of birds all the way up the stairwell.

"Whoa!" said Blaise, teetering backward. He crouched down and touched a brightly colored spot on the floor. "I almost stepped on that, whatever it is. Wait, it's a ladybug. Not a real one, a painted one."

Sunni knelt down beside him. "Look, there's another one over here."

"Who made all this?" Blaise found a painted spiderweb almost hidden in a corner.

"I will explain in a moment," said the man.

"Are you an actor?"

"An actor? No. This house was built in 1753, so we wear period costume to enrich the visitor's experience."

"Cool," said Blaise.

"My name is Throgmorton. I conduct tours here." The man slid an enameled watch from his vest and studied it. "We shall begin in a moment. Please wait here."

Throgmorton closed his watchcase and disappeared down a staircase. He returned with two pairs of oversize felt slippers and handed them each a set.

"Put these on, please," he said. "Over your footwear."

Tittering under their breath, Sunni and Blaise slipped them over their sandals, the felt tickling their bare toes. Sunni was about to do a quick moonwalk when she caught Blaise staring at something behind her. The blissful look in his eyes alarmed her somehow, and she whirled around to see what he was looking at.

A girl stood motionless near the top of the stairs. It was as if she were floating in the blue expanse, held up by a few clouds.

She was dressed in a billowing silver gown, and her pale blond hair was pulled up into an elaborate arrangement of knots and twists. Without a word, she gathered up her skirts and glided down the stairs, like a goddess descending from the heavens to join the mere mortals on earth.

Chapter 2

*T**he girl was smiling at him. At him! And she was gorgeous.*

Throgmorton was saying something, but Blaise was lost in her jade-and-ocean eyes.

The girl giggled.

"Blaise!" Sunni was trying to catch his attention. "Will you get a grip?"

"What? I'm listening."

She glared at him. "At last."

"Are you ready?" Throgmorton repeated.

"Sorry," said Sunni. "We are ready. Really."

"Then we shall begin. My daughter, Livia, and I will show you the house. No cameras or recording devices, please. Please do not touch the walls, and do not eat or drink while you are here."

"Am I allowed to draw?" Blaise tapped his sketchbook, casting a sidelong glance at Livia to see if she was impressed.

A flicker of interest lit Throgmorton's impassive face, and his daughter smiled her approval of this idea. "You may draw, yes, if it does not take too long. And we will be interested to see what you make."

Blaise stuck his pencil behind one ear and opened his sketchbook to a fresh page.

"We'll never get to the park now," Sunni muttered.

Throgmorton bowed deeply. "Welcome to our tour of Starling House. This was the home and workshop of the artist Jeremiah Starling. He was born in 1723 and died in 1791, an eccentric who did not always fit into the art establishment of his time. But today we recognize him as the genius he was. This house was his canvas. Every room is filled with surprises and little visual jokes, like the ladybugs on the floor."

He herded them into the front room on the ground floor. "The dining room."

A huge tiled fireplace and mantelpiece overlooked an oval table and wooden chairs. In alcoves on either side of the fireplace were sideboards laden with crockery and candlesticks. Tall cake stands of sweets and confectionery rose up into the alcoves like fruit trees ready for harvest. Portraits of gentlemen and ladies gazed from the walls. A birdcage in one corner contained a brightly plumed parrot, and in another corner a cat was curled up behind a chair draped with a Turkish carpet.

"As you can see," said Throgmorton, with a knowing look, as if he were playing a familiar game, "this room contains only a table and chairs."

Sunni peered at the alcoves and realized that not only were they painted, but so were all the fruits, plates, and candlesticks.

"It's an illusion. This wall is completely flat," she said. "There's no recess here at all. It just looks like one."

"And the portraits were done straight onto the wall. The frames, too," said Blaise, his pencil flying across his sketchbook. "And that birdcage."

"This is what the French called *trompe l'oeil*," said Throgmorton. "It means 'fool the eye.' Starling went out of his way to trick and entertain the viewer with his paintings."

"Trump loy," repeated Blaise, his best attempt at a French accent still sounding American. "I've heard of that before. . . ."

"Aw, Blaise, come look at the cat," said Sunni, kneeling down to see the painted tabby close up.

But Blaise did not move. Livia was standing close behind him, her gown brushing against his leg.

"Your hand is so quick," she said. She had a melodious accent that was hard to place.

"Th-thank you," he stammered. It was wonderful and yet awful, having her watch him draw. He dreaded making a mistake or smudging something.

"Where are you from?" asked the girl.

"A town called Braeside in Scotland. Well, Sunni's from there—I'm not, I just live there." Blaise was sure he was babbling, but he couldn't stop. "I'm American. My dad is, too. He's a professor and he had to go to a conference in London, so we came with him for the weekend—well, three days, actually, because we got Friday off from school—"

"Do you wear that same dress on every tour, Livia?" Sunni interrupted, still studying the cat. "You must be roasting hot in it."

"I have many dresses." Livia did not take her eyes off Blaise. "And I always feel fresh."

"Really? Is it true people didn't wash much in the olden days?"

Blaise stopped drawing. "We're not in the olden days, Sunni."

"I was just wondering, that's all." Sunni shrugged.

"Continue drawing, please," Livia said. "It's almost finished!"

Blaise made a few more marks on the sketch and held it out at arm's length. Livia clapped her hands.

"Bravo!" said Throgmorton. "You are very composed under scrutiny. That is an admirable quality in a young man. Let us see how you do in the next room."

Sunni came over to look at Blaise's sketch.

"Let's see it," she said, her hand out, but Livia had already begun guiding Blaise toward the hall, murmuring, "I love artists."

"I'm not an artist yet. But I want to be one," Blaise said.

"What is your name?" she asked.

"Blaise."

"Like the blaze of fire," said Livia. "You have a very *powerful* name."

Powerful! Blaise walked a bit taller.

"Watch out you don't combust." Sunni folded her sunglasses with a sharp snap and shoved them into her bag. "His name is spelled B-L-A-I-S-E, and it's got nothing to do with fire."

Livia stopped short, and Sunni tripped against her.

"I am sorry," said Livia, turning to her with wide eyes. "I did not notice you there."

"No problem."

"What is your name?"

"Sunni."

"Ah, like the weather." Livia tilted her head in a most winsome way.

"No, it's Sunniva, actually, after a Norwegian saint."

Livia let out another "Ah," and turned back to Blaise. "You will adore this," she said, steering him toward a back room.

Sunni slid after them in her felt slippers, stone-faced.

Throgmorton was already in the room, holding a worn book in his hand. Sunlight filtered in from the solitary window onto walls lined from ceiling to floor with shelves, each tightly packed with books.

"The library," said Throgmorton, closing his book. "Would you care to count the number of books in this room?"

Sunni met his eye. "One," she said. "It's in your hand."

"Correct," he said with a smile. "You begin to understand. All the books are painted onto the walls, except for this one."

"Didn't Jeremiah Starling own any books?" asked Sunni. "Or any plates to eat from? Or real candlesticks?"

"Yes, but most of them are gone now." Throgmorton flicked a dead fly from papers strewn on a desk. They did not rustle or shift, painted as they were on the wooden surface. "Sold or passed on."

He raised his eyebrows at his daughter and beckoned toward Blaise, who was at work on a new sketch.

"Blaise," breathed Livia, "may my father look at your sketchbook, please?" Before he had time to object, she drew it away from him.

"Uh, sure." Blaise held his pencil in midair for a moment.

Throgmorton leafed through the sketchbook, his lips pursed. Livia hung on his arm, pointing out things she liked. A smile blossomed on Throgmorton's face, growing as he moved on to the next page, and the next. He stopped at one drawing and tensed with concentration, but just as Blaise was wondering what had caught his attention, their guide gestured to him.

"You make beautiful drawings," said Throgmorton, handing the sketchbook back. "And your hand is swift. I am very impressed."

"Thank you."

"And you take this sketchbook with you wherever you go?"

"Yes. I draw pretty much everywhere."

"Everywhere," Throgmorton repeated. "And everything."

"And from memory," said Blaise, watching Livia stroke a platinum curl into place. "When I have to."

Out of the corner of his eye he caught Sunni frowning. *What's her problem now?*

"To the second floor, please," said Throgmorton. He led Blaise through the hall and up the staircase, high into the painted sky, followed by Livia, who hoisted her gown to climb and revealed delicate slippers with suede soles. Sunni was last.

Upstairs, the grand sitting room was decorated from floor to ceiling with ornate pillars, marble busts tucked away in arched recesses, and grinning cherubs, all painted to look three-dimensional. The floor was a complex grid of colored geometric tiles. There were a few good-quality chairs and a table set with a real china teapot and cups.

Livia glided over to the fireplace and gazed up at a cherub. "This is my favorite room."

"I don't like it as much as the others," said Sunni.

Livia's smile did not slip. "Why not?"

"It's cold. As if no one is ever allowed in because they might leave a speck of dirt somewhere."

"I do not see anything wrong in having a beautiful, clean room," said Livia with a tinkling laugh. "You prefer a dirty one?"

"No, that's not what I meant—"

Livia suddenly approached Blaise and tapped him playfully on the elbow. "I caught you! Father, look, Blaise is drawing me!"

"Well, you were standing still. . . ." Blaise blushed to the roots of his floppy dark hair, but it was just as much with pleasure as embarrassment.

Sunni's lip curled as she watched Livia dance away with the sketchbook again and thrust it under her father's nose.

Throgmorton glanced at the sketch and said, "No one could do justice to my lovely Livia. But it is a good start. Shall we continue the tour?"

"I'll put the sketchbook away if I'm going too slow," said Blaise.

"No!" Livia hugged it to her chest. "I want Blaise to finish my portrait."

"Now, now," her father said. "We will see whether he has time. He may be obliged to hurry off somewhere else."

"You're not hurrying off, are you, Blaise?" Livia asked. "Do you have time to finish my portrait?"

"Sure. We're not in a hurry."

"We need to get to Tottenham Court Road," Sunni said. "Your dad said he'd be finished early today."

"But not yet," said Blaise. "We've got tons of time."

Throgmorton's face brightened, as if an idea had just come to him. "In that case, perhaps you would be interested in . . ." His voice trailed off, and he shook his head. "Perhaps not."

"What, Father?" Livia held Blaise's sketchbook close. "What were you going to say?"

"Well, my dear, I was thinking of a visit to the Academy," said Throgmorton.

"Yes, yes, Blaise must see it! He wants to be an artist, and he will love the Academy."

Sunni jumped in to ask, "What is it?" but Livia ignored her.

"Father," Livia said, "I think Blaise should stay to see the Academy *and* finish my portrait."

"Should he?" Smiling, Throgmorton eased the sketchbook away from his daughter. "Then, of course, Blaise *will* stay."

Chapter 3

I f you wish to see the Academy, that is," Throgmorton said to Blaise, almost as an afterthought, handing back the sketchbook.

"Uh, what's the Academy?" Blaise finally found his voice.

"An art school—but only for the best, the most talented pupils. The Academy teaches young people the secrets of the Old Masters. It is so exclusive, students are admitted by personal recommendation only."

"Really?"

Sunni could see a familiar alertness come over Blaise, like a hunter sensing he was near an elusive treasure.

"The Academy is not for everyone," said Throgmorton. "It is only for those willing to work hard and learn from the Master."

"I'd love to go to a school like that," Blaise said.

"You are the sort of young man who would make an ideal student," Throgmorton said. "The Master will be delighted to meet you."

"Right," said Blaise, his eyes wide.

"And we can discuss your drawings in depth," Throgmorton said. "I have a number of thoughts about them, as will he."

"That would be so amazing." Blaise beamed.

Sunni waved her hand. "Hello? I'm here, too, you know, Blaise."

"Aw, sorry, Sunni," he said quickly. "Sunni wants to be an artist, too. She's excellent at drawing."

"Oh, yes?" said Throgmorton. "You have a sketchbook you can show us?"

Sunni shook her head. "I didn't bring it today."

"That is a pity." Throgmorton shrugged and turned away.

At that moment, Sunni wasn't sure what made her more angry: this tour guide and his daughter treating her like she was smaller than Jeremiah Starling's ladybugs or seeing Blaise's soppy grin whenever Livia hurled herself at him in her flashy gown. Watching the way his eyes now followed Livia, with all her shining hair and slender grace, Sunni couldn't blame him. But deep down inside, her feelings were buzzing around and around like an outraged wasp caught under a glass.

As they left the grand sitting room, Sunni wanted to pull her slippers off and throw them. But she took a deep breath and said, "Mr. Throgmorton. Art means more to me than anything. I love to draw."

"But I think you only love to draw *sometimes*." Throgmorton smiled. "When there is nothing more interesting to do."

"I know I don't draw all the time, like Blaise does," said Sunni, trying to keep her voice even. "He's special that way. But it doesn't mean I'm not good at it."

"True," Throgmorton said. "But why are you telling me this?"

"Because I'd like to see the Academy, too."

Throgmorton glanced at Sunni and then at Blaise.

"Of course," he said after a moment. "You are welcome to."

He hurriedly guided them through the small sitting room and two bedrooms on the third floor. Blaise put away his sketchbook to save time and hunted for all the painted illusions in each room, like the combs on a dressing table and the rack of long-stemmed pipes on a mantelpiece.

They climbed up the last flight of stairs to the top of the house, winding around toward a small landing below a ceiling painted with blue sky and clouds. There were only two rooms on this floor. One was a small bedroom for servants, plainly decorated and of little interest.

Throgmorton swept them into the other, larger room. "The Cabinet of Curiosities," he announced. "Jeremiah Starling's workshop."

Starling had made this room into an airy space with windows spilling light onto the wooden floors, neatly organized worktables, and chairs. There was another paneled door, similar to the one they'd come through, that looked as if it connected to the servants' bedroom next door. But when Sunni got closer to it, she smiled to herself. Jeremiah Starling had managed to fool her again—the door was another *trompe l'oeil* painted onto the wall.

The shelves and showcases that lined the workshop's walls were filled with open drawers of artifacts and relics, leather albums and inlaid boxes. There were conch shells and cowries, pieces of amber, feathers and tiny skeletons.

Stuffed birds stood on top of the cupboards, their glass eyes gazing into the distance.

On every bit of available wall space hung small framed paintings of landscapes, animals, and people at their everyday business.

Otherwise, the ceiling and walls were covered with neatly pinned animal specimens. Starfish, crabs, snakeskins, small sharks, dried scorpions, and lizards formed an orderly pattern over their heads. In the center, suspended upside down from the ceiling, was a large stuffed crocodile.

But none were real. They were all painted, every last one.

The only sunlight came from two small windows — the other four were illusions, delivering a bright sky that never changed, whatever the weather.

"Look how Jeremiah Starling painted those dragonfly wings, Sunni," Blaise said, examining a case of insects. "How long do you think it took him to do all those little facets?"

"Hours and hours," said Sunni. "I wonder which blue he used to get that blue-green."

"Cobalt maybe? Did they use cobalt back then? We'll have to ask Mr. Bell when we get back to Braeside," Blaise said, mentioning their favorite art teacher. "Boy, he'd love this house. . . ."

"Blaise." Livia seated herself on a chair and struck a demure attitude. "Work a bit more on my portrait."

All Sunni could think was how much Livia looked like a sickly sweet china figurine from some stuffy museum collection.

Blaise whirled around. "That's a great pose. How long can you hold it?"

"As long as you wish." Livia's eyes flicked toward Sunni, who made a point of studying other painted specimens nearby while taking deep breaths to calm herself down.

Suddenly her phone let off a loud burst of drums and guitars. Sunni dragged it out of her bag and answered in a low voice. It was her stepmom, Rhona, worrying about something and wanting to know exactly when Sunni would be back in Braeside the next day.

Throgmorton loomed next to her. "Please take your device outdoors. This is a quiet house." He guided her to the landing. "My apologies. I should have made that clear before."

"I have to go all the way outside?"

"Yes, please." Throgmorton rested both hands on the banister and waited there till she was downstairs.

"Who were you talking to?" Rhona's voice buzzed in her ear.

"A tour guide in a museum. I have to go outside to talk on the phone."

"I've never heard that rule before—what museum are you in?"

Sunni muttered, "You wouldn't know it. And it doesn't matter anyway because we're leaving soon. If I can tear Blaise away, that is."

"How is he?"

"Fine."

"Is Mr. Doran with you?"

"No, we're meeting him in a while." Sunni kicked off

the felt slippers, opened the big main door, and wedged one in it so she could get back inside. She felt better as soon as the summer air touched her skin.

"I don't like you wandering around London alone," said Rhona in a peevish voice.

"I'm not alone, and I'm absolutely fine. Honestly, Rhona, I am fifteen now, you know." She glanced up at the top floor of Starling House and sighed. "Mr. Doran trusts us, unlike you."

"That's uncalled for, Sunni. You know very well why I'm concerned. After what happened in February . . ."

"I know, I know. Sorry." Sunni walked back and forth in front of the house, half noticing the blue plaque on the wall commemorating its famous resident, Jeremiah Starling.

LONDON COUNTY COUNCIL

Jeremiah Starling
Artist
1723 - 1791

Lived here all his life.
He rebuilt this house in 1753
after it was destroyed on
14th September 1752.

"Look, I need to go. How's Dad?"

"He's great and sends you hugs."

"Okay, me too. And Dean?"

"Right where I can see him, playing his Skeeterbrain game."

"Typical."

"I'll tell him you said hello."

"Yeah, okay. Bye, Rhona."

Then Sunni called Blaise's dad and left a message. "Hi, Mr. Doran, it's Sunni. We got caught up at some old museum that Blaise wanted to see. We'll be there as soon as we can."

She turned off her phone, reentered Starling House, and shoved her feet back into the felt slippers.

Sunni padded upstairs and peeked around the door frame of the Cabinet of Curiosities. She was irritated to see Blaise still drawing Livia in his sketchbook. Neither of them noticed her there.

Suddenly Throgmorton moved into view and said, "Blaise, we must go now."

"Go where?"

"To see the Academy."

A pang of mistrust made Sunni hang back to hear more. Blaise paused. "But Sunni's still outside."

"You are very considerate but, sadly, we cannot wait for her."

Sunni was tempted to burst in and tell him what she thought of that, but something still kept her back.

"I'd feel pretty weird going without Sunni," said Blaise, his brow furrowed. "Besides, she'll be back any minute—"

"No, Blaise," Throgmorton interrupted gently. "We can see the Academy now, at this moment, but not later. Visitors are invited in only at certain times."

"I can't leave Sunni."

"You do not have to. The Academy is under this very roof. Through that door."

Puzzled, Blaise swung himself around to look at the corner Throgmorton was pointing to. "But that's a painted-on door. Isn't it?"

Livia laughed and shook her head.

Sunni's heart began thumping. Blaise was right; it was painted to look exactly like a brown-wood paneled door with a brass handle, just like the real door they had entered. What was going on?

"It is a real door," smiled Throgmorton. "Come. I cannot wait to show you the Academy." He led Livia toward the corner, out of Sunni's view.

"But—"

"Only a short visit, Blaise. You will return here before your friend does."

"I don't know. . . ."

Sunni shook herself into action and entered the Cabinet of Curiosities as Livia's tinkling voice chided, "Why do you look so worried, Blaise?"

His face lit up with that besotted grin. "I'm not worried, Livia. Everything's okay now." He threw Sunni a cool glance as he deposited his sketchbook in his messenger bag. "Finally. What took you so long?"

"Hold on," Sunni spluttered. "I had to go all the way outside, you know."

But Blaise had already turned and walked toward Throgmorton and Livia, who gestured for him to leave his slippers behind.

Somehow while Blaise had turned to talk to Sunni, the painted door had opened. Blaise was following Livia through it, past Throgmorton's outstretched arm. Sunni shed her slippers and hurried after them, still not quite believing they were walking through what she had thought was only paint on a wall.

Throgmorton's arm twitched as she approached, but his face was expressionless. Sunni couldn't help feeling the tour guide saw her as Blaise's tiresome sidekick, tolerated but unwelcome.

She paused before the door, still suspicious of its solid timber and the brass handle. She peered through, half expecting to find a walk-in cupboard or a hidden stairway, but she could see nothing beyond except golden flames flickering in darkness.

A razor-sharp twinge of misgiving made Sunni hesitate, even though Blaise had already gone through, but Throgmorton's hands clamped onto her shoulders and propelled her over the threshold.

Chapter 4

The momentary darkness gave way to scores of small glowing lights. Blaise stepped into a candlelit room filled with people and furniture.

"Where are we?" he asked Livia. "How can a whole other room be here? There were only two rooms on the top floor."

"No, this room is also on the top floor of Jeremiah Starling's house." Livia's face was half in shadow, but her smile gleamed. "It is a special room."

Blaise looked puzzled. "So are we somehow between the Cabinet of Curiosities and the servants' bedroom?"

"In a way," she answered. "The door leads to another part of the house. It is the only way to enter it."

Blaise peered at their surroundings. The worktables, timber floors, and windows were similar to the ones in the Cabinet of Curiosities, and there was an open door in the opposite corner. But this room was a jumble of furniture, objects, and artwork, crowded with six teenage boys working on tables and at easels. They wore loose shirts and breeches, their lank hair tied back.

Daylight filtered in through the rippled glass of two windows and a crude skylight, but even so, there was an array of lanterns on every ledge and surface. The candle tallow's acrid smell made a heady mix with beeswax, stale air, and a pungent substance boiling in a crockery casserole on the hearth.

There were a couple of shabby shelves stacked with paint jars and jugs of brushes and tools, with small animal skulls, chunks of rock crystal and conch shells scattered between them. The candlelight caught the glass eyes of real stuffed birds and reptiles looking down on them from the top shelf. On the wall above the specimens, a decorative border of proverbs was painted in spidery letters: *He that will eat the fruit must climb the tree. Willful waste makes woeful want. The Devil finds work for idle hands to do.*

The boys had stopped in the midst of their work, as if stunned by the sight of visitors. Their eyes moved over the newcomers, eventually coming to a stop on Sunni's summer dress, which revealed her bare shoulders and calves. She crossed her arms over her chest and hid behind Blaise.

Throgmorton stepped forward. "I bid you welcome to the Academy of Wonders. These are six of the finest pupils in the land, being expertly trained in the noble arts of drawing and painting." He turned toward the boys. "Gentlemen, have your manners flown out of the window? Please greet our visitors."

The seated pupils scrambled to their feet. They bobbed their heads and collectively murmured something unintelligible.

"Return to your work now, gentlemen," said Throgmorton, clapping a hand on one boy's shoulder and murmuring, "Well done, Toby," as he examined his drawing.

"*This* is the art academy?" Blaise asked. It looked more like a living historical reconstruction for visitors; there was no electricity source that he could see, no plastic containers or felt-tip pens, nothing that said twenty-first century—and nothing that fulfilled his idea of an exclusive art school.

"Yes. As I told you before, the pupils are taught to paint and draw in the style of the great masters."

"And to dress like them, too, by the look of things," Sunni muttered.

"This has to be a setup. I bet they're just pretending for the tourists," Blaise whispered to her, disappointed, but not wanting any of the boys to be offended. He said to Throgmorton, "This is an amazing place. It seems really authentic. Can we look around?"

"Yes, of course. Please observe the boys' skills and craftsmanship at your leisure." Throgmorton gestured to Livia, who held her skirts away from the charcoal dust and wet paint smears as she made her way to his side, surveying the room with a placid smile.

"And we're still in Starling House?" Blaise asked uncertainly.

Livia chided him with a teasing air. "I told you— we are!"

"Okay." Blaise moved toward the easel closest to him, where a boy of about his age was working, illuminated by a cluster of candles in a fixture on the wall. He was painting a horse. It was an exact copy of another painting in a gold frame propped up nearby.

Sunni shadowed Blaise. "I still don't get it," she

whispered. "This room shouldn't exist. You can't just stick a room in between two others!"

"I know. I don't see how it's possible," Blaise answered in a low voice, becoming transfixed by the boy's confident hand. *He's really painting that horse.*

"And that door—how did it just materialize out of paint?"

At Sunni's words, the boy glanced up at them with a small crease of worry between his eyebrows.

"No idea." Blaise glanced back at the door they had just come through, which was now completely closed. This wasn't the first time he'd seen a painting come to life, but he was mystified at seeing another one here.

"It was a real door, for a few minutes anyway," whispered Sunni. "But now it's a painting again."

"I don't get it either." Amazed by the boy's painting abilities, Blaise said in a loud voice, "That is an awesome copy. I can't draw horses to save my life."

The boy smiled but kept his eyes on his work.

"You shall learn to, Blaise," called Livia, the dancing candlelight giving her hair and silk dress a golden sheen. "And you shall paint my portrait as well."

"It stinks in here," Sunni said, interrupting Blaise's brief vision of Livia in a big fancy picture frame.

"Oil paints," said Blaise. "They smell."

He squeezed in between some tables, where two younger boys were copying landscape drawings. "Hello. I'm Blaise. How old are you? Twelve, thirteen? I couldn't draw like that when I was your age."

The boys shrugged and smiled shyly.

"Thirteen," said one. His quill pen fell into his lap and a black ink patch bloomed on his breeches.

"Sorry—" Blaise started.

The boy just shook his head, picked up the quill, and started up where he had left off. Blaise noticed that his baggy breeches were covered with stains and rips. *Must be his work clothes.* He glanced behind him. Sunni was standing near a window, peering down at the street, an incredulous look spreading over her face.

Throgmorton addressed the eldest-looking boy. "Toby, where is the Master?"

"He is gone to the colorman's shop for paints, sir," the boy answered.

"I see. When did he leave?"

"Some time ago, sir." Toby didn't meet his eye. "The Master said he wouldn't be long, because Jacob needs vermilion to finish."

Throgmorton strode over to a boy with wavy blond hair, who was sketching out a new drawing. Next to him was a nearly completed copy of a landscape painting.

"Ah, Jacob, admirable work." Throgmorton peered at the copy and then at the splotches of pigment on Jacob's wooden palette. "Wait a moment. Here is a pearl of vermilion hiding amongst the other reds! Surely that is enough to finish this painting."

"Yes, sir."

"Get on and finish it, Jacob." He pointed up at a proverb painted on the wall that said *Procrastination is the thief of time,* his shadow looming large behind him. All the boys shifted uncomfortably in their seats.

Jacob dropped his charcoal stick and, with a quaking hand, picked up a fine paintbrush.

Sunni murmured into Blaise's ear, "You've got to see something. Come to the window. Now."

Heavy footsteps could suddenly be heard coming upstairs. The climber hummed as he went, then let out a belch.

Blaise gave Sunni a searching look and turned toward the windows, but just as they were about to move, Throgmorton said, "At last. The Master has returned."

The sound of the Master's panting reached their ears before he came into view. When at last he careened through the door, nearly tripping over the hem of Livia's dress, he was propelled by a gigantic sneeze.

"My word, Starling," said Throgmorton acidly, "you make a splendid entrance."

The man gave a perfunctory bow to Livia, pulling a three-cornered hat from his head. He deposited a leather satchel on the floor with a thud.

"And your esteemed daughter, sir, makes a charming obstacle," he replied, though nothing about the look he gave Livia suggested he found her charming.

Livia's smile held, but her nostrils flared as if something offensive had wafted by. "Good day, Mr. Starling," she said.

Blaise's bewilderment grew. *Starling?* If this was an actor impersonating Jeremiah Starling, the organizers of the workshop reconstruction had scraped the bottom of the barrel. The man had sneezed something horrible over his cravat. Dark flecks dotted his chin as well, and, most disgustingly, one clung to the tip of his nose.

"Good day, madam. Another parcel from your dress-maker awaits you downstairs. Or was it from the cobbler?" The man shrugged. "You receive so many parcels."

"Sir," said Livia without looking at him, "you seem to have ejected your tobacco. . . ."

Starling gave two almighty snorts and fished a dirty handkerchief from his pocket. After a quick dust over his chin and nose, he batted stray shreds of tobacco off his cravat and smiled.

"Father," said Livia. "May I go downstairs and see to my parcels?"

"Of course, my dear."

"And I shall order tea for us." She beamed over her shoulder at Blaise and hurried away.

"We have guests, Starling," said Throgmorton. "Two young art lovers, Miss Sunniva and Master Blaise."

Starling raised his eyebrows at the sight of them and, like the boys, seemed taken aback by Sunni's dress.

"And this," Throgmorton went on, "is the Academy's tutor, Jeremiah Starling, master draftsman and painter."

Sunni's and Blaise's mouths hung open at this information.

Jeremiah bowed low and shot a barbed glance at the guide. "Visitors of a most singular variety. How extremely unexpected."

"There was no time to inform you," Throgmorton replied.

"Excuse me, sir," Blaise managed to speak. "I thought this was visiting time. You said we had to come now."

"That is correct. But remember, Blaise, you arrived without an appointment, and we were not expecting anyone else today." Throgmorton extinguished a dying candle with his thumb and forefinger. "We very seldom invite visitors for, as I told you, the Academy is exclusive."

"Wait," Sunni said. "You're an actor, right? Impersonating Jeremiah Starling?"

It was Jeremiah's turn to gape. "I am no actor, miss, nor impersonator!"

"B-but Jeremiah Starling is . . ." Sunni stammered. "Well, he's dead."

"Egad. I may be many things, but dead is not one of them." Jeremiah glared at Throgmorton. "You should inform your guests more accurately, sir."

"Mr. Starling is as alive as I am," Throgmorton said. "As you can see."

This has to be some sort of performance for us, Blaise thought. *Jeremiah can't be alive. He died in 1791. Throgmorton said so.*

"You appear to be disappointed. Perhaps you would have preferred to meet my corpse." With a snort, Jeremiah shoved a stool aside. "See to my satchel, Toby. The bladders are fit to burst."

Toby unbuckled the satchel and carefully pulled out two full pigs' bladders. On a corner table, he punctured one and moved it over a selection of glass vials and small bags, squeezing a dollop of thick bloodred liquid into each.

"Have no concern," said Jeremiah, observing Sunni

and Blaise's shocked expressions with amusement. "'Tis but vermilion pigment, freshly mixed for me at the colorman's shop. The other bladder will piss blue paint. Toby is decanting the colors into jars and small bladders tied up with string."

Throgmorton looked displeased. "I believed you mixed your own colors, Starling, to ensure their quality."

"I have little time for that, sir," said Jeremiah. "The boys and I are kept mightily busy with our work and need much paint. Besides, the colorman does an admirable job—as fine as I would do myself, if not better."

"I will confer with you about the purchase of pigments later, sir." Throgmorton turned to Blaise. "Please show Mr. Starling your drawings. I am sure he will have much to say about them."

Still half watching Toby empty the second bladder, Blaise found his sketch of Livia.

Jeremiah nodded at it curtly. "A passable likeness of your esteemed daughter, sir."

Jeremiah Starling, *a dead guy*, was insisting he was alive, carrying around pigs' bladders of paint, and commenting on his sketchbook. And Throgmorton had brought them to a room so well hidden that Blaise had lost his bearings. Plus, a bunch of teenage boys were acting as if they'd never seen a girl's legs before.

Throgmorton pulled the sketchbook away from Jeremiah and leafed to a page toward the front. "What is your opinion of this?"

When Blaise saw which drawing the guide was interested in, another worry tightened his chest. It was a sketch he had done last winter, when he, Sunni, and her step-brother, Dean, had been transported into an enchanted Renaissance painting made by artist-magician Fausto Corvo. Blaise had made scores of drawings of the fantastical worlds inside the painting. But because he had sworn to protect its secrets, he had avoided sharing the sketches with anyone but Sunni, Dean, and their art teacher, Mr. Bell, the only adult who knew what they had been through.

"Those aren't very good," said Blaise, and reached for the sketchbook. But Throgmorton was quicker and held it back.

Jeremiah wrested the sketchbook away from him. "On the contrary, they are impressive."

"Blaise." Sunni was at his side and he could hear a warning in her voice. She was always scolding him for carrying the sketches around. If she had her way, that particular sketchbook would be under lock and key. A little voice inside him wondered whether she was right after all, but he nudged his elbow against hers for reassurance. By the look on her face, he realized the sketchbook wasn't the only thing upsetting her.

"I have seen this drawing before," said Jeremiah. "Or one very like it."

"I copied it," said Blaise.

Jeremiah let out a grunt of approval. "And the name of the artist who made the original?"

Blaise could barely say the name out loud. Even that somehow felt like a betrayal. "Fausto Corvo."

"That is it! Corvo." Jeremiah slapped his knee. "From

Venice, was he not? Now, Venice, there's a city. Magnificent, I am told. I cannot place the accent in your speech, Blaise. Are you from the West Country perchance? Bristol?"

"America," said Blaise.

A hoarse whisper circulated around the room.

"The Colonies." Jeremiah leaned forward. "Egad, you are a well-traveled young man."

"Quite," said Throgmorton, tapping the sketchbook with his forefinger. "Now, Blaise, tell us about these other sketches."

Alarm spread through him again. Throgmorton seemed very eager to know about the drawings he had done of Arcadia, the land inside Corvo's magical painting.

"Those?" Blaise wracked his brain for an explanation that wasn't an out-and-out lie. "Just doodles."

"Doodles?" Jeremiah laughed. "What, pray tell, is a doodle?"

Blaise wondered how long he would have to keep up this game. It was getting annoying — and worrying.

"A little sketch of nothing important. Shapes ... faces ... funny animals. Your hand just sort of draws what it likes." He caught several of the boys half grinning at one another, as if they knew just what he meant.

"Ah. Such as . . ." Jeremiah thrust a quill pen into some brown ink and lazily drew a dog prancing on its hind legs, wearing a plumed hat. "This?"

"Um, yes. And no. That's way too good for a doodle."

Throgmorton scooped up the book and held out another page of sketches. "Of all things, your hand *chose* to draw a chariot and these strange beasts?"

Blaise answered warily, "Yes." There was no way he would tell them he'd seen those things painted on a palace wall in Arcadia.

"Do you know what any of them are?"

"That's Apollo in his chariot. And that's a phoenix and a python. . . ." Sunni broke in, her voice tremulous. "We learned about Greek and Roman mythology at school."

"Ah!" Jeremiah turned to her. "By your speech, miss, I would reckon you to be from the north—" he began, but was cut off by Throgmorton.

"I think, sir, that it is now time for a lesson. Miss Sunniva and Master Blaise shall join in."

Yet again, a rush of whispers buzzed among the boys.

"Gentlemen?" Throgmorton whirled around and looked at them one by one. "Have you some opinion you would like to share with us?"

"No, sir," said Toby.

"The boys have no opinions, Mr. Throgmorton, except upon the best use of quills, paintbrushes, and pigments," said Jeremiah, with a sharp sniff. "Robert, Samuel, shift those tables and make room." He fished two threadbare shirts off a peg and handed them to Sunni and Blaise. "It pains me that I have nothing better to offer you, miss, but we are unused to ladies in the workshop, as you see."

Sunni pulled one greasy sleeve over her bare arm and tried not to grimace. The shirt had not touched soap in a long time, if ever.

Starling hung up his coat and rolled up his sleeves. "Toby, your assistance with the pot, if you please."

The pair crouched down to the hearth and hoisted the bubbling casserole onto some bricks scattered on the floor nearby. Throgmorton dusted off an empty seat and sat down to watch.

"I shall show you how we prepare the glue"—Jeremiah used a wad of rags to protect his hand and pulled the lid off—"straining out the bones and skin."

A pungent steam cloud enveloped Jeremiah and Toby, who recoiled for a moment from its heat. The smell rolled through the workshop like an ill wind.

"Bones and skin of what?" asked Blaise in a small voice.

"In this particular mixture, rabbits," said Jeremiah, wiping his brow. "Though oft-times goat parts come cheapest. Necks, feet, and skins."

"What's it for?" Blaise grimaced at a chunk of gristle that had landed by his feet when the lid rose.

"To mix with gypsum and chalk for the making of gesso." Jeremiah stirred through the foul casserole and fished out a tiny bone. He threw it into a graveyard pot already half full of bones and cartilage. "We must coat the surface of our paintings with it before we begin work."

He held out a long-handled wire strainer with hard dried bits of something gray stuck to it. "Which of you shall start?"

Sunni yanked Blaise back a few steps toward the windows. Her face was white and covered with a sweaty sheen. "Can I talk to my friend for a minute, please?"

"As you wish," said Throgmorton, watching her closely.

Starling shrugged and handed the strainer to Toby.

Sunni turned her back to the others so they could not make out what she said. "This is out of control. I think that man really *is* Jeremiah Starling."

"He can't be," whispered Blaise. "Throgmorton told us he died. . . ."

"Yeah, I know. But look outside," she murmured. "And don't be obvious!"

Blaise strained to see out of the window from the corner of his eye, but he was too far away. "What? I can't see anything."

"Everything is wrong. We've got to get out of here. Now."

Chapter 5

"Miss Sunniva," called Throgmorton. "You are missing Master Starling's demonstration."

"I'm sorry. We have to leave." She took off the work shirt and dropped it onto a stool. "Blaise's father is waiting for us, and we're late already."

Sunni made her way to the painted door. She studied the wall, hoping that the solid panels and metal door handle might reappear, but they did not.

"Mr. Throgmorton," she began, anxiety pulsing through her.

"Miss Sunniva," he answered, "not that way. Please come with me. And you, Blaise." He took a step toward the open door in the opposite corner of the room.

Sunni hesitated. "Why are we leaving through that door? We came in through this painted one."

"Please come along."

"Where does he want to take us?" she whispered to Blaise.

"I dunno. Do we go?"

"Don't think we have a choice." Sunni turned away from the painted door but stood still.

Throgmorton raised his arm like an outspread wing, sending the candles flickering. "Come."

The boys kept their heads down. Toby and Jeremiah stirred the glue pot intently, until the painter lifted his head. "I advise you to go with Mr. Throgmorton."

"Stay close together," said Sunni as she and Blaise threaded their way through the tables and easels.

Reluctantly, they followed Throgmorton down the stairs.

"What did you mean that everything's wrong here?" whispered Blaise.

"Out the window," Sunni whispered back. "Nothing's right." She might have believed that the workshop was a recreation for tourists, but not the world outside. She'd seen London's old rooftops beyond the rippled glass windowpanes and had had a clear view of Saint Paul's Cathedral dome. It was by far the tallest building, with no sign of any high-rise offices, construction cranes, or air traffic above it. The passersby in the street below were dressed in period clothes like Throgmorton and Livia.

"What do you mean, nothing's right?"

"No skyscrapers, no cars," said Sunni huskily. "Everyone out there's wearing old clothes and wigs."

On the second floor, Throgmorton opened a door for them, smiling. "Please."

Inside, Livia rose from a dark-green wingback armchair. "You are very welcome."

She guided Blaise by the arm to a matching chair opposite hers, but let her father offer Sunni the hard-looking sofa. They were in a formal sitting room that had no trace of *trompe l'oeil* trickery. A chandelier lit the room with a blaze of beeswax candles. The busts on the mantelpiece were real, and the small table by Livia had an array of playing cards spread across it in a game of solitaire.

"Mary is bringing tea for us," said Livia.

A servant girl struggled in with a large silver tray holding teacups and a pot. She gawked at Sunni and Blaise as she laid it down on a table beside Livia and scurried out after a nod from Throgmorton.

Livia's hands fluttered over the tray, pouring and stirring. She extended a china cup toward Sunni but did not get up from her chair. "You must be very thirsty."

"No, thank you." Sunni sat stiffly on the edge of the sofa.

Blaise shook his head at the offer of tea. "Where are we?"

"Jeremiah Starling's house." Livia's laugh chimed out.

"Where are all the *trompe l'oeil* murals?" Blaise asked tersely. "I don't see them anywhere."

"He has not painted them yet," said Throgmorton.

Sunni jumped in. "What do you mean, he hasn't painted them *yet*?"

"You met Starling. He's a young man, and this is his old childhood home. One day he will build a new house on this land. He'll fill it with murals and it will be known as Starling House." Throgmorton pointed at a few framed landscape and portrait paintings on the parlor walls. "Those are the sorts of paintings he has been making during the past few years."

"This can't be real. He can't be Jeremiah Starling," said Blaise.

"I have told you the truth." Throgmorton showed a flicker of displeasure. "He is Starling."

"You told us he died in 1791," said Sunni.

"That is also true."

Blaise said, "Jeremiah Starling can't be alive and dead at the same time."

"He is for us. You have traveled back to the time when Jeremiah Starling was twenty-nine years old," said Throgmorton. "You are in the year 1752."

1752 — where had she seen that date before? Sunni couldn't keep her hands still in her lap. "The painted door. It's the crossing point, isn't it?"

"Yes, it is an astonishing door," said Livia, sipping delicately from her cup. "It connects our time and yours by the slenderest sliver of space and time."

"But why us? Why bring us?" Blaise nearly shouted.

"To show you the Academy," said Throgmorton. "You agreed to it."

"We didn't agree to go back to 1752!"

Throgmorton shrugged. "That is what one must do to see the Academy. And you have not even left Phoenix Square. We are still in the same location. Starling House is not the only house that has ever sat on this land. Other houses were here before it, including this one. We have stretched a little hole in the skin of time and crawled through to it."

"You can't just make an opening in time!" Blaise interrupted.

"How do you think you got here then?"

Blaise murmured, "I don't know."

"You control the painted door," said Sunni. "How?"

"It is just an ability I have. Far too complex for you to understand," replied Throgmorton.

"W-what are you?" asked Sunni.

"An ordinary man." Throgmorton's mouth twitched. "A mere mortal."

Silence fell over the tea party, but Sunni's and Blaise's eyes didn't leave Throgmorton's face.

"So," Sunni said at last, "we're sitting here in this room, but somewhere right around us, right now, across a closed-up hole in time, is the other Starling House with all the murals, on the date we left it?"

"Yes."

"And the only way back is through that painted door."

"Yes."

"And you'll take us back through it now, since we've seen the Academy," said Blaise.

The words hung there while Sunni and Blaise waited for his answer. When it came, Throgmorton delivered it without a flicker of doubt.

"No."

The air crackled with Sunni and Blaise's outrage.

"You have to!" Sunni cried.

"My father is waiting for us." Blaise leaped to his feet. "You can't stop us from going home."

"I can." Throgmorton strolled about the parlor with his hands clasped behind his back. "And I will. The door is now closed."

"I don't understand *why*!"

"Because I wish it." Their captor said this as if it were the only explanation anyone could require.

Sunni fidgeted on the hard sofa. "You can't keep us here!"

"My father has never brought anyone else across to our time. Only you," said Livia. "It is a great honor, so do not be angry!"

"Honor!"

"You have met Jeremiah Starling," said her father. "And seen his Academy, full of the most astounding boy-artists in this century or any other. This is what you wished for."

"No. We didn't wish to be kept here!" said Sunni, shaking with fury.

"You have no choice," said Throgmorton. "I have decided you will stay and be pupils at the Academy. You are highly qualified applicants."

Blaise's hands were clenched into fists. "You can't force us to do anything! I'm not going to be your trained monkey."

Livia appealed to him with wide eyes. "Do not be this way, Blaise! Please."

"How am I supposed to be then? Your father is keeping us here against our will."

"You will like it here. I promise," she said. "You want to be an artist, don't you? Now you will be."

"Trade our freedom so we can draw better?" Sunni jumped in. "No chance."

"You do have a choice," said Throgmorton. "Accept what

I offer you, or I will have you sent to prison for thieving from this house."

"You'd do that to us?" Sunni could barely get the words out. "Why, what's the point? Why not just send us back where we came from?"

Throgmorton's mouth was pinched. "You will stay here with us as well-behaved pupils or go to prison."

"That's no choice. We're in prison either way." Blaise thumped the arm of his chair.

Livia nestled her teacup close and bit her lip. "This is not a prison."

Sunni scowled at her and Blaise just turned away.

"Forgive them. They do not understand yet, my dear, but they soon will." Throgmorton squeezed his daughter's shoulder and said softly, "There is sleeping room for two more pupils in the Academy, but it is difficult to hide a girl amongst boys. People will ask questions."

"What you are talking about?" Sunni asked.

"You will need to disguise yourself as a boy, Sunniva. Sometimes visitors come to see the workshop, and they will notice a girl pupil."

"What!"

"Father, I think there are some cast-off breeches that will fit her," said Livia. "They are men's but can be tied tighter around her waist."

"Will you see to it, my dear?"

Livia shook her platinum curls. "Yes, Father. This will be most amusing, Sunniva, like dressing for a masquerade!"

"No way—" Sunni began.

"You would prefer to spend time in Newgate Prison? For that is where burglars end up," Livia said gaily.

Sunni mumbled something and shot a look at Blaise.

"You said something, Sunniva?" Throgmorton's face was impassive.

"I said you have no right to do this."

"I have *all* the rights in this house," said Throgmorton. "Livia, my dear, take Sunniva to your chamber."

"Come with me!" Livia pulled Sunni up and frog-marched her out of the parlor.

"Walk properly, Blaise! You are not a wild animal." Throgmorton steered him up the stairs and into the Academy workshop.

Blaise's rage continued to come out with every footstep. He kicked against the stairs and shrugged off his kidnapper's hand.

Throgmorton pulled him to a halt outside the workshop door. "Leave your childishness outside the Academy. It does not suit you."

Blaise snorted.

"Stop your work, gentlemen," said Throgmorton as he entered the workshop with the sullen boy in his grip. "Blaise is to join you as a fellow pupil."

"Is he?" Jeremiah looked puzzled.

"May I have a word, sir?" Throgmorton let go of Blaise

and strode into the corridor. Jeremiah grumbled and followed, with a gesture to the group to continue working.

Blaise dodged candles and easels as he ran to the painted door. His hands trembled as he worked his fingers over the illusion of a door handle and along the door's false edges, looking for an indentation. There were some barely visible curved scratches in the paintwork, but otherwise all he could feel was the flat coolness of plaster.

Desperate, he implored the boys, "How do I get out through this door?"

Six heads shook from side to side. No one answered.

"But you saw us come in! How did Throgmorton make the door open?"

One of the younger boys, Jacob, said, "The door comes alive when he wills it to."

The others shushed him and glanced toward the corridor to make sure the two men were nowhere near.

"Jacob!" Toby shook the boy by the shoulder. "Do not speak of that, now or ever."

"Why can't he speak about it?" Blaise growled.

"Do not ask. The less you ask, the better for you."

Raised voices and a clattering of shoes pulled their attention away.

"Strewth!" cursed Jeremiah. He burst angrily into the workshop and flung his arms in the air. "Blaise, you are one of us for now. I shall not pollute the air with any useful advice except this. Keep your mouth and ears closed to anything but artistic instruction. Draw when I say, eat when I say, sleep when I say, and not before."

He stormed out again. There was banging and scraping from next door.

"The Master is making you a sleeping place with us," Toby murmured, clearing broken bits of charcoal and chalks away with his arm. "Here, this will be your table and stool."

Jeremiah blustered back into the workshop. "Follow me, Blaise."

The room next door was a maze of small, narrow cots with little space between them. Jeremiah yanked a wooden chest from under one bed and pulled its contents out. Two rough white shirts, two pairs of breeches, and a few pairs of dirty, once-white stockings lay there, along with a nightshirt and three scrunched-up undergarments.

"Wear these clothes. They belonged to a boy who is gone away now," said Jeremiah. "And do not pass judgment upon their fit or fashion. We have no use for such nonsense."

"Mr. Starling, I am not supposed to be here," Blaise pleaded. "I need to get home."

"It is not for me to say."

"You must realize we don't belong here! Throgmorton's put us in your Academy against our will."

"Your will has no importance here," said Jeremiah gruffly. "You are to be a pupil of this Academy in accordance with Throgmorton's wishes for as long as he requires it."

"But this is *your* art school!"

"I instruct whomever is placed in front of me." Jeremiah scooped up the clothes and thrust them into Blaise's arms.

"Unless they prove to be incompetent at learning and are taken back from whence they came."

"So if we're terrible students, he might let us go."

"Do not contemplate it!" Jeremiah gave a short laugh. "Throgmorton wants you here for his own reasons and will not release you until he is satisfied."

Blaise picked up a stocking that had slipped to the floor. It was stretched into the shape of its previous owner's foot, dark with grime at the heel and toe. "I'm supposed to wear this?"

"The dirt will hardly be noticed once the shoe is upon your foot." Jeremiah nudged a pair of worn shoes from under the bed. "Place your belongings in that trunk."

"Whose clothes were these?"

"A boy who is no longer with us," said Jeremiah, unable to look Blaise in the eye. "Or so I presume."

"You don't know where he went?" Blaise was appalled that he could smell the departed boy on the clothing he held. "Was it because he was 'incompetent at learning'?"

"No on both counts," muttered Jeremiah, growing visibly agitated. He dug around in his vest and coat pockets till he found a pewter snuffbox.

"What do you mean?"

Jeremiah gave the snuffbox's lid a few taps, opened it, and sniffed a pinch of tobacco into both nostrils. His face relaxed somewhat. "Questions draw unwanted attention, Blaise. I have already given you my humble advice, but I think you have need of more. So hear this: do what you can in this house to extend your life rather than shorten it."

Chapter 6

Sunni's sundress and sandals lay in a pile on the floor of Livia's bedroom.

"I think you make an excellent boy, Sunni," said Livia. "Your face has a plainness to it that works very well for this purpose. But what shall we name you?"

A servant, Mary, was trying to tie a bit of fabric around Sunni's waist to make the breeches fit better, but Sunni clawed at the fabric. "You think your father is right to keep us here? Why don't you say something to him?"

"I will not." Livia reclined on her four-poster canopy bed. "He is my father."

"I wish I could see *my* father, but I can't, because *yours* is keeping me here. Please, Livia, you must know how the door works. Help us go home."

Livia gazed at herself in a silver hand-mirror. "You will become used to it here."

Sunni cried out in frustration. "Don't you have any feelings at all? Do you ever think about other people?"

"Forgive me, Sunniva, but I am trying to help you."

"Really. How?"

"By helping you to fit in. Did you not notice how the Master's pupils stared at your bare shoulders and legs? It was not because your features are particularly good, but because they were on show for all to see. This cannot be the sort of attention a proper young lady would wish for."

Sunni's mouth hung open. "Are you joking? You're thinking of my clothes, and I'm thinking of my life!"

"Clothes are important." Livia pursed her lips. "Young ladies do not attend boys' art academies. You must impersonate a boy so you do not call attention to yourself. Gossip might spread, and then what might happen?"

Yeah, someone might realize your father has prisoners in his special Academy. Sunni glared down at her drooping stockings and scuffed shoes with one buckle missing. Mary had rolled up the sleeves of the man's white linen shirt and tucked in its long tail, but it was still too big, especially after she had bound Sunni's chest in a tightly wound piece of muslin to make her as flat as a boy. Angry tears filled Sunni's eyes, but Livia took no notice and prattled on.

"You must practice walking and talking like a boy. Your voice is already deep for a girl, but you should lower it even more," said Livia. "A lady's voice should be high and light, like a tinkling bell. Yours is neither, but it will be suitable for a boy's voice."

Sunni wiped her eyes and said nothing. She would get nowhere with this girl, so what was the point of even trying? Better to find out how to open that painted door and get away from these people on her own.

At last, Mary stopped fiddling with the breeches' waistband and anchored Sunni's wavy hair at the nape of her neck with a scraggly bit of ribbon.

Livia dismissed the servant with a wave and smirked. "What a fine fellow you are."

Disgusted, Sunni picked up her dress and sandals from the floor. She slung her bag across her chest and said, "I'm keeping my clothes because I *will* be going home."

Livia shrugged. "Let us go and see how handsome Blaise looks in proper boys' clothing."

Blaise's head was splitting. He couldn't get enough air, and his skin was slick with sweat. *How are we going to get out of here?*

He took a breath. *You can handle it. You got out of Corvo's painting when you never thought you would. You fought off plenty of enemies there and figured out the way home.*

But fighting Throgmorton won't open the painted door. He cradled his head in his hands.

Jeremiah Starling appeared at his side with a jar full of long goose feathers.

"Choose one," he said quietly. "They are all good."

Blaise stared, dull-eyed, at the feathers.

"By doing something useful, you will chase melancholy away." Jeremiah thrust the jar into Blaise's face.

He pulled a feather out and shrugged.

"Very well," said Jeremiah. "Now we strip off the barbs and shorten the shaft." He laid the feather down on a wooden board, and with a small, sharp penknife, the Master sliced and nipped it into shape. A few deft cuts later, he had carved an angled drawing tip, ready to receive ink.

"The goose's loss is our gain," he said. "Now choose another feather and make one yourself, as I have."

The pounding in Blaise's head started to recede, and his panicky feelings moved out of focus. Somehow, watching Jeremiah work brought him a moment of calmness. He went at his own feather with care, teasing the downy feathers from the shaft and excising them with the knife.

"Mr. Starling," said Livia, standing with Sunni at the workshop door. "This is Jack, your new pupil."

Sunni's face went pink at this. "What?"

"Jack Sunniver."

Blaise's small shoot of tranquillity withered. Seeing Sunni, rumpled in her sagging breeches, with her missing shoe buckle, made him curse himself for dragging her to Starling House and going through the painted door without question. Livia was gazing at him, approving of his eighteenth-century outfit, and he cursed himself again for following her.

The Academy boys gaped at Sunni's transformation. But none of them was bold enough to point or titter. Instead, they turned to see what the Master would make of this.

"Jack Sunniver, you say?" Jeremiah crossed his arms over his chest. "A *boy* like yourself probably prefers to be called by his surname, eh? Shall we call you Sunniver then?"

"He is called Jack," Livia protested.

"Madam, you may call him Jack when he is outside my domain," said Jeremiah. "When he eats his gruel or sleeps in his quarters, you may feel free to interrupt him. By the way, where are *his* quarters? For there is no room with the others."

"The servant's room by the kitchen, Mr. Starling."

"Lucky lad, Sunniver. Mistress Biggins shall look after you." Jeremiah ushered Sunni toward the goose feathers. "And your friend Blaise shall now instruct you on how best to cut a quill pen." He glanced over his shoulder. "Good-bye to you, miss."

With a toss of her head, Livia vanished downstairs.

"Welcome, Blaise and Sunniver," said Jeremiah. "You are Academicians now, and as far as it is any outsider's business, you have both been with us for some time. You are orphans of the parish, found by Mr. Throgmorton, just like the other boys. No outsider shall know any other details but this." He swiped the back of his hand across his nose. "Gentlemen, we make nine altogether. A fine number. Now let me hear the sound of nine at their work."

The boys settled down, and Jeremiah began sketching out a painting on a large easel in a corner.

"Take a feather," Blaise said to Sunni. "And watch what I do."

She plucked the first one she saw and sat down next to him, her back rigid. The feather fell from her grasp and landed on the floor, but she made no move to retrieve it.

"I know, I don't feel like doing this either." Blaise picked up her feather and asked in a gentle voice, "Are you okay?"

"Not really. I can't see how we're going to get out of here. Livia won't help us. I pleaded, but she wouldn't listen."

"That doesn't surprise me. I tried the door, but I don't

have any idea how to open it, and none of the boys knows exactly how Throgmorton goes through it," he murmured.

"Your dad will be out of his mind worrying, let alone my dad and Rhona. *Again.*"

"Yeah."

"I can't believe this." Her voice rose. "Why are we here? Doesn't he have enough boys to choose from in his own century?"

"Sunniver!" Jeremiah interrupted, with a pointed look.

"Sorry, Mr. Starling." She began whispering. "Why would Throgmorton bother to kidnap two random kids that wandered into a museum? None of this makes sense."

Blaise laid his hand protectively on his sketchbook, which never left his side. "If I hadn't shown him this, he never would have invited me in here. He was pretty interested in some of my sketches from Arcadia."

"You're right." Sunni sat up. "He was."

"You think that means anything?"

"I don't know." She sighed. "And I haven't got a clue how we're going to get away from him either."

Blaise looked around. Starling was busy, and the boys were hard at work. "So what do we do?"

"Play along with this Academy stuff and find out how the door works."

"Yeah, and fast." Blaise scratched one of his filthy stockings.

"You don't look too bad in those clothes," muttered Sunni.

"You don't either," he said. "You wear pants most of the time anyway."

"Huh?"

"I mean—"

"So you think I look like a guy even when I'm not trying to."

Blaise put his hands up. "That's not what I meant."

"Just show me how to make that stupid feather into a pen," said Sunni, fidgeting in her makeshift muslin corset and itchy breeches, "and don't you ever dare call me Jack."

"Yeah, right." Blaise picked up her feather and began slicing into it.

"Blaise." Jeremiah's voice boomed. "Show me that quill."

"It's not done yet, sir."

"That is because your mouth is working harder than your hands. Quiet labor, Blaise and Sunniver, at all times!"

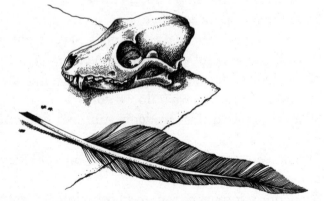

In the gathering gloom of nightfall, the candle flames in the Academy of Wonders became bright jewels against the dim walls. The boys lit more lanterns and rearranged the lights nearest their worktables, settling down again after a brief meal of bread, cheese, and cups of tea in the kitchen. The cook, Mistress Biggins, had shooed them away before they could even finish swallowing their second cup. There had been no sign of Throgmorton or Livia, and every door in the quiet house was shut, but as Mary and the cook bustled to prepare a lavish evening meal, a current of excitement spread from the cellar kitchen to the Academy workshop.

After several rounds of snuff and a barrage of sneezes, Jeremiah rapped on a tabletop for the boys' attention. "Make not a sound tonight, lads, not one sound. There will be guests in the dining parlor, and Mr. Throgmorton warns you not to spoil their pleasure."

"What sound? It's already like a tomb in here," whispered Sunni, working her quill pen in more curves and lines on yet another sheet of paper.

"Except for my stomach rumbling." Blaise squirmed. "Bread and cheese isn't going to cut it for me. How can these guys live on that?"

"Look at the size of them. They'd dry up and blow away if the sun ever hit their skin."

Blaise tried to check the time, but there was only a pale patch on his wrist where his watch had been. It now lay with his other belongings in the trunk under his cot. "Excuse me, Mr. Starling?"

Jeremiah ambled over, cradling a stoneware bowl filled with small animal skulls. He picked through them with care, making sure the jawbones did not become separated.

"A question?" He peered over Blaise's practice sheets and nodded. "You handle the pen well."

"How much longer do we work tonight?"

The boys all glanced up.

"Answer him, Robert." Jeremiah selected a blunt-nosed skull, perhaps of a dog, and laid it in front of Blaise.

"We work until first sleep," said a dark-haired boy with very few front teeth. "Then we awake and work on till second sleep. We rise with the morning light, break our fast, and work again."

"Thank you, Robert," Jeremiah said, placing a delicate specimen in front of Sunni. This skull was small enough to fit in her hand. It brought a lump to her throat wondering what animal it had been.

"First sleep?"

"We have a few hours yet till then," said Jeremiah. "And we wake again at midnight."

Blaise exhaled noisily and exchanged a look with Sunni. "Where we come from, people sleep through the whole night, unless they're worried or sick. I can sleep for ten hours straight—even longer on weekends."

"Ten hours," Toby murmured. "I have never slept so long."

"Nor I," said Samuel. The other boys murmured agreement.

"A waste of time," Jeremiah said. "One can complete a drawing in the space of time between first and second sleep. You shall see. Sunniver and Blaise," he continued, "you may try drawing these creatures' skulls with ink now. But remember, draw first with charcoal, then brush the excess away." He put down his bowl of skulls and dragged a clean sheet of paper onto Sunni's table. "Let me show you."

He picked up a tiny stump of charcoal that had rolled onto the floor and began sketching out Sunni's specimen on the paper. He made a sweeping line with his right hand, then changed hands and kept drawing with his left. He mumbled as he went along, "Make the overall shape with a light hand. . . . Refine it. . . . This curves in here. . . . The eye socket. . . . Mark the teeth in last. . . . Take care not to press too hard."

Jeremiah looked around and noticed that his pupils were secretly watching him. "Very well, you imps. You have seen me do this many times before, but it will not harm you to see it once more."

The boys gathered around and watched the Master draw, leaning on each other's shoulders, chins cupped in their hands. It was the first time Sunni had seen some of them smile, and she guessed that this was as close to fun as they got.

Jeremiah eventually whipped the paper off the table and shook it, blowing off the excess charcoal. He took up Sunni's quill pen and drew over his sketch. When it was finished, he left it to dry and threw a feather down on top of it. "You may dust off charcoal lines with that."

"You is a right genius, Mr. Starling," said a deep male voice somewhere near them.

"Hear, hear," drawled another voice.

All heads jerked up to see two men in dark clothing looming behind them.

Chapter 7

The first man was tall and slender, with a long nose and chin. The other was slight but well proportioned, with a smirking face. Both had ebony-colored hair pulled back tightly under their three-cornered hats.

"Egad," Jeremiah erupted. "The two of you shall stop my heart dead one day!"

"Apologies," said the smaller man, tipping his hat with one black-gloved hand and revealing a parcel tucked under his other arm. "Delivery."

"Yes, yes, thank you, Mr. Sleek," grumbled Jeremiah, leading the men away and whispering something to them as they went.

The tall man gnawed on a fingernail and pointed to a large wrapped parcel against a wall. "Brought you a rather a significant delivery tonight, Mr. Starling." He tripped over the *r*'s in his words, morphing them into soft *w* sounds.

"Thank you, Mr. Fleet."

Sunni and Blaise stared after Fleet, who had the look of a greyhound ready to bolt on command, and the feline Sleek, who moved smoothly and silently beside him. In their dusky clothes of no nameable color, they brought the night's darkness in with them.

"Who are they?" Sunni whispered to Toby.

The boys had scattered back to their seats, but Toby was seated close by.

"They work for Mr. Throgmorton. They bring us artworks to copy for our learnin' and take them away when we are finished."

Sleek tilted his head to study Sunni and Blaise. His smirk made Sunni feel that he had figured out her secret within five seconds, but when he shifted his gaze to Blaise, his expression did not change.

"New apprentices," Sleek said, raising his forefinger in greeting and touching it to the brim of his hat.

"Rather different from the others," Fleet observed. "What poorhouse did he find these in?"

"I have not been told," Jeremiah said. "Their origins matter not to me."

Sleek raised his eyebrows and did not remove his gaze from the pair.

"Odd."

"Odd?" Fleet repeated. "What is odd, Sleek?"

Sleek tapped his forefinger against his lips. "Well fed."

"Aye, they is rather well fed, now you mention it," said Fleet.

"Mr. Throgmorton is selective in his new apprentices," Jeremiah said abruptly. "Now, show me the specimens."

Fleet unwrapped the cloth that protected his painting and threw it over his shoulder. He just managed to hold both edges of the wide gilded frame and gave the painting a critical once-over.

"Not a mark on it," Fleet said, leaning it against the wall. "Painted by the French master, Caradas."

Jeremiah peered at the portrait of a young man in musketeer's clothing and examined the signature. A brief cloud of anger crossed his face as he pulled the cloth off Fleet's shoulder and draped it across the painting, tucking it in firmly at the back.

"Does the picture vex you, Mr. Starling?" asked Fleet.

"Not in the least." Jeremiah took the other package from Sleek and unwrapped it, revealing a small drawing of a lady with pearls woven through her braided hair.

"Italian," said Sleek, brushing his gloved hands together.

"Florentine," Jeremiah added. He gently covered up the lady and placed her on a high shelf away from the candles and paints.

"Has you anything needing to be taken away, Mr. Starling?" asked Fleet.

"I do, sir, as it happens." Jeremiah moved toward three loosely wrapped paintings propped against a wall. "The Flemish angel is not ready, but that still life may go. Pray also remove the drawing of the sleeping shepherdess. Jacob will soon be finished working upon the Tuscan landscape, now that he has enough vermilion paint."

Fleet lifted a cloth covering to reveal the Flemish angel, and Sunni's pulse quickened. "I recognize that painting," she whispered to Blaise.

"So do I. We saw it in the National Gallery yesterday."

"How did those two get hold of a famous painting?"

Fleet scooped the packaged artworks up and handed the smallest to Sleek.

"Mr. Fleet, Mr. Sleek, our business is concluded," said Jeremiah. "Please see yourselves out."

But neither man moved.

"Old Slaughter's," said Sleek with a glint in his eye.

"Aye! I nearly forgot. But Mr. Sleek misses nothing," said Fleet. "You was discussed at Old Slaughter's coffeehouse last night, Mr. Starling."

"By whom?" asked Jeremiah, fumbling for his snuffbox.

"By all who was there, Mr. Starling. All the gentlemen remarked upon your rather long absence from their company and drank your good health."

"What else was said of me?"

"No more than that," said Fleet. "There wasn't nothing else said, was there, Sleek?"

His companion shook his head. "Nothing."

"How did you come to be at Old Slaughter's? That is hardly your sort of . . ." Jeremiah stopped. "Did you say anything to them? Anything of me?"

Fleet stroked his long chin. "Nay, of course not, Mr. Starling. We was just passing by and heard the jabber."

"Discretion," said Sleek with his finger to his lips.

"Aye, discretion," said Fleet. "Secrets is always safe with us."

With that, he and Sleek gave the boys a parting glance and slipped out of the workshop, arms wrapped around their packages. Sunni and Blaise waited for the sound of shoes on stairs but heard nothing. It was as if the two men had sprouted wings and floated down the stairwell, making no noise and barely causing the candles on the landing to twitch.

Sunni and Blaise managed to make five halfhearted drawings under Jeremiah's watchful eye. At times, fear gripped Sunni and she battled to keep it under control. She kept telling herself to be cool and alert, in case a chance of escape came, and concentrated on drawing obediently. From skulls to shells to horned beetles, she had drawn and redrawn, erased with the feather, and inked in with her quill pen. Even so, she constantly checked the painted door, praying it would rematerialize and they could make a dash for it.

Eventually Sunni's eyes swam in the warm lantern light and her chin dropped to her chest. She awoke with a jerk, looking around to see whether anyone had noticed. But all the boys, Blaise included, were engrossed in their work, and Jeremiah was downstairs, attending Throgmorton's dinner.

When her resistance to sleep finally broke, she slumped forward and the quill rolled out of her hand. The next thing she knew, Gus and Toby were standing over her.

"You'd best go down to Mistress Biggins," said Toby. "She's made you a bed near the kitchen."

Her mouth was parched, and a red lump was coming

up on her middle finger, where the quill pen rubbed as she drew. "See you at midnight, I guess."

"We need to talk," Blaise whispered as she passed.

"I know. Later." Sunni wound down the stairs, perking up at the sound of laughter and voices from below. The door to the dining parlor was ajar, its interior glowing with candlelight. The room hummed with men's voices, punctuated by ladies' laughter.

She hovered by the door. *I could just go in and tell them we're being held prisoner. But would they believe me over Throgmorton?*

Just as Sunni was getting her courage up, Mary burst from the dining parlor, laden down with dirty tureens and plates.

"Take something!" the servant girl hissed, a greasy sweat across her forehead.

Sunni took the most precariously balanced bowls from her and led the way to the kitchen. She nearly toppled down the uneven stairs at the bottom of the house and picked her way along a short, dingy corridor. Edging carefully into the kitchen, she placed her burden on the first clear surface she could find.

Two familiar figures sat in wooden chairs on either side of the blue-and-white tiled hearth, one warming his mantislike legs and the other smoking a long-stemmed clay pipe, his eyes following the shapely cook. The packages they had taken from Jeremiah leaned against a bit of wall underneath one of the shuttered subterranean windows.

"'Tis the new apprentice," said Fleet. "Or is you rather the new maid?"

"Both," said Sleek, his pipe smoke curling up toward the low ceiling.

"I wish he was the new maid," said Mistress Biggins, as she laid out jellies, syllabub, and potted cheeses on the large table. "Mary is obliged to do the work of three and does not even manage to do the work of one."

The heat blasting from the fire and oven sent Sunni cowering to the far wall. The sideboards were heaving with picked-over skeletons of pigeon and carp, bowls still green with slicks of pea soup, and the discarded peelings from potato pudding. To Sunni, the smoke-stained ceiling seemed to grow lower and lower, as if it would flatten them all.

"Mary!" said Mistress Biggins. "Upstairs with all this—now!"

The serving girl hung her head and began ferrying the sweets upstairs.

"Boy," said Fleet. "What do they call you?"

Do I tell them the truth? Under the men's scrutiny, she lost her nerve.

"Sunniver," she murmured.

"Singular name." Sleek puffed his pipe.

"Which parish is you from?"

Panic slithered into Sunni's stomach. *Parish—what's that?* Hoping this was just an old-fashioned way of asking where she was from, she replied in her best imitation of an English accent, her tone lowered to sound more boylike. "Outside London."

Sleek gave his companion a knowing look.

Fleet leaned forward on his bony knees, poised to ask more questions.

Mistress Biggins interrupted before they could continue. "This boy needs his bed. Come with me, Sunniver."

She took a candlestick and bustled Sunni out of the kitchen to a nearby door in the dingy corridor. They entered a cavelike room, the single flame barely illuminating a couple of rickety cots and a cold hearth. As in the kitchen, the bottom half of its window was below ground level and dankness hovered in the air.

"That's your bed, the far one. Mary sleeps in the other."

"Where do you sleep?" Sunni asked, hoping this hearty, rosy-cheeked woman would be nearby.

Mistress Biggins laughed. "There is no room for me in this crowded house. I lodge but a few streets away."

She set the candle down on an upturned crate next to Sunni's cot and plumped the bedding. "I'm to wake you before I leave. Mr. Starling's orders."

Sunni hesitantly sat down. Dampness wafted up from the covers and made her want to gag. From under the bed Mistress Biggins pulled out a chipped china pot that would serve as her toilet.

"Thank you," said Sunni miserably.

"Pleasant dreams, Sunniver." The cook pulled the door shut, and Sunni was left in the dim light of the sputtering candle.

She yanked the bedding off and shook it till her arms ached. If any vermin were hiding in the mattress, they'd soon be squashed; she went over every inch, top and bottom, holding the candle close to the stained fabric. Last, she peered under the bed and, finding nothing but torn spiderwebs in the corner, she remade the bed and lay down on it, fully clothed. Hot tears came, and she punched the rancid pillow.

All trace of tiredness was gone, replaced by anger and a need to do *something* to get home.

She sat up. The dampness tickled at her throat, and the food smells from the kitchen teased her half-empty belly.

The two men and Mistress Biggins were having a lively conversation in the kitchen. Sunni wiped her face and crept out of the room, inching along the wall of the corridor till she came to the open doorway.

"Sleekie and I work for her father," she heard Fleet say, "not for her."

"Little madam," added Sleek.

"My word," said Mistress Biggins. "You do not know the half of it. A more spoiled creature than Miss Livia you have never met."

"Impertinent," said Sleek.

"Precisely," said Fleet. "Do you know, she scolded us for appearing in this house today?"

"But why?" asked the cook. "You come here to do business."

"I imagine she didn't want them dinner guests to see us. We nightsneaks is of such low status, and they is Persons of Quality." Sunni could hear the sneer in Fleet's voice. "Though nobody'd ever heard of Mr. Throgmorton and Miss Livia before they turned up."

"And they appeared with no warning," said Mistress

Biggins. "I found them at the breakfast table with Mr. Starling one morning. No explanation then, and none since. I do wonder where they came from so suddenly."

"And Starling took them in!"

" 'Twas money," Sleek said.

"Aye, Sleekie. Throgmorton had ready money. Where from, you and I may both wonder."

Mistress Biggins agreed with a long *"Mmm."*

Fleet went on, "Why, if them Persons of Quality had an inkling of our business with the gentlemen in this establishment, they'd never be seen here again."

Sunni's ears pricked up, but Fleet changed the subject, so she sneaked back into her room and blew out the lonely candle by her bed. Desperately hoping that Biggins, Fleet, and Sleek would stay in the kitchen and that she would not bump head-on into Mary, Sunni tiptoed upstairs. The hall was empty. She hurried to the front door and pulled on it, but it was locked. She put her head to the dining parlor door, but when guests began getting up from the table with a scraping of chairs, she sprang away.

Sunni ran up the stairs just as the dining parlor door opened. She dived out of sight on the landing and darted to the top floor as silently as she could.

The boys were tidying up and extinguishing candles in the workshop before going to their beds in the next room. Blaise flexed his drawing hand and rubbed his eyes.

"Blaise." Sunni hurried in and dragged him to the painted door. "Come on." She ran her hands over the wall, as he had, and pounded on it in frustration when she could find no way to pry it open.

"I told you it was closed." He touched the wall once more just in case.

Sunni faced the other boys. "You all know how this works, don't you? You must! And you know we don't belong here either. Blaise and I have to go back through that door, and you have to help us."

"Keep your voice down. They won't tell you, because they don't know," said Blaise. "Besides, they're scared to talk."

"Scared? Of what?" Sunni threw her arms out wide. "Go on, why don't you run away from the Academy then, if you're scared?"

Robert murmured something, and though the other boys shushed him, he kept talking. "We can't go. Mr. Throgmorton's paid the parish for us."

"He's put a roof over our heads and food in our bellies," said Toby, giving Robert a warning look.

"What's the parish?" asked Sunni.

"The poorhouse," said Samuel. "Where we was all raised from babies. Mr. Throgmorton came looking for boys who was good at drawing, and he chose each of us."

"If we is clever at our work, we can stay here," said Jacob.

Toby's eyes flashed. "Instead of rag picking or sifting the Thames mud for lost coins."

"But he paid *money* for you. That's wrong!" said Sunni. "You're human beings."

The boys said nothing until Toby murmured, "It's the way of things. You do not understand."

"I understand that you all have to draw night and day. You never seem to stop working."

They all shrugged.

"Do you ever leave this house?"

Silence.

Sunni wrenched one of her sleeves up to show her tanned arm. "You never feel the sun or the rain? Or run about outdoors?"

One or two heads shook.

"We still have much to learn," Toby insisted. "Mr. Starling has taught me everything, but there is always more to do here."

"Copying artwork that Mr. Fleet and Mr. Sleek bring in." She pointed at the newly arrived painting of the musketeer. "Do you know where they got that from?"

More silence.

"How do they get these paintings?" asked Sunni. "Fleet and Sleek seem to be able to supply them with no problem."

The boys hung their heads and Blaise said, "Like the Flemish angel painting. It's *famous*."

Will, who had never spoken up before, raised his head. "I am copying the angel. But Mr. Fleet and Mr. Sleek will take it back where it come from, like all the others. They says so. We just borrows 'em to copy for our learnin'."

"Borrow them from where? You don't just 'borrow' well-known artwork," said Sunni.

Will shrugged, shrinking away from her furious questions.

"It's okay, Will. You're not to blame," said Blaise. "We're just trying to figure out what's going on here."

"Do not ask questions," said Toby.

But Sunni ignored him and picked up the copy one of the younger boys was making. "Are you allowed to keep the copies you make? Do they belong to you?"

"Nay, we do not keep them," said Will earnestly.

"Will!" Toby hissed.

"Let him talk," said Blaise. "What happens to your copies when you're done?"

"There's nothing wrong in saying it, Toby," said Will. "Mr. Throgmorton takes the copies. He takes 'em away." His eyes darted momentarily toward the painted door.

Toby grabbed his arm. "Are you mad? Say nothing more, Will!"

"He doesn't need to." Sunni tapped the wall. "You all slave away making drawings and Mr. Throgmorton takes them away through this door, doesn't he?"

There was rustling behind them, and everyone turned, startled.

Livia stepped from the shadowy hallway, regal in a deep rose–colored gown. "Jack Sunniver, what are you doing here?"

Sunni's lip twisted. "Nothing."

"Come away from that wall. Your bed is below, and you are nowhere near it."

"I was just going."

"That is a lie. I spied you running up the stairs."

"I couldn't sleep." Sunni stormed past her and ran down the stairs.

"What were you telling Jack Sunniver, William?" asked Livia, her expression mild.

"Nothing, Miss Livia." Will's eyes were huge in his thin face.

Livia's short laugh was like a windowpane shattering. "Never lie, William. Dishonesty always hurts someone in the end."

Chapter 8

The stale-smelling bed was too short for his lanky frame, and the mattress sagged in the middle, but Blaise fell asleep almost immediately. For a brief, anguished moment, he wondered again about the boy whose bed this had been and if he and Sunni would ever escape, but, with the urge to sleep so great, his questions just drifted away.

The painted door kept appearing in his dreams, opening and closing for everyone else, but never for him. Just as he thought it was about to allow him through, he felt a hand shake his shoulder.

"Blaise, it's midnight," whispered Jacob, his fair hair shining in the lantern light. "We rise now."

Blaise rolled over and looked around the dark room. It smelled of sleep and unwashed bodies. No light came in from the small windows. The night sky was solid black, with no electric street lights to tinge it amber.

The other boys were already up and filing out of the bedroom. He could hear them beginning work in the Academy on the other side of the wall.

Jacob lingered by Blaise's cot. "You are truly allowed to sleep all night where you are from?"

"Yeah."

"Does everyone sleep so much?"

"No," said Blaise, thinking of his dad, who got up early to go running every morning, and feeling another twist of sickness in his stomach. He'd hardly thought of his dad with everything that had happened. By now, he would have reported them missing, after having waited for hours on Tottenham Court Road.

"What is it like where you are from?" Jacob asked as Blaise pulled off his nightshirt and dragged the breeches, shirt, and horrible stockings back on.

"Oh." Blaise half smiled. "Where would I start? There's too much to tell."

"Mr. Throgmorton found you there?"

Blaise tied his hair back into a short ponytail with a bit of string. "Yes, unfortunately."

The boy looked around to make sure no one else was listening. "I wonder what he does with our copies after he takes them through the door."

"I have no idea. He didn't have any with him when we met him."

Jacob sighed. "We work so hard to make the copies well, and as soon as they are finished, they are taken away."

"I know. I would hate that." Blaise sensed an opportunity. He lowered his voice. "You were the one who said Throgmorton makes the painted door come alive. You've seen him do it, haven't you, Jacob?"

After a moment's hesitation, the boy nodded. "Once only."

Blaise's heart jumped. "How did he open the door?"

"H-he drew on it," Jacob whispered. "With red."

"What did he draw?" Blaise tried to keep his voice calm.

Jacob drew an arc in the air. "I know not. Just a shape—like this."

Blaise remembered the curved scratches in the painted door's surface. "What did he use to draw? A paintbrush?"

"A stone knife, I think," said Jacob, "It was reddish and there was something crimson he dipped it in."

Cold spread through Blaise, as if he had been dipped in an icy sea. "Did he say anything while he was drawing?"

"No."

"Where did the red liquid come from? The workshop?"

"From a vial under his shirt."

Blaise's heart sank. How would they ever get this red substance, whatever it was, from Throgmorton? "Do any of the other boys know more than you do?"

"No, only what I told you." Jacob took a backward step toward the door, his face creasing with worry.

"It's all right." Blaise held the boy's elbow and said earnestly, "I will *not* tell anyone, especially Toby."

Jacob relaxed at this, and they hurried into the workshop together. The boys were lighting lanterns and sitting down to their work.

"Strewth!" came a familiar curse from a far corner of the room. "Toby, is it midnight already?"

"Yes, sir."

Jeremiah lay fully clothed in a corner, half covered by dusty bedding and sprawled across a pile of lumpy-looking sacks.

"Egad," he muttered, and sat up. The candlelight seemed to bother him, and he shielded his eyes. "'Tis as if I left Throgmorton's dinner table only a moment ago."

"That's where he sleeps?" Blaise whispered to Jacob, incredulous.

Jacob gave a quick nod.

"But this is his house, isn't it? Why doesn't he sleep downstairs in a bedroom?"

"Do not speak of me behind my back." Jeremiah got to his feet, looking unsteady. "Yes, this is my house!"

Blaise backed away from Jacob, so as not to bring Jeremiah's anger onto him.

"My father built it thirty-five years ago. It is the only home I have ever known, and the only home I shall ever know. Nothing—no one—shall force me from it."

"I'm sorry," said Blaise. "I didn't know—"

"Mr. Throgmorton and his daughter are my, er, lodgers and stay downstairs," said Jeremiah. "That is all you need know. My living arrangements are no business of yours."

"I—I'm sorry. . . ."

"You remember what I told you. Keep to your work."

Blaise sat down at his table and stared at his pile of ink drawings. He sighed. The last thing he wanted to do was pick up that quill pen again.

"What's going on?" Sunni appeared in the workshop, late and bleary-eyed, from her own bed in the cellar.

"Don't talk right now," Blaise said through clenched teeth. "Someone's in a bad mood and taking it out on us."

Sunni dipped her quill in the inkpot and started

scratching away on the corner of one of her practice sheets. A huge black blob rolled onto the paper and she groaned. "This pen is terrible."

"Have you honed the quill, Miss—er, Sunniver?" grunted Jeremiah. "Instruct him, Toby."

The Master sat down heavily in his seat and rubbed his bloodshot eyes. "There is no use in a blunt tool. We must have sharpness at all times."

With that, he let his eyes close, and his chin fell to his chest.

A distant church bell rang two o'clock in the morning. Sunni paused from her work to examine the lump on her middle finger. It was so sore from drawing, she could hardly bear anything to touch it.

Jeremiah snored in his chair. Toby had already warned them not to wake him.

She studied the boys' wan faces. All of them worked without complaint, barely stopping to stretch, except for Blaise. For the first time ever, even he seemed to need a break and couldn't stop fidgeting and yawning.

So he's not a perpetual drawing machine, she thought, stifling a yawn herself.

She couldn't stop glancing at the painted door, half expecting Throgmorton or Livia to step through it at any moment. But she knew they were both downstairs, having waved off their dinner guests an hour and a half before.

As she drew yet another sketch, holding her pen so it would not press on her raw finger, she thought of Dean, tucked up in bed at home in Braeside with her dad and Rhona. But would they actually be sleeping or awake, worrying about her? Sunni had managed to disappear—again—and no doubt her stepmother would lock her up and throw away the key after this.

From down below, slow footsteps climbed the stairs. A lantern cut through the gloom, illuminating Throgmorton's figure at the workshop door.

"Blaise. Jack Sunniver," he said. "Come with me."

They followed Throgmorton in silence as he led them into a dark-paneled study on the ground floor. The atmosphere was chilly, with no embers glowing in the hearth or candles on the mantelpiece, and was stagnant with spent tobacco.

Throgmorton gestured for them to sit and locked the door. He set the lantern on a small table littered with half-empty glasses of port wine and a discarded pipe. The gentlemen must have sat here talking and laughing after dinner, but they had taken everything light and jolly away with them when they went home.

"How is your instruction progressing?" Throgmorton asked softly.

Play along, Sunni told herself. She forced her face into a pleasant expression. "I've learned about making a quill and drawing with ink."

"Me, too" was all Blaise managed before he had to yawn.

Throgmorton pushed the lantern closer to Sunni and

Blaise, lighting their faces and sending his own farther into the darkness. "You are not used to working properly. Life is very easy in your world. And you have great opinions about work, about what is too much or too hard. I am speaking to you, Jack Sunniver."

Sunni met Throgmorton's gaze.

"You have been especially busy not working this evening. Instead you have been exploring, listening at doors, asking questions, demanding things," said Throgmorton. "I was not expecting this kind of behavior from my guests."

"I'm not your guest—I'm trapped in this house," she said. "Though it's more like a sweatshop, isn't it? With slaves copying artwork that you take away from them."

"You have a loose mouth, Jack Sunniver."

"That's not my name."

Sunni could sense Blaise tensing and willing her to shut up, but it was too late.

Throgmorton released a long breath. "It is your name now, Miss Forrest."

A sharp shock ran through Sunni at his mention of her surname. She had never told it to him or anyone else there.

"How do you know my—?"

"Blackhope Tower," said Throgmorton, crossing one leg over the other. His shoe buckle glinted sharply in the candlelight. "You know the place."

"What?" Sunni gasped. "Who *are* you?"

Throgmorton did not answer. "Of course you know Blackhope Tower, the castle built by Sir Innes Blackhope. And all who can read newspapers or see those magnificent devices, the television and the computer, know about you." He gave them a nod. "You are famous for vanishing there in the Mariner's Chamber, a room that was already notorious because skeletons would appear from nowhere on the tiled labyrinth in its floor."

Sunni knew exactly where the skeletons had come from, but she was not going to tell him.

"You were only in the Mariner's Chamber to see Fausto Corvo's painting, *The Mariner's Return to Arcadia*," said Throgmorton. "But you happened to discover Corvo's once-secret password, *chiaroscuro*." He let the Italian word that meant "light and dark" roll off his tongue in an exaggerated way.

Sunni cringed at hearing this man say it aloud. Of course she had talked openly about the password that connected the tiled labyrinth with the painting's hidden world. Since the labyrinth's power had been closed down, there hadn't been any reason to hide the password. Not that she, Blaise, or her stepbrother, Dean, had dared to divulge any of the painting's *real* secrets; they had sworn to protect them. But now she wished she had kept the password to herself.

Throgmorton continued. "Then both of you, and the other boy, Dean, vanished from the Mariner's Chamber with no explanation. People became obsessed with the mystery of the missing children. When you finally reappeared, you told a fantastic story—that you had entered Corvo's painting by walking the labyrinth and repeating the word *chiaroscuro*. Some believed you, but many others thought you had invented the tale."

Though she was tempted to contradict him, Sunni kept

silent. Their predicament had shifted again, and she was trying hard to keep up.

"I believe your story. I have no doubt that Corvo endowed that labyrinth with magical powers when he designed it. He was suspected of sorcery, and because of it he escaped from Venice, never to be seen again," said their captor.

Blaise burst out, "So would I, if some power-hungry guy had put a bounty on my head and sent his spies after me."

"Who are you talking about?" Throgmorton asked.

"Soranzo," Blaise muttered.

"What do you know of him?"

"Soranzo went after Corvo because he wouldn't sell him some paintings he wanted. If it hadn't been for him, Corvo wouldn't have had to run. Soranzo ruined his life."

"You know many things about Corvo," said Throgmorton, not moving a muscle.

"No more than anybody else. Everyone knows he was chased out of Venice in 1582."

"I disagree. You know things no one else does. And I have been waiting for an opportunity to speak with you about them. Destiny brought you to Starling House yesterday."

"No, a man with a beard brought us there," Sunni said. "He spoke to us in a café. Some coincidence."

"It was no coincidence," Throgmorton replied smoothly. "He is my associate."

"What do you mean?"

"He had been following you for some time before

bumping into you in the café. He knows your town, Braeside, very well."

Sunni shuddered. "That man was in Braeside?"

"Yes. When he learned you were coming to London with Blaise's father, I knew we would meet. I saw to it."

"You set this up!" Blaise said, charged up with anger. "Sunni and I didn't come to Starling House to talk about Corvo."

"But now that you are here, we will discuss your adventure."

"No."

"What did you say?" Throgmorton's eyelids lowered.

"No. There's nothing to tell you, or anyone else. We told everything we know to the police, and that's as far as it goes."

"Fausto Corvo's painting, *The Mariner's Return to Arcadia.* You know it very, very well." Throgmorton's hand twitched. "You entered that painting and saw things inside it that you drew in your sketchbook."

Sunni pressed her lips into a tight line. Blaise was sitting forward, his jaw clamped shut.

"It was rumored that Corvo went to Blackhope Tower, where Sir Innes hid him. It would make sense for him to have concealed himself in *The Mariner's Return to Arcadia,*" Throgmorton said. "Did you see Fausto Corvo when you were inside that painting?"

"No," said Blaise and Sunni as one.

"I see," said Throgmorton. "Then how did you come to draw him, Blaise?"

Sunni cursed to herself. Why did Blaise have to carry

that sketchbook around with him? She'd told him umpteen times that he'd either lose it or damage it, but he refused to put it aside until he had filled all of its pages with pictures.

"I didn't draw him." Her friend's voice was edgy.

"His portrait is in among your drawings."

"I copied that from a self-portrait he made."

Throgmorton frowned. "I do not know of any self-portrait like your sketch. Are you certain you did not draw it from life?"

"Yes, I'm sure," Blaise muttered.

"From memory then?" asked Throgmorton.

"It's partly copied and partly from my imagination. Not that it's any of your business."

Throgmorton peered at them from the half dark. "I think Sunniva has a bad influence on you, Blaise, encouraging you to lie. But I also think you are the sort of young man who would lie only to protect others."

Sunni bristled at being described as a bad influence. "You have no idea what sort of person I am."

"Nor am I interested. I only want the truth about what is inside Corvo's painting. Now."

"We're not telling anyone anything. There's nothing to tell." Sunni stood up. "Take us back to our time, Mr. Throgmorton."

Blaise jumped to his feet, too, and picked up the lantern, shining it in the tour guide's face.

Throgmorton's eyes were fixed on them, cold blue like shadows on icebergs. "Sit down."

"No, take us back through that door upstairs," said Blaise.

"Sit down!" Throgmorton's command emanated from somewhere deep in his chest, as violent as a crack of thunder and just as unnerving.

Shaken, Sunni sat back on her chair, and Blaise put the lantern onto the table.

Their captor's face returned to impassive calmness. "This is a serious business. Do you think I would have brought you to this time if it were not?"

Sunni and Blaise remained silent.

"You know far more than you admit. You have seen paintings come to life before! And Blaise has drawn symbols and creatures in his sketchbook that could only be recognized by few learned men from the distant past. He may deny it all he likes, but I know he copied them from what he saw inside *The Mariner's Return to Arcadia*—including Corvo's three lost magical paintings."

Sunni's face twisted. "So you know about *them*, too. Why am I not surprised?"

He gave Sunni a cool look. "I brought you against my better judgment. But you are here now and will make yourself useful."

"What does that mean?"

"You admit you know about the three lost paintings: *The Chalice Seekers, The Jewel of Adocentyn,* and *The City of the Sun.* It is said that Corvo hid the deepest, most powerful secrets of the universe below their surfaces. Tell me their exact location, how to find them, and how to get out of the painting."

"You're wasting your time," Blaise said. "The labyrinth is closed down now. It's over. There's no way back in."

Throgmorton's eyes glinted. "The labyrinth is only closed in *your* time."

"You want to go into the painting yourself!" Sunni said, horrified.

"And to return safely, for my daughter's sake."

"I've got nothing to say to you." Her face was set.

"Will you be more sensible, Blaise?"

Blaise just shook his head, glowering.

"So be it." Throgmorton rose and smoothed out his long overcoat.

"You will remain pupils of the illustrious Jeremiah Starling at the Academy of Wonders. For the other boys, this is luxury compared to life on the streets. But for you, it will be hell. When you are so tired and hungry you cannot go on, you will be eager to tell me everything you saw inside *The Mariner's Return to Arcadia*."

"You can't keep us here! You haven't bought us like you have the other boys," cried Sunni.

"Stay in that chair, girl, and do not move." Throgmorton clamped one hand onto Blaise's arm and steered him to the door, which he unlocked with his other hand. "In this house, you *are* my property, though you, Sunniva, have far less value than Blaise and his sketchbook. You are expendable to me, but perhaps not to him. If he values you, he will soon reveal what I want to know—or you, too, will vanish without trace. Just like the boy who once wore Blaise's clothes."

He pulled Blaise into the hall and locked the door behind them with a hard click.

Chapter 9

B laise was asleep when a rising chorus of gasps and cries yanked him into consciousness. He sensed movement nearby and heard something scraping along the floor. Rough men's voices came out of the darkness, and then what sounded like a sharp slap on skin.

He lay still, huddled against the wall of the boys' bedchamber, watching a dim light travel across its cracked surface. It vanished, and the sound of boots and bumps faded away down the stairs. Blaise slowly turned toward the boys.

One was sobbing into a pillow, and another was cursing, trying to light a lantern. A tiny light finally burst into life, and Toby held it to a candle's wick. His forehead was creased with anguish.

Blaise whispered, "What's going on?"

Robert and Jacob hovered above Toby like ghosts in torn nightshirts.

The eldest boy ignored Blaise and said, "Back to bed, both of you."

"But where's he gone?" whimpered Robert, gnawing on one knuckle as he and Jacob crawled back into their beds.

Toby could only shake his head.

Blaise leaped up and crept into the workshop to see what he could from the windows, which overlooked the square. In the light of a single lantern over the entrance below, he saw dark figures in action.

Toby stood, pale-faced, at the workshop door, the other boys behind him. "Get away from there, Blaise."

"Not till I see what's going on. Put that candle down on the floor, Toby, or behind something, so they don't see me here," Blaise said in a low voice. "There are three men and a cart with a horse. They're loading something onto it. A sack. One of them is tying it up at the end." He let out a hoarse cry. "One of them just hit the sack with a stone or something!"

Toby buried his face in his hands.

Blaise had a horrible feeling he knew what was inside the sack. One of the men had jumped on the cart and was holding the sack down, while the other two swung onto the driver's seat. The cart rolled away into the night.

He jerked away from the window and herded Toby and the others back into the bedroom. "Tell me what happened."

Toby pointed to one of the beds wrenched out of its place. The sheets had been torn away, and there was only an indentation where Will had slept.

The boys gathered around the bed, clutching their arms tightly across their chests against the chill air and the shock.

"Somebody tell me where Will's gone," Blaise said.

"They've taken him," said Toby.

"Who has?"

"Them strangers," whispered Gus. "They takes boys and they don't come back."

Blaise looked under Will's bed. A small trunk was there, untouched.

"His things is still there," said Toby. "But he's gone for good. Just like the others."

An icy bead of sweat snaked down Blaise's spine. *The others.* How many boys had left behind dirty stockings like the ones hanging from the nail by Blaise's bed? Throgmorton's threat to Sunni echoed in his head. *You, too, will vanish without trace.*

"Where's he been taken?" Blaise didn't want to know but had to ask.

"To the country."

"Country as in forests and mountains?"

"Yes. Though I've never seen it." The boy angrily scrubbed a tear off his cheek.

"But why?" Something Jeremiah had said passed through Blaise's head. *Boys incompetent at learning are taken back from whence they came.* Will had not been incompetent. He was making copies as well as any other boy. "Did Will come from the country?"

"No, he came from Spitalfields parish, here in London."

"I can't believe Jeremiah Starling would send him away."

No one answered this at first.

"Mr. Starling don't send boys away," Toby muttered. He didn't have to say who did.

"Will's a good artist," said Blaise, his blood rising. "He shouldn't have had to go."

"No, he shouldn't have." Toby's face twisted. "And he wouldn't have, if it had not been for Jack Sunniver."

The diffused candlelight emphasised the hollow shadows in the boys' faces, hardening their features.

"She . . . Sunniver kept asking questions," said Robert. "And Will answered."

Gus and Samuel nodded in agreement.

"So? You were all talking! I asked you questions, too, before that." It was all Blaise could do to avoid looking at Jacob and risk giving anything away about their conversation.

Robert's voice dropped to the barest whisper. "But because of Sunniver, she overheard Will say that Mr. Throgmorton takes our work away through the door."

"She?" repeated Blaise, confused. "Sunni heard Will—"

"I do not mean your friend," whispered Robert, eyes riveted on the door.

Blaise flinched when he realized who Robert did mean. *Livia.*

Sunni lay awake, listening to the sound of Mary's even breathing—and the scratching sound coming from under her bed. Cockroach, mouse, rat? Her neck was stiff from lying so still in her muslin binding—and from the bruising Throgmorton had given her when he "guided" her back down to this dank room.

When he'd returned from hauling Blaise upstairs, he'd

said, "You will no longer speak to Blaise. Not even to ask him to pass you salt at meals. If you do, I shall lock you in your bedchamber until you are removed from this house."

Throgmorton had gone on, his face a mask of mildness. "If Blaise cares for you, he will tell me everything. If that is not enough, perhaps Livia can convince him." He had smiled at her. "You may have noticed that Blaise is susceptible to the persuasive charms of my daughter. Fifteen-year-old boys fall very hard into love."

Sunni had winced inside but had held herself as still as she could.

Throgmorton had moved to her side and taken the nape of her neck with one hand. Like a cat with a helpless kitten, he had pulled her up from sitting and steered her down the stairs, pushing her into her room and locking the door.

Mary hadn't stirred, even when Sunni had tripped over something and fallen against the wall. She'd felt around for her candle and managed to light it, before rolling onto the rickety bed, fully clothed. The nightshirt she had been given smelled even worse than her shirt and breeches.

The scratching under her cot started up again, and something small and ratlike darted across the flagstones and out of the light. Sunni leaped across the room and huddled against the locked door.

"What are you doing?" Mary stared at her sideways from under a floppy nightcap.

"Something was scratching under my bed. A mouse," Sunni said gruffly.

Mary rolled over toward the wall and sighed. "Is that all? I would never sleep if I worried about all them creatures living here." Her voice trailed off into steady breathing again.

Sunni lay back down on the bed, her insides churning. *Would Throgmorton really get rid of me? Who was the vanished boy whose clothes Blaise was now wearing?*

She heard a low rolling sound from somewhere outside the house and footsteps in the hall above. Her sharp ears caught the sound of the main door opening and a vague murmur of voices. A herd of feet ascended the stairs and went out of earshot.

When the herd returned, it was anything but quiet. A party of men seemed to half stagger along the floorboards, grunting to one another. The main door was locked behind them, and the rolling sound eventually moved away.

It no longer surprised Sunni that this house was active around the clock. Even the vermin didn't sleep. When the scratching began again, she held the pillow tight, grappling with deeper worries.

At dawn, the boys filed into the kitchen and ate gruel made from water and oatmeal. Blaise, who hated oatmeal, gobbled down two bowls of it and three cups of weak tea fortified with sugar.

No one spoke. Gus, Samuel, Robert, and Jacob barely

ate, and Toby did not even come downstairs. He had insisted on staying to make Will's bed and tidy his clothes away into the trunk underneath it.

There was no sign of Sunni.

Mistress Biggins called Blaise back into the kitchen as he shuffled toward the stairs. She handed him a broomstick and said, "At last we have a tall boy in the workshop. Climb the stairs and get rid of all the cobwebs you see in high places. I shall take a tumble if I try to do it myself, and Mary is useless." She tied a bonnet onto her head, took a basket in hand, and left him to go to market.

Blaise walked past Sunni's room, his head bent under the low ceiling, and tried opening the door. It was locked. An irritated voice came from the other side.

"About time," Sunni said. "Why do I have to wait till all the others have finished eating?"

"Sunni, it's me."

"Blaise! Don't let Throgmorton see you trying to talk to me. He's warned you, too, hasn't he?"

"Yeah. But we've got to make a plan. Now."

"Go on," she said.

"If we don't figure a way out soon, he'll get rid of you. I mean it."

"You're not going to tell him anything about Corvo?"

"No, but I'm not going to let anything happen to you, either." Blaise clenched his fist against the door. "I'll try to buy us some time, but we'll have to work fast to find another way out of this. We've got to try to get help from anybody we can, starting with the servants."

"What if they refuse?"

"Then we might have to run away."

"But the painted door is the only way home, and it's here!"

"I know." He paused for a moment. "Don't ask the boys any more questions. Something horrendous happened last night—"

The floorboards creaked above his head.

"I gotta go." Blaise scurried up to the ground floor and ran straight into Fleet and Sleek.

"Are you off for a ride on that broomstick?" asked Fleet, and Sleek snorted into his hand.

"I'm clearing cobwebs for Mistress Biggins."

"Are you, now?" Fleet stood about two inches taller than Blaise and made a point of looking down his long nose at him.

Sleek snorted again and pointed toward the steps down to the kitchen. "Breakfast."

"Momentarily, Sleek," answered Fleet. "I'm rather curious about you, young sir. Which parish is *you* from?"

Blaise leaned on the broomstick. "I'll tell you if you answer a question from me."

"I admire your approach. It depends upon the question."

"Do you know why three men would carry a sack out of this house in the middle of the night and take it away on a cart?"

"Does we know anything about a sack, Sleek?"

"Nay," said Sleek, clamping a pipe between his teeth.

"Could be anything inside a sack," said Fleet. "Laundry . . . rubbish . . . anything."

Blaise straightened himself up. "What if there was something alive in the sack?" he asked. "The boy called Will disappeared at the same time."

Fleet frowned. "I do not know him. 'Tis nothing to do with us."

"I'm not saying it is. I just want to know where they would take a boy—and why," hissed Blaise.

Sleek chewed on his unlit pipe and nonchalantly strolled up to the parlor door, giving it a soft rap. When no one answered, he opened the door and checked inside. Without a word, he tiptoed to Throgmorton's study door and did the same. After a further swift dance along the hall, glancing at staircases up and down, Sleek nodded to Fleet.

"Well, 'tis only a *guess*, but it could be the sack-'em up men took him down to Smithfield Market," said Fleet in a hushed voice, still looking round. "'Tis convenient for Saint Bart's Hospital."

"What do you mean?"

Fleet leaned close to Blaise's ear. "There's various drinking establishments in Smithfield where a healthy boy might be sold. To anatomists. You get my meaning?"

Blaise's mouth hung open. "I'm not sure . . ."

"Saint Bart's surgeons," Fleet said breathily. "The anatomists. They needs cadavers for experiments. For cutting open to see inside."

Pure horror hit Blaise as if an icy dissection blade had been dragged across his own chest.

All he could utter was "But Will's not dead."

"Yet," said Sleek mournfully.

Blaise sagged and Fleet grabbed hold of his arm to prop him up. "The other boys said he'd been sent to the country."

"Hear that, Sleekie? The *country*—that's a good one," said Fleet. "You listen, young sir. Questions get answers, and answers ain't always what we wish them to be. But we carries on, aiming for the top of the stinking heap, and takes a lesson from the unlucky ones who fall by the wayside."

"Aye," agreed Sleek, one ear cocked for footsteps.

"Will wasn't *unlucky*," said Blaise. "He just told us a bit of information, and now—"

"There's the lesson. Say nothing. Watch and listen."

Blaise took hold of Fleet's free arm. "You've got to help us go back where we belong. We're trapped here against our will."

Fleet peeled Blaise's hand from his sleeve. "That is a rather enormous request. Our employer would not take kindly to it at all."

"You're right. Forget I even asked you."

"Worry not. We keep secrets. 'Tis our stock in trade." Fleet gazed up at the ceiling. "Spiders has been busy in the nooks and crannies. Best get on to them now."

When Sunni was finally released from her locked bedroom, she quickly ate breakfast and climbed upstairs to the top floor. Morning sunlight poured into the Academy of Wonders, but the boys, who had already started work, seemed to be toiling under a dark cloud. At first Sunni could not make out what had changed from the night before, and when she saw the empty table and easel, confusion rolled over her. Who was missing?

She looked around the room and took an inventory of the boys. Will, the boy with bright hazel eyes, was not there. Not sure what to make of this, she moved to her place beside Blaise.

Jeremiah strode into the workshop, puffing from a swift climb up the stairs. His skin was gray and covered with stubble.

"Sunniver," he said briskly, pointing at Will's table. "That is where you will work from now on."

It was as far away from Blaise as could be. *Throgmorton's idea*, she thought.

"Where's Will?" Sunni asked. Blaise gave her a warning glance and went back to his drawing.

Jeremiah squeezed his eyes shut as if in pain. "William has left us to go to the country."

"In the middle of the night?" she persisted.

"That was when his transport departed."

Sunni noticed Blaise shudder at Jeremiah's words. She carried her stack of ink sketches to her new table. It was odd to sit in the absent boy's seat, and the more she sat there, the more unsettled she became. She saw that Toby's chin crumpled every time he glanced at her, and Robert kept wiping his eyes. Worst of all, Blaise would not look at her. It was as if she were not even there.

"Gentlemen," said Jeremiah, finally turning around. "The weather is fine this morning, and we will build a green-wood fire in the back courtyard. Toby, go downstairs and start the blaze."

He dug around under his table. It was piled with old books, folios, broken bits of sculpture, and scrunched-up papers. At last, he found what he was looking for and laid several tattered books on Sunni's desk. When he opened the top one, a reek of mildew made her turn away.

"This book has been unloved for too long," said Jeremiah. "We shall give its pages new life today." He pulled a tiny pocketknife from his waistcoat and, with a quick slice along the book's spine, its blank first page came free in his hand. "Now you attempt it."

Jeremiah had Sunni lean over the book and use her weight to hold it steady. Hesitantly, she drew the blade down the edge of the second page and yanked it out.

The Master nodded his approval. "Now we must make this edge match the other three." He lightly ran the blade up and down the raw cut edge of the paper till it was soft and its corners were rounded. "Now cut as many blank pages as you can from these and prepare their edges."

Jeremiah dropped a pile of books with Blaise and gave him the same lesson. Sunni watched her friend go through the motions, his mouth drooping, and desperately wished she could talk to him.

Throgmorton appeared with Livia at his side. He wore a waistcoat of indigo blue and a wig of deep chestnut, making his cold eyes all the more disconcerting. Livia's moss-green dress was embroidered with leaves, and diamonds sparkled from her earlobes.

"Good morning, Mr. Starling," said Throgmorton.

Sunni thought she heard Jeremiah answer, "Is it?" under his breath, but he returned the greeting with a perfunctory bow before turning back to Blaise.

"Why is that one not yet finished, Mr. Starling?" Throgmorton nodded at Will's copy of the Flemish angel.

"Because, sir, the boy is gone and cannot finish it."

"Then another must do it. Now."

Jeremiah bounded over to where Sunni sat. "These boys have only two hands." He snatched up Will's painting and set it onto his own easel. "I shall finish it myself."

"As you wish," Throgmorton said, moving languidly among the tables and looking over the boys' shoulders. "And as soon as possible, if you please."

Livia swished to Blaise's side and peered at what he was doing, her dazzling smile on show. But it dropped ever so slightly when he kept his head lowered.

Sunni smirked to herself, watching the girl position herself at different angles to catch Blaise's attention but getting nowhere.

"Eyes down and finish your work, Jack Sunniver," said Throgmorton, standing just behind her. He leaned forward and leafed through the papers she had cut from various books.

She scraped the knife along the paper's edge, her lips pressed together hard. When she finished, Throgmorton's hand caught hold of her page and pulled it away. From his waistcoat, he pulled a small shard of red stone, its tip curved into a point, then he rubbed it along the paper's edge. As he did this, he observed Sunni with his hooded eyes.

"How did you sleep, Jack?"

"Fine."

"I am delighted." Without warning, he ran the razor-sharp blade down the middle of the paper and severed it in two.

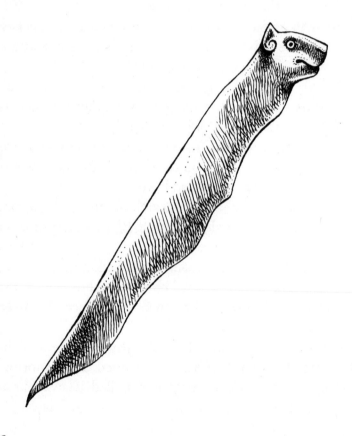

Chapter 10

The walled courtyard was so small that there was barely room for Toby and Sunni, let alone a small fire in an iron brazier. Toby prodded the flames and lifted his face to the sky, drinking in the sunlight. Sunni was struck with the thought that he wouldn't be half bad to look at if he was a little heavier, smelled a bit cleaner, and had teeth that weren't brown.

"Pass me a sheet of your paper." Toby held it in the smoke, letting it become darker and darker before turning it over.

"Why are we doing this?"

"To tint the paper," said Toby. "And make it look old."

"It already is," said Sunni.

"Not old enough. We want this paper to look two hundred years old."

"Then what?"

Toby handed her the perfectly aged paper. "We will copy a picture on it."

"Don't you ever draw anything *you* want to?"

"Copying is the way we learn. We see how a master artist made a drawing and we try to make ours the same. Mr. Starling says this is how artists have always learned."

"I know that. But why do all this extra work to make paper look old?" Sunni asked. "Unless you want to fool people into thinking they're authentic originals from the Renaissance or something. It sounds crooked to me."

Toby tensed and tipped his head toward the window behind her. "Take care. That's *his* study."

"You know what I'm talking about, don't you?"

"No," said Toby, his voice hardening. "You ask too many questions and bring trouble into the workshop."

"I don't want to make trouble. That's the last thing I want. I like all of you."

"It is already too late." He poked the fire and would say nothing further.

When Sunni had finished tinting her loose papers, she laid them carefully inside a leather folio for protection. Toby told her to go back to the workshop and send Blaise down.

She could hear a man's spluttering cough coming from the front parlor, but she dared not listen at the door this time. As she started up the stairs, she was interrupted by a gravelly voice.

"You. With that folio."

Sunni pressed herself against the stairwell wall and turned. A stout, red-faced man in a grand wig had staggered out of the parlor.

"What have you in there?" he called.

She lifted her chin and spoke clearly. "Just papers, sir."

"Let me see." He lurched toward her, bringing the stench of alcohol with him.

Sunni untied the strings and opened the folio, recoiling from his pungent breath.

"Humph." The man waved the folio away. "Who are you?" His voice was slurred.

"I'm one of Mr. Starling's pupils."

"Have you seen Mr. Throgmorton?" The man stamped his foot and then yowled in pain. "I am a busy man, and he's kept me waiting for half an hour. Summoned me saying he has urgent information about two nightsneaks stealing paintings, and then leaves me sitting here."

Sunni's ears pricked up. "I don't know where he is, sir. Should I fetch Mistress Biggins for you?"

"Why would I want anyone called Mistress Biggins? No, boy, you tell Throgmorton he will have to come along to see me himself. I cannot seize the thieves until formalities have been followed." The man paused to expel a wheezing cough. "And certain fees paid. And documents submitted. And so on."

"Yes, sir."

"I shall take my leave then. If Throgmorton wishes to find me, he may visit the Saracen coffeehouse in Leadpurse Lane. Pray tell him Mr. Justice Wright will be at business there."

"I'll tell him, sir," Sunni said, stealthily crossing her fingers.

"Now unlock this door so I may go," grumbled Mr. Justice Wright, hobbling away unsteadily.

But by the time Mr. Justice Wright got to the front door, Sunni had already raced to the next floor, a plan forming in her mind. She ignored his outraged shouts and let Mary scurry up from the kitchen to let him out.

Blaise wished Livia would just go away, but she insisted on watching him dissect the smelly old books. For dissection was what he was doing—and it was what some surgeon was going to do to Will, if he hadn't already. He threw the small knife down in disgust.

Livia touched the back of his hand with one delicate finger. "You look tired."

He shrugged her hand away and began smoothing down the paper edges. "I don't sleep too well when I'm trapped in a place."

"I will see that you get extra food for supper," she whispered.

"Don't bother. I'll have the same as everyone else."

Livia bit her lip and withdrew her hand. As she did, Blaise noticed a red scratch across her palm. "Have I offended you, Blaise?"

Yes, he wanted to shout. *You reported to your slimy father and he got rid of Will. And you act like Throgmorton's doing us a big favor by keeping us here.*

"How do you expect me to act when I can't get out of this house?"

"Can't get out?" Livia looked at him with wide eyes. "I thought you liked me. But you now want to get away from me."

"You don't get it, do you?" said Blaise with an irritated sigh. "It's not all about you."

Sunni burst into the workshop, her face smeared with soot, and emptied her folio.

"Barbecued paper," she announced for Blaise's benefit, holding up a sheet.

Jeremiah examined Sunni's smoked paper. "Excellent. Blaise, carry your paper down to the fire and do the same."

Livia accompanied Blaise downstairs, then flounced into her bedroom and shut the door. He couldn't care less that he had put her lovely nose out of joint. Something ugly lurked below her perfect skin and made her beauty drain away. Even so, Blaise was confused by his own shifting feelings, made worse by exhaustion. His heart had beat like a tom-tom at first, ready to jump out of his chest at the sight of Livia, but now there was no buzz at all, just aversion and distrust.

It was a relief to stand by the fire with Toby in companionable silence, smoking the papers. When Robert joined them with a huge sack of refuse to burn, they took turns feeding rubbish into the brazier and enjoying the smell of smoldering wood in the late-summer air.

Blaise noticed how quiet the surroundings were. No planes or cars, just the sound of passersby and the wheels of an occasional cart. When Toby doused the fire, Blaise felt his heart sink at having to go back inside.

The morning passed into afternoon. Another simple meal and several anemic cups of tea later, Blaise found himself back at his worktable with a large bound album of drawings in front of him.

"Copy one of these on your tinted paper," said Jeremiah, tapping his snuffbox for his after-lunch snort.

"Who drew these, sir?"

"I did."

"What are they copied from?"

"They are not copies. They are originals, done from life." Jeremiah let out a snuff-ridden sneeze.

"Mr. Throgmorton told us you made the paintings in the parlor, too. They're beautiful."

Jeremiah's shoulders slumped. "Beauty means little when there are bills to pay. If I could but spend my days making beautiful paintings, I would be content, but I cannot live on it."

Blaise was heartened by Jeremiah's willingness to talk. "Aren't there people who would buy them?"

"Not enough," said Jeremiah bitterly. "My work is not fashionable, so I must take what I can get." He tossed one of the boys' copies aside, and it landed facedown on the floor. With a sigh, he picked it up and dusted it off.

"Please don't give up, sir," said Blaise in a quiet voice, gazing over at the painted door. "You painted that, too, didn't you?"

"Yes, last year. I decided to attempt mural painting," said Jeremiah, wiping his nose. "Though now I am sorely tempted to hide it with white paint and be done with it."

"No, please don't do that," said Blaise, alarmed at the thought of losing their only way back. "It's an amazing painting. You could paint murals in people's houses and make a living that way."

"More like that hellish door? By heaven, I wish I'd never painted it."

"Then why did you, sir?"

"To make my workshop wall look symmetrical and balanced. It seemed important at the time." Jeremiah frowned. "How wrong I was."

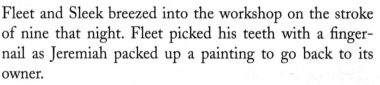

Fleet and Sleek breezed into the workshop on the stroke of nine that night. Fleet picked his teeth with a fingernail as Jeremiah packed up a painting to go back to its owner.

"I never did find out where you was from," Fleet said to Blaise.

"America," Samuel breathed before he could be shushed.

"My word," said Fleet. "There once was a gang of gents who pressed me greatly to join His Majesty's Navy and see the Colonies. But I outran the rogues."

Sleek let out a guffaw.

"Mr. Fleet," said Jeremiah. "If you would be so kind as to take this painting away forthwith." He shoved the package into Fleet's hands.

"Is all well, Mr. Starling?" Fleet inquired. "You seems rather agitated this evening."

"No more than usual, sir."

Sleek doffed his hat and led Fleet out the door.

Sunni's heart was pounding. She could not let the pair get away. "Mr. Starling, I need to—you know."

Jeremiah looked puzzled. "You need what?"

She nodded down at her knees pressed tightly together. "The chamber pot."

"Egad, go on then, Sunniver." The Master turned red with embarrassment.

Sunni leaped away and followed Fleet and Sleek. She caught them on the second-floor landing, where it was dim and deserted. The two phantoms seemed as comfortable in the dark as in the light.

"Mr. Fleet, Mr. Sleek," she said, panting. "Wait."

"Yes?" came Sleek's voice.

"Are we alone here?"

"Does we need to be?" Fleet's voice was low.

"Yes," said Sunni.

"We is alone. Sunniver, ain't it?"

She nodded and tried to catch her breath. "I think you're in danger."

"Is that so? What danger?"

"Throgmorton is going to turn two thieves in to someone called a 'Mr. Justice.' He might have done it already."

Fleet gave a short laugh. "What?"

"Details," said Sleek.

"I'll tell you the whole story, but on one condition. You have to help Blaise and me escape from this house."

Fleet scoffed. "Escape? Is this because of the boy called Will? Throgmorton ain't going to have you killed as well. Not unless you gets too curious about things."

Sunni had stopped listening after the word *killed*. "Will's dead?"

"We has already explained it to the boy Blaise."

"Throgmorton's banned us from speaking to each other." Sunni felt tears brimming. Now she knew what "trouble" Toby was talking about. "We're here because he kidnapped us to get information. He's threatened to get rid of me, too, because he only needs one of us to tell what we know."

Fleet sucked in his breath. "Thereby obliging Blaise to give up information and save your skin."

"Yes," she whispered.

"What information?" asked Sleek.

"It doesn't matter! Don't you want to know what's going to happen to you?" Sunni swallowed back her tears.

"Aye," said Fleet. "May as well hear it."

"Throgmorton's going to name two 'nightsneaks' who steal art. This Mr. Justice is going to arrest you. You're nightsneaks, aren't you? I heard you call yourselves that when you were talking to Mistress Biggins."

"Sharp ear holes," said Sleek.

"Quite. What does you think, Sleekie? Is Sunniver telling the truth? We knows already that he and Blaise is desperate for our help, being here against their will as they claim."

"Details," Sleek repeated knowingly.

"All right," said Sunni. "His name is Mr. Justice Wright, and he's fat, with a huge wig. He limps and stinks of drink. He said Throgmorton should find him at the Saracen coffeehouse in Leadpurse Lane. How's that for details?"

"Majestic." Fleet let out a frustrated groan. "Throggie has squeaked to the Law, such as it is. In our case, that is gout-ridden Wright."

"Will you help us escape?"

The nightsneaks hesitated.

"Are you going to help us or not?" she asked again. "I've told you the truth."

"I believe you. Throggie has sold us out, all right," said Fleet through gritted teeth. "After all we done for him."

"Dog!" said Sleek.

"Something is up, Sleekie. Throggie suddenly wants rid of us. Cleaning his nest of rotten eggs, no doubt, in case a bad smell sticks to him. We must go to ground for a while."

"But you could take him down with what you know," said Sunni.

"Who will the Law believe?" Fleet asked ruefully. "A gentleman like Throggie, with money to buy witnesses, or a pair of rogues such as us?"

He dragged Sleek into a huddle in a corner. After a brief discussion, Fleet said, "We is in your debt for warning us of this treachery, and agree to spring you from the house, Sunniver. We shall see you off in the right direction, but you is on your own after that."

Sunni smiled and caught the glint of their teeth smiling back. "Good."

"Very well, Sunniver. You two has one chance to bolt and it is tonight. Throggie and his daughter are out but shall probably not be for much longer. Sleek and I daren't return here after today. Wright's men will be waiting if they ain't already." He turned to Sleek. "I have half a mind to take the musketeer picture with us, Sleekie, as payment for our troubles."

"Pah!" his companion said.

Fleet burst into laughter. "Aye, better to leave it here. Perhaps Wright shall see it and land Throggie himself in the broth!"

"More likely Jeremiah Starling will be caught with it," said Sunni.

Fleet grew solemn. "Sadly, you is right, Sunniver. Throggie has set it up so that others take the blame. Pray that Starling hides the blasted painting well." Then he slapped Sunni on the shoulder. "What sharp ears you has, Sunniver! Though you bring bad news, you is a lad of hidden talents. Talents that will be useful, no doubt."

Chapter 11

Just before first bedtime, Sunni screwed a scrap of paper into the tightest bullet she could, tidied her table, and took some rubbish to a sack by the workshop door. When she got close enough to Blaise, she launched the tiny note toward him.

She nearly croaked when it bounced off his neck and fell to the floor. But luckily, Blaise had felt it and scooped it up in one unnoticed move of his hand. Years of note-passing at school had made him good at sneaky reading under desks. Within a few moments, he gave Sunni a nod and tore the paper scrap into tiny bits.

She trudged downstairs. All she could do now was pray that Blaise could get himself to the ground floor without alerting anyone. The boys and Jeremiah would be nodding off soon, with any luck. Sunni knew Mary would already be sound asleep, since she didn't have to wait on the Throgmortons that evening, and Mistress Biggins would have left for home.

When Sunni had told the nightsneaks that she hoped they could get into the house, they had just laughed.

"We come and go as we please," said Fleet. "To Miss Livia's annoyance."

When she reached the ground floor, Sunni crept into the front parlor. She pulled back one of the shutters and peeped outside. The lamp over the front door flickered, revealing the dark, empty square. Lamps glowed over the other houses' entrances and in their windows, but few people were about. There was no sign of Throgmorton or his daughter. Sunni had hardly seen more than a glimpse of the outside world till now—and in a short time, she would be in it, for better or worse.

She descended into the subterranean corridor leading to her bedchamber. When she pushed open the door, she was dismayed to see Mary waiting up for her. The maid rolled out of bed and hastily locked the door from the inside, holding the key tight in her fist.

"Mr. Throgmorton's orders," she said. "So you cannot wander about in the early hours."

"It's the mice under the bed," Sunni said. "I can't sleep when they're scratching."

"Hit 'em with your shoe." Mary pulled the chamber pot from under her bed, revealing a dead creature already there.

Sunni recoiled in disgust. "Aren't you going to get rid of that?"

"In the morning."

"But what if you need to go in the night?"

"The creature won't mind. It's dead," mumbled Mary with a shrug, hunkering down under her bedding. "Blow the candle out when you is ready to sleep."

Sunni found her bag and made sure all her belongings were stuffed inside. She wedged it beside her pillow and blew out the candle.

She took a deep breath and asked, "You know the workshop, Mary?"

"I am ordered to stay away from it," came Mary's muffled voice. "Mr. Starling says I would knock something over or trample on a drawing."

"What about Mistress Biggins? Does she ever go up there?"

"Nay, never. She rules the kitchen. Mr. Starling rules the workshop."

Sunni sighed. *So much for the servants knowing anything about the painted door.*

"Good night, Mary," she said, but the maid answered with a snuffling snore.

Sunni lay in the dark, her fingers closed over her bag's strap, and waited for the nightsneaks. Each second seemed like an hour, and as they ticked past, her stomach fluttered. *What if they aren't coming? What if leaving this house is a big mistake?*

Eventually, clicking and rustling came from the keyhole, and after a few agonizing seconds, someone pushed the door open an inch. A single flame crackled into life and illuminated Sleek's face. He nodded once and extinguished the light.

Sunni eased herself out of bed and tiptoed across the room. She followed Sleek upstairs to the back door and into the pitch-black courtyard, where he bundled her into the far corner, away from Throgmorton's study window.

The late-August air was mild, with undertones of autumn, but Sunni shook with nerves.

"Where are Blaise and Mr. Fleet?" she whispered, craning her neck toward the back door.

Sleek held his gloved forefinger to his lips and shook his head.

With a thump and a low curse, Blaise finally tripped out of the back door, and Fleet pushed him unceremoniously toward Sunni and Sleek.

"Go!" he commanded huskily.

Sleek guided the pair through a door set into the high courtyard walls. With several long-legged strides, Fleet followed and locked the outer door behind them.

Sunni glanced up at the top floor of the house to see if anyone was at the boys' window, before Fleet yanked her away. Sleek led them all down a narrow alley that snaked along the back of the fine houses. There was little light, and the path was littered with rubble, decaying food, and something underfoot that squelched like mud but smelled much worse. Sleek moved as if he could see everything before him, dodging small carcasses and broken crockery with ease. Fleet stayed at their heels, ensuring that no one followed them.

Sunni slipped once, and immediately Blaise's warm hand took hers. He said nothing, and neither did she, but she hoped he could feel how happy this made her.

When they were a good distance from Jeremiah's house, Fleet broke his silence.

"That is that, Sleekie. Our business with Throgmorton may be finished, but he will not be finished with us when he learns we has stolen his two golden eggs. By eggs I mean you, Blaise and Sunniver. He will come after you, swift and terrible, as soon as he finds you has left the nest."

Blaise decided that the thing he would remember most about this London was the sour stink of it. The overripe foulness of the streets made him gag, and when a woman emptied a chamber pot from a top window, nearly catching him in its spray, he bent over and retched, much to the nightsneaks' amusement.

Sleek guided them through interwoven back streets without the use of a lantern. He felt his surroundings as he went, touching corners of buildings and counting doorsteps to himself under his breath. When they passed other pedestrians carrying lights, he and Fleet both shied away, lowering the brims of their hats and veering into the shadows till they had passed. Once or twice they had to navigate around people huddled in doorways or the stiff bodies of dead cats.

They moved away from avenues of grand stone houses into a neighborhood of crooked wooden ones, whose upper floors overhung the street, making the uneven paving stones even darker and more treacherous.

At the end of a narrow lane, warm light blazed a welcome. As they neared the glow, Blaise could see Sleek grinning back at Fleet.

"Safe now," he announced.

A tattered wooden sign painted with a green dragon hung outside the house. The windowpanes were opaque with grime, and the door groaned as Sleek opened it.

A haze of tobacco smoke hung under the tavern's low ceiling beams, swirling in accompaniment to a mournful fiddle's drone and many raucous voices. Just visible in the choking mist, heads swung around to take note of who had entered. When these heads recognized Fleet and Sleek, they winked or nodded and went back to their mugs and pipes.

Fleet steered Sunni and Blaise toward a table at the back, half hidden by its tall wooden benches. Before Sleek even sat down, he had his pipe jammed between his teeth and was lighting it with a candle from the table.

"Grub," he said, smiling, when Fleet returned with bowls of pea soup and hunks of rough bread. "Eat."

The landlady brought joints of stringy beef and two tankards of ale for the nightsneaks. They set upon their food like pariah dogs, gnawing and slurping and smoking in between. Neither spoke until they had sat back against the benches, grinning and wiping their mouths on their sleeves.

"This is the Green Dragon," said Fleet. "The safest house in Saint Giles for nightsneaks, lowlifes, and desperadoes like yourselves. No questions asked, no answers offered. You is allowed in under our wings, but any stranger seeking us shall be sniffed out at the threshold and barred from entry. Throggie shall not show his face here."

"Nor Livia," said Sleek.

"By jingo," Fleet exploded. "We is well shot of her."

"Not half," muttered Sunni.

Blaise looked at his empty dishes. "I can't think straight when I'm still hungry."

"You has them long hollow legs, like me. We had better keep you fed then. Jenny!" Fleet waved at the landlady for more food. "Nightsneak work has need of fast feet and clever brains."

"Thanks for helping us," said Blaise. "But why did you change your minds? You told me you couldn't."

"Sunniver learned Throgmorton was about to betray us to the Law," Fleet answered. "We came to an arrangement. One good turn deserves another."

Blaise turned to Sunni. "When did you find that out? While you were down smoking the paper on the fire?"

"Yeah. I'll explain later," she said, eyeing Fleet. "Right now I want to sort out what we do next. You said you'd see us off in the right direction."

Fleet scratched dried food off his chin. "So we shall. But you is weaker than newborn kittens at this moment, with nothing in your purses and a price on your heads, no doubt. These streets shall feed on you and drag you under unless you is taught skills forthwith."

"What skills?" Sunni mopped up soup with a crust of bread.

"Lifting, nimming, snatching."

"Forking, angling," added Sleek.

"Aye, all of that. Robbing, to put it simple," said Fleet, drawing his hand up from under the table. Sunni's sunglasses were dangling in his fingers. He looked at them curiously and perched them on his nose, looking like an eccentric rock musician in vintage clothes.

"How did you get those?" Sunni snatched them off his face and looked around to find her bag open on the bench next to him.

"Skills," said Sleek as he handed her bag back.

"There's other interesting, inexplicable things in your satchel," observed Fleet, a look of wonder on his long face.

"My bag's private," said Sunni, incensed. "Leave it alone."

"Secrets is safe with nightsneaks." Fleet put both hands up. "You has very odd things in there, made of odd materials. You comes from somewhere else, do you not? Somewhere strange."

Blaise swore inwardly. Thieves were the last people he wanted to share their secret with, no matter how trustworthy Fleet claimed they were. But what choice did they have now?

"We're not from this time," he said.

"The odd things ain't old, so you ain't come from the past. Is you by any chance from a future time?"

"Yes," Sunni said grudgingly.

Fleet's eyes practically popped out of his head. "Travelers in time, eh? No wonder Throggie wants to keep hold of you for information. Boys who can tell the future? You could bring down kings and start wars!"

"Aye!" said Sleek, the pipe nearly falling from between his clenched teeth.

"I'd make a terrible fortune-teller," Blaise said. "We didn't learn much about English kings at school. I can't tell one from another, except for King Arthur."

"How did you come here?" Fleet's body was tensed against the table, and Sleek puffed on his pipe, his hands trembling with excitement.

Before Blaise could answer, Sunni said, "Throgmorton lured us through the painted door in the workshop."

For once, Fleet was speechless.

"And we have to go back the same way, but we don't know how."

"Starling?" Sleek asked.

"If he knows anything, he won't admit it. Throgmorton controls him. None of the boys know either." Sunni hung her head. "Maybe Will wouldn't be . . . gone, if I hadn't asked questions."

"You didn't know that would happen," said Blaise.

Fleet finally stopped gaping. "Aye, Blaise is right. Other Academy boys has gone before Will did. And perhaps it was his time anyway, with or without you here."

"Is that supposed to make us feel better," Blaise asked, "knowing that Throgmorton sold Will off to be dissected in a science experiment?"

As soon as he saw Sunni's stricken face, he realized she didn't know *where* Will had gone. He grasped her shoulder and murmured, "Oh, man, I'm sorry."

She shook her head and said to the nightsneaks, "Where's that food?"

An uncomfortable silence fell over the table. When the second helpings arrived, the nightsneaks solemnly gave Sunni and Blaise the lion's share. Blaise sensed they wanted to ask more questions, but they held back.

Fleet cleared his throat and said, "What will you do?"

"Try to find someone who can help us open the painted door and get past Throgmorton."

"No easy thing," said Fleet. "Throggie is crafty, as Sleekie and I know only too well."

"We have no choice," said Sunni.

"You has other things to learn, too, or you shall not last long here."

"Stealing," said Blaise, licking his soup bowl clean with his tongue, as the nightsneaks had done with theirs.

"How else shall you survive? Everyone needs ready money," said Fleet, "to climb to the top of the dung heap."

"I'm not stealing," said Sunni. "We'll find another way."

"When you've found it, enlighten us. Unless you intends to dig ditches or haul muck for a pittance, in which case Sleek and I ain't interested."

Blaise nudged Sunni with one elbow. "Maybe he's right."

"Him up there in heaven will forgive you," said Fleet. "You is only doing it to preserve yourselves—and return where you belongs."

"All right, all right," Sunni said quietly. "Whatever it takes to get home."

"We starts in the depth of night." Fleet threw a few coins on the table and rose. "Jenny will give you a place to lock up your belongings, and then later we goes nightsneaking."

"What is this nightsneaking, anyway?" asked Blaise.

"Hunting," said Sleek, as suave as a tomcat.

"Nightsneaks prowl in the dark, seeking what there is to have and who to have it from. We never takes from those that have little. Sometimes we stays in lanes where only fools dare go. Other times we finds ways into houses, for there is always a way, when backs is turned. A false delivery, a humble inquiry of the servant—then, squeak, in through the door. We knows the good places inside to wait undisturbed. When the house is silent and full of sleepers, we strike. Then it's out quick with the night-soil men hauling the household's dung, or with the laundress come at dawn to take the filthy clothes away."

"No one's ever caught you?"

"Never," said Fleet. "For Sleekie and I was given rather valuable talents when we was born. Eyes sharp as a fox's, ears keen as a dog's, and feet clever as a cat's. We see everything, but nothing sees us. We blend into a mob like phantoms into fog."

Jeremiah Starling awoke to find Throgmorton standing above him with a lantern.

"Egad, man, you shall bore holes into me, staring in that way!" exclaimed Jeremiah, scrambling up to sitting on his makeshift bed in the workshop. "For a moment I thought you were an apparition!"

The lamplight played across Throgmorton's flattened nose, sending odd shadows dancing on his face. "Why are the boys not at work? It is ten minutes past midnight already."

"Another few minutes' sleep shall not harm them. Not after the night they endured and the loss of William from the workshop."

A nerve twitched near Throgmorton's eye. "William is not the only loss."

"What do you mean?"

"Two more beds are empty. Blaise's and Sunniver's."

Jeremiah fell back against the wall. "How is that possible? This house is locked every night."

"I suspect Fleet and Sleek took them."

"What?" said Jeremiah.

"The nightsneaks melt through doors, Starling. No lock is too much for them. You know this."

"We must confront them when they return!"

"They will not be back," said Throgmorton. "I am finished with them. I am shutting the business down, and with it goes all connection to Fleet and Sleek."

"When did you decide this?" Jeremiah's mouth hung open.

"The evening before last. During our after-dinner smoke, my guests repeated a description of the thieves seen stealing the Caradas musketeer painting and the drawing of a Florentine beauty the night before." Throgmorton's lip curled.

"Egad" was all Jeremiah managed to say.

"I passed this rumor on to magistrates this morning," Throgmorton said.

"You informed upon your own men—?"

"They are not my men."

Jeremiah quivered with disbelief. "W-what will become of the Academy? And all the paintings Fleet and Sleek have left here?"

"I have it all in hand, Starling," said Throgmorton. "My mind is now fixed on something more important— apprehending Sunniver and Blaise."

"I cannot fathom why they are so important to you— why you risked bringing them here," said Jeremiah.

"It is none of your business, Starling."

"Not my business? Nothing is ever my business, even though you rely on me to oversee the work that keeps you and your daughter in such fine clothes!" Jeremiah struggled to his feet and faced Throgmorton.

"If it had not been for me, you would not even be under this roof. You would be in debtors' prison, dying a slow, grinding death." The lantern sputtered at Throgmorton's words.

"That would be more honorable than making starving boys forge stolen paintings," sputtered Jeremiah. "And having to pretend they were sent to the country when they vanish." His face flushed dark red. "And having you take ownership of the house my father built with his own hands. I regret the day I painted that infernal door, which allowed you and your daughter to enter from whatever underworld spawned you!"

Throgmorton's sudden blow to Jeremiah's jaw knocked the artist sideways. He tripped backward onto his rough bed and lay there, chest heaving.

Throgmorton rubbed his hand. "So, I have made you dishonorable? When I saw that you were in trouble, I bought your debts and saved your home. All I need to do is sell the debts to someone who is less softhearted than I. Then you and the boys will be thrown out into the street."

Jeremiah whispered, "Your hand of friendship conceals a dagger."

Throgmorton's eyes closed into slits, like a lizard's. "I am going out to hunt for Blaise and Sunniver. If you or any of the boys encounter them, or hear any rumors of them, come to me immediately. A manhunt has already begun for the nightsneaks."

"They will implicate us!" cried Jeremiah, looking with horror at the musketeer painting propped against the wall. "The stolen artworks are in my workshop!"

"Stop fretting," Throgmorton said. "No one will believe what nightsneaks say. I have paid magistrates and 'witnesses' enough to make certain of it. When they are captured, Fleet and Sleek will hang from the gallows at Tyburn."

Chapter 12

The previous owners may be dead and buried for all I knows," Jenny declared, rooting through a pile of lost-and-found clothes at the Green Dragon. "Or floating in the River Thames. Does that put you off, gents?"

"No." Sunni examined the black stockings and three-cornered hats the innkeeper had found for her and Blaise to wear as camouflage when out in the night. "They might still be alive."

"You is an optimist, I see," said Jenny, perching a hat on Blaise's head for size.

Blaise looked like he would say yes to anything at that point. His constant yawning and the violet circles under his eyes convinced the nightsneaks to let their two charges flop out early in the "Nook," as Jenny called the large open room full of snoring travelers and locals sleeping on improvised beds.

"We rise at three," said Fleet. "No later."

The hearth rug smelled of rancid dog fur and whatever had been wiped off the soles of guests' shoes. Sunni put her bag under her head and slept in fits and starts with her back against Blaise's knees. Fear woke her again and again, every time she heard a noise. But even the vandals and burglars around them needed sleep when they were not marauding and made no move from their beds. Fleet and Sleek were stretched out against a wall, their hats pulled down over their faces, completely still.

Sunni could not settle. She shook Blaise gently until he lifted his head to look around.

"Wha . . . ?" he groaned.

"We need to plan," she whispered, turning over and pulling herself close so they were face-to-face. "Now, while everybody's asleep."

"Okay."

"Where are we going to go?"

"To find someone who can help us open the door, if that someone even exists." Blaise touched her wrist. "I didn't tell you. One of the boys said he saw Throgmorton open it by drawing a shape on it. With a stone covered in red stuff from a vial hidden under his shirt."

"What?" She breathed out. "He had a sharpened stone in the workshop. It sliced my paper in two like a knife through butter."

"Was it stained red?"

"Faintly."

"So we've got something to go on," he said. "Sort of. It sounds like he uses some kind of magic."

Sunni sighed. "How do we find a magician?"

"Fleet and Sleek. They already know we've done the impossible and walked through a painted door. We just say we need a magician's help to get home."

"Okay."

The next thing she knew, Blaise was asleep again. She snuggled close and drifted away herself.

When the bells of a distant church tolled three, Fleet nudged them awake. Fully decked out in their new gear of dark hats, coats, breeches, and stockings, Sunni, Blaise, and the nightsneaks left the Green Dragon's dim public rooms, passing the orange embers in the fireplace.

The quartet huddled in a black alley, awaiting the arrival click of heels on paving stones. A rain shower had left a slick of moisture over everything but had cleared away to leave the sky open and full of stars.

"Not much moon tonight," Fleet observed. "But enough starlight to move around well. On a dull night, you must use your hands and ears and nose to pick out the way through the dark."

Sleek hissed for them to be quiet. "A glim."

A lantern wended its way down the lane, held aloft by a boy of about twelve. As he got closer, they saw that he led an unsteady young man in fine clothes.

" 'Tis Smithy," whispered Sleek.

Fleet explained, "Smithy is a link-boy, hired by gents to guide them home with his lantern—we calls 'em glims. At other times, Smithy changes into a moon-curser and lifts valuables from his squires' waistcoats."

"Moon-curser?" Sunni shook her head. "Link-boy?"

"You shall learn, Sunniver. Stay in the shadows and watch. We has decided Smithy will play moon-curser tonight, with the assistance of me and Sleekie."

When Smithy came near the alley, the nightsneaks stepped out and raised their arms in greeting.

"Why, Smith, 'tis a pleasure to see you," said Fleet with a quick wink at the boy, who stopped short and glared at him.

The tipsy young man with him jumped back and exclaimed, "Do not accost us, sir! Be on your way."

"You misunderstand, sir." Fleet put on a serious face and bowed. "We is here to warn our friend of danger. Footpads is nearby, and the night watchman is all up in arms."

"Footpads!" said the young man, weaving back and forth, his eyes rolling in his head.

"Aye. They like nothing better than to bleed innocent young gentlemen of their money, so take care." Fleet stroked his chin thoughtfully. "Shall I demonstrate how they ensnare their victims, so you shall not be caught out?"

"By heaven, would you?" cried the drunk.

Fleet gestured to Sleek, who moved to the young man's side. "One rascal speaks to you, genial and close up, like my friend there. While his crony comes up from the back, like this, and is upon you!" Fleet mimed stabbing movements with an imaginary blade.

"Vile! I am glad you warned me, sirs!" The drunk staggered away from Fleet and his invisible dagger, stumbling into Sleek, who kept him upright. They all had a convivial chuckle.

"Safe home then, sir," said Fleet, saluting the pair and winking again at Smithy. Once the light had dwindled in the distance, Fleet and Sleek danced into the alley.

From his deep pocket Sleek produced an elegant watch and an engraved snuffbox, both glinting in the starlight against his black-gloved hand.

"You picked his pocket while you stood next to him," Blaise said. "Right?"

"Nay, the goods was lifted in the moment he fell against Sleekie," Fleet said. "The man never felt a thing but Sleekie's helping hands, when his valuables was snatched. He thanked us!"

"Smithy didn't look too happy," said Sunni.

"He will when he gets his share later." Fleet glanced around them at the empty lane. "Eyes and ears bright at all times, lads. Or else bigger fish may happen along and see us as dinner."

Sunni shuddered. Fleet was right—she did feel vulnerable in these predatory streets. "I can't do this."

"Me neither," said Blaise.

"But you saw how easily Sleekie nabbed the silverware," said Fleet. "Snatching works well in pairs. When you two is on your own, one can engage the gentleman or lady, while the other plucks the goods from a purse or pocket."

"No," said Sunni. "I've changed my mind."

"We shall take our leave then." Fleet threw his arms up in the air. "Perhaps you shall do better alone."

Sleek pocketed his booty and began to walk away.

"Wait!" Blaise blocked his path. "Sunni, er, Sunniver, are you sure?"

"Yes. Look," she said to the nightsneaks. "All we want you to do is tell us where we'll find a magician. Then we can look after ourselves."

"Magician!" Sleek exclaimed.

"We think Throgmorton must have used some sort of

magic to open the painted door. The only way we can go back to our time is if we find someone who can help us do the same," said Blaise.

"Aye, of course," said Fleet slowly, as if this made all the sense in the world. "Magic." He paused and looked inquiringly at Sleek, who nodded. "We only knows of one place where magicians gather. But there is a problem."

Sunni and Blaise groaned in unison.

"You must pay money to see them. Not much, but you have none. And the first magician you meet may not be the right one, and then you needs more money. And in the wait for the right one, you must eat and lay your heads down."

"I get the point," said Blaise. "Can't you lend us some money?"

"Lend?" Sleek snorted.

"Aye, if we had plenty to spare, but we do not," said Fleet. "Sleekie and I must go to ground, and we needs every shilling."

"Then we're stuck," said Sunni angrily. "We have no choice but to be pickpockets."

Blaise shrugged. "If it's the only way we can get quick money, we'd better just do it."

She kicked at the ground and grumbled, "All right, all right. But how do we get money for the stuff we take?"

"We fences it for you with people we knows and takes a small commission for our trouble." Fleet cocked one ear. "Hear that? It's the watch, and he's coming this way. This is your chance."

A lone, thin voice moved nearer, droning, "Four o'clock,

the sky is clear." A man came into view, walking slowly along the lane, a lantern in one hand and a long pole in the other.

Sleek laughed silently at the sight of him and nudged Fleet.

"Old Slipper, the night watchman. A more easy target you could not wish for." Fleet pushed Blaise toward the corner of the alley. "See how slow he is."

"But he's an old man," Sunni protested.

"Pah! Old Slipper is tough as iron. You cannot injure him," said Fleet. "Go on, which of you shall divert him and which shall do the lifting?"

"I'll do the talking," said Blaise. "Sunniver's got smaller hands than me."

"Thanks a lot," said Sunni.

Fleet nodded. "Good stratagem. Your Colonial way of speech will throw Old Slipper off balance, Blaise."

Sunni started shaking her head. "How am I supposed to take something from him without him feeling it?"

"Diversion," said Sleek.

"Keep his attention on Blaise," added Fleet. "Seek his pocket watch. It will be in his waistcoat or his coat pocket. Ask him the time and you shall see which."

"I don't know."

"Look, if we screw up, just run for it," said Blaise, shifting his weight from one foot to the other, as if he were warming up for a race.

"I don't believe this," Sunni said, her brow furrowed.

"We've got to eat." Blaise readied himself, hat pulled down over his forehead. "Come on."

He yanked her out into open view of the watchman, who was trying to relight a street lamp.

"Sir!" Blaise called, smiling nervously. "Did I hear you call the time?"

Old Slipper turned suspiciously. "Four o'clock and the sky is clear."

"Are you sure? It seems later to me."

The watchman scooped his pocket watch from his coat and squinted at it. "You is right. It is gone one quarter past four."

"Thank you very much," said Blaise. "My friend and I are new in town, from the Colonies, and we don't know our way around."

"The Colonies," the old man said, his eyes round. "Which one?"

"Massachusetts," said Blaise. "Boston." He gestured at the pole. "Can we help you?"

"No, no." Old Slipper lit the end of the pole and aimed its flaming tip toward the wick above them. "Are the Colonies as rough and lawless as they say?"

Sunni moved in behind the watchman and steadied the lower end of the pole for him. Old Slipper looked around at her and shrugged.

"Not Boston, sir," said Blaise, watching intently as Sunni inched closer to the man's back. "Boston is as fine a place as you would ever want to see . . . almost as good as London."

Old Slipper strained upward, leaving his wide pockets vulnerable to incursion. With a deep breath, Sunni dipped her hand in and withdrew the old man's pocket watch.

Horrified at what she had done, she nearly dropped it. When it was safely inside her pocket, she backed away from the man and let go of the pole. Blaise scrambled to her side, and they made for the alley.

"I doubt it is as splendid as London," muttered Old Slipper as he finally managed to light the streetlamp. But there was no answer. He looked around and the two Colonists were gone.

By the time he looked for them down the nearby alley, it was empty, too. The four thieves were already on the hoof to Bandy Lane and the welcoming lights of the Green Dragon.

"By jingo!" said Fleet. "That was well done, boys. Clever brain, Blaise, and clever fingers, Sunniver." He put out one hand. "Let me see the booty."

When Sunni fished the pocket watch out, she could not hand it to Fleet fast enough. It was a sad, dented object. Somehow the sight of it broke Sunni's heart in a way that a brand-new watch would not have.

"Old Slipper might've had that since he was young," she said, her lower lip sagging. "It might have been his father's or grandfather's."

"Or he might have bought it from a pawnbroker for ten shillings. I doubt we shall get much more than that for the thing," said Fleet. "He might even have lifted it himself, off some poor drunk in the street."

Sunni shook her head, rejecting these explanations.

"Or Old Slipper might be King George himself, come down from his palace to light lamps in the night!" Suddenly Fleet took hold of her shoulder and stopped her dead. "We can imagine stories till the sun rises, Sunniver, and find reasons not to do the things that must be done. It don't change the fact that you and Blaise will now have a few shillings to make your way with. And Old Slipper ain't hurt or starving, is he?"

"No."

"At worst he cannot shout out the time all night, for he will not know it till he finds a new watch. And for that, the citizens of these streets heartily thanks you!"

He and Sleek guffawed as they rapped on the Green Dragon's door. A surly watchman let them in with a nod, and as they strolled into the tavern, the other thieves grinned welcome.

"See?" said Fleet, saluting them. "You is one of us now."

Chapter 13

The sun was already high in the sky when Blaise awoke. Someone had covered him with a moth-eaten blanket. It gave off a cloud of dust when he shrugged it aside, revealing Sunni stirring awake by his feet.

Blaise pulled his hat over his face, so no one would talk to him quite yet. The next thing he knew, two hard things bounced off his hat and onto his chest. Jenny was tossing bread rolls into the Nook and cackling at the snoring men in the back.

"No use going out in the day, eh, gents?" The landlady laughed. "You is all far handsomer in the dark."

Sunni was already sitting up, gnawing on a roll. "So do we think this is an improvement on the Academy?"

"At least they let us sleep here." Blaise let out a yawn.

Jenny called to them, "Gentlemen waiting for you downstairs, boys."

The tavern on the ground floor was already heaving with customers and seemed no different from the night before, since the grimy windows let in so little sunlight.

Fleet and Sleek were in discussion with two other men.

"Good day, boys." Fleet pulled two stools up to their table. "Straight to business. Here are Mr. Simpkins and Mr. Jute."

Mr. Simpkins, a sallow man with tufts of hair sprouting from his ears, counted out a selection of coins from a pouch. "Ten shillings for the pocket watch. 'Tis only worth nine, but I gave you an extra shilling as it comes from Old Slipper, which amuses me greatly."

Sleek smiled and moved one silver coin away and into his pocket. "Commission."

"Merely half a crown," Fleet assured Sunni and Blaise. "For our guidance in these matters." He siphoned off some copper coins and made them into a small pile. "This goes to Jenny, for your grub, bed, and clothes."

"Mr. Jute and I," said Simpkins, "will be happy to dispose of your unwanted goods in future, lads."

Blaise brushed the rest of the money off the table and dumped it into a tattered pouch he had discovered in his coat pocket. "Thank you, sir."

The two men left the table after handshakes all around.

"What can we get with this money?' asked Blaise. It didn't look like much.

Fleet smiled. "One shilling buys four suppers, and you has seven shillings left."

"So we won't starve anyway," said Blaise. "But I hope we won't be here long enough to need twenty-eight more suppers."

"Aye, but grub ain't your only expense. You pays for your sleeping places. And other special costs perchance."

"Magicians," said Sunni.

"Good point," said Blaise. "When do we start magician hunting?"

Sleek knocked his pipe against the bench. "After dark."

"I'm glad I don't have to wear these things again," Blaise told Sunni back in the Nook that evening as he threw the filthy white stockings into a corner for someone else to find and use. After a slow afternoon of eating and dozing, he was anxious to get going.

Sunni's face fell, and he knew she was thinking of the boy who'd owned the stockings. "Do you think Throgmorton will punish the boys because we got away?"

"I hope not. Better not to dwell on it," he said, packing his belongings into a worn leather satchel he'd gotten from Jenny. It blended in better than his twenty-first-century messenger bag. "You okay?"

She shrugged. "I don't know. Stealing Old Slipper's watch really got to me."

"Look, I'll do the lifting from now on, so you don't have to. And I know it doesn't make stealing right, but if it looks like we're getting out of this place, we can give all the money to people here that really need it."

Sunni tied her hair back. "Yeah, I guess."

Blaise leaned over to push a stray lock from her face. At that moment, he felt his old feelings for her come rushing back, but two things kept him from acting on them:

the worry that Sunni might push him away—and the fact that everyone around them thought she was a boy.

He pulled back quickly just as Sleek appeared, beckoning for them to come downstairs.

"Who are these magicians you talked about?" Sunni asked when they were seated in the tavern.

"Don't know them to speak to," Fleet said, tearing apart the carcass of a roast chicken. "They works their wonders in demonstrations to the public."

"What are they called?"

"Various names. They comes and goes," said Fleet. "Mysterious gents with unusual ways, often learned in foreign places. Perhaps one will have the knowledge you needs."

Sunni asked a question that had been nagging at her. "How long have you known Throgmorton?"

"More than a year. 'Twas in spring, eh, Sleekie?" Fleet said. "That's when he appeared and the Academy began."

Sleek shrugged and nodded.

"The boys started in spring last year?"

"Aye."

"And you've been working for Throgmorton all that time?"

"Aye."

Blaise gnawed on his chicken drumstick and said, "What's he going to do without you two?"

Fleet thought for a moment. "I suppose he shall find others to 'borrow' the paintings. Sleekie and I has been discussing this of late. Before Throggie informed upon us, we was already feeling a shift in the wind."

Sleek narrowed his eyes. "A chill."

"It *was* a chill wind, Sleekie. As if Throggie's Academy business is winding down. For the last few weeks, we has felt uncertain of the future."

"Did he say anything to make you think that?" Blaise asked.

The nightsneaks snorted and Fleet said, "Nay, why should he? We was but hired hands."

"You know the real reason the boys copy the artworks, don't you?" Sunni asked.

"Nothing to do with us. We borrows 'em and, after a time, we returns 'em to the owners' houses as if they never left."

She sniffed. "I think Throgmorton is selling the copies."

"By heaven," said Sleek, winking at Fleet.

"Imagine," said his companion.

"The boys draw on old paper smoked to make it look older," said Sunni, thinking back to the fire in the courtyard.

The pair offered no further information.

"Where do Throgmorton and Livia come from?" asked Blaise.

"That is a mystery," said Fleet, sipping at his tankard of ale.

Sunni remembered overhearing the nightsneaks' conversation in the kitchen. "They just appeared at Jeremiah's, didn't they?"

"Aye," said Fleet. "Out of thin air, Mistress Biggins said."

Out of thin air, Sunni thought. *Did they arrive through the painted door, too?*

Blaise let out a frustrated laugh. "And they act like they own Jeremiah's house."

"Perhaps they does," said Sleek, loading up his pipe.

"No, I don't think so," said Blaise. "Jeremiah said his father built that house and no one would ever force him out."

No one would force him out, Sunni repeated to herself. But they knew something had forced Jeremiah out. Otherwise he would not have had to build another house to replace it, the one he later filled with his murals.

She remembered the blue plaque on the front of Starling House. It had said something about the house being rebuilt. There might have been a date but, to her annoyance, she couldn't remember it.

Sleek's hand waved in front of her face.

"Are you with us, Sunniver?" Fleet asked. "I was saying, let us hope Starling ain't forced out. He has always been a gentleman to us."

Sunni shook herself back into the present. "Yes, I hope he'll be all right."

"Sleekie, I think we must show them the way to the magicians now," said Fleet, dusting crumbs off his coat.

Blaise grinned and pushed his empty plate away.

"We're ready," Sunni said, hugging her leather satchel.

All the clothes and possessions belonging to her twenty-first-century life were hidden in it.

"Sleekie and I will disappear after we leaves you," answered Fleet. "If we is taken, you will be, too."

"And vicey-versey," added Sleek, patting his hat onto his head.

"Wait. We'll have to get back into Jeremiah's workshop to go through the painted door," said Blaise. "You came and went from his house as if it had no locks at all. How do we get in?"

"Aye, well. Sneak inside when Mary is taking in clean laundry or sending the dirty away with the washerwoman, just before sunrise," said Fleet. "The girl is half-asleep and leaves the door hanging open. Or when Biggins arrives or goes, if you diverts her attention and slips in before she locks up. You is clever enough and shall think of a way."

"What if there isn't a way?" asked Sunni. "They're bound to be on the lookout for us."

Fleet put one hand on her shoulder. "You has had a bit of nightsneak learning. You will find one."

"Aye," agreed Sleek, puffing blue smoke rings toward the Green Dragon's ceiling.

Sunni looked doubtful.

Fleet sighed and began fishing around in his waistcoat. "'Twill cost me dear to get another," he said as he laid a key on the table. "Made by a crooked locksmith known only as Lucifer." He pushed it toward Sunni. "This skeleton key will spring any door in Starling's house."

"Thank you." Blaise put two shillings on the table. "It's probably not enough, but it's all we can spare."

"Special costs," Sunni quoted with a melancholy smile.

"Aye, well . . ." Fleet stared at the coins, then shoved them back at Blaise. "Keeps your money. You shall need every farthing of it."

Rain pelted down upon Bandy Lane, turning it into a sea of rubbish floating along the gutters. A few feeble candles blinked from the upper floors of the houses, but except for the Green Dragon's glow, the lane was dark. None of the residents had bothered to light the lamps above their doors.

Fleet led the way, loping across streaming puddles and kicking dead rats out of their path.

Sunni scanned doors and windows as they went along, unable to shake the feeling that hidden eyes were following them. She kept looking over her shoulder but saw nothing. When they crossed the junction, she looked back one last time, assuming the street would still be deserted. It was not.

The dark shape of a man stood in the gloom. He was still, like an animal sensing prey nearby. Sunni couldn't see his face, but she knew he was watching them.

"Someone's behind us," she hissed to the others.

"Do not run!" said Fleet. "Go swift, but calm. And follow close."

He quickened his pace and made a sharp turn into a back lane. Once they were out of the man's view, he whispered, "Good eyes, Sunniver. It may be something, or it may be nothing. Make haste now, boys."

They moved stealthily from alleys to streets, aiming to outrun the man tailing them. Sunni glanced at every face they passed, looking for inquisitive eyes intent upon tracking them. But the people hurrying past took no interest in anything or anyone except escape from the lashing rain.

The nightsneaks finally pulled Sunni and Blaise into a quiet corner.

"This is as far as we goes. 'Tis no use being seen together," said Fleet. "You carry on through the back streets: next right, second left, and first right again until you comes into Piccadilly. Find the theater at number 24, where magicians conjure wonders for ladies and gentlemen at three pence a ticket."

"Thanks for everything," Sunni said, panting, still watching for the dark figure who had followed them.

"Maybe we'll see you again at the Green Dragon," said Blaise.

"Not if oglers is nearby watching for us—and for you. Best not to return there. Sleekie and I will disappear now."

They shook hands all around and Blaise checked that neither of the nightsneaks had picked his pocket at the same time.

With a grin, Fleet turned away. "To the top of the dung heap, Sleekie."

Sleek raised one black-gloved finger to the brim of his hat before the pair slipped away into the night.

Chapter 14

Sunni and Blaise stood for a few moments, saying nothing.

Then Sunni shivered, her jacket sodden with rainwater. "I know they're thieves and everything, but they did look after us. Now there's no one."

"I know."

"I feel like they've dumped us." Sunni wiped a drip from the end of her nose. "Though I know they didn't."

"But that was the deal. No use crying over it now."

"I'm not crying. It's the stupid rain!" She kicked at a stone, and her wet shoe flew off into a deep puddle.

Blaise turned away, his mouth hidden behind his hand, which made things even worse.

"Stop laughing," Sunni said, outraged.

"Your shoe . . . The way it flew off . . ."

She limped to the puddle and fished out the shoe. Water drained from the inside, and she shoved it back on her foot with a squelching sound.

"Hilarious."

"Sorry." Blaise snorted into his fist. "I can't help it."

"Give me a break. You look as ridiculous as I do."

"I know," he said. "I'm glad no one at home can see us."

"You're glad they can't see your stick-insect legs in tights," said Sunni. "I'm glad they can't smell us."

"Speak for yourself."

"Yeah, I stink. And so does everyone else."

"I'd kill for some toothpaste." Blaise stuck out his tongue and then his serious face returned. "Come on, let's get out of here."

They threaded through the back streets Fleet had directed them to, keeping their hats lowered and satchels safe. Every time someone bumped into them, they hastened away. Just before reaching the dark expanse of Saint James's Park, they turned into Piccadilly and found number 24, which housed a shabby theater.

Blaise looked around. "Is the coast clear?"

"I think so."

A few well-dressed people struggled out of carriages and sedan chairs, adjusting their wigs before entering the theater, but most people were on foot. Sunni and Blaise joined the queue and paid their coins to a man who looked unimpressed with their streaming wet clothes leaking onto the floor. When they stepped into the small theater, another man pointed them toward the cheapest benches.

The room was heady with the smell of humanity, tobacco, and candle wax. No one seemed in a hurry to sit down. Ladies wandered about to speak with one another, and men smoked together in clusters.

"'Monsieur Farlowe's Spectacle, presented by Monsieur Farlowe himself, Celebrated Magician, including Neptune's Grotto, Mister Jollity's High-Wire Walkers, and Madame Morency's Menagerie,'" Sunni read aloud from the playbill. "It says here that Neptune's Grotto presents a tableau of living mermaids, centaurs, and other monsters thought previously to be mythical. This ought to be interesting."

"Sounds like a freak show," Blaise said.

He bought them two small pies, and they jammed them into their mouths, then wiped their fingers on their breeches like the men around them.

There was still a dull chatter of voices as lamps were extinguished and the theater went dim. Torches danced beside a bloodred curtain. At last the audience grew quiet, until there was only a hush of whispers. A small orchestra fired up its violins and horns, sending a strange lullaby soaring into the smoky air.

"Look," whispered Blaise. "There are empty spaces in front. Let's go."

"What if they chuck us out?"

"Nobody's paying attention. Come on!"

They hurried forward, hunched over, and slipped into a block of empty seats. Almost immediately, a young, well-dressed couple slid into the seats in front of them. The man looked right and left and announced to the woman, "I might have known they would be late. We came from farthest away and arrived first."

"Wait, Henry," said the woman. "I see them coming now."

Half a dozen men, chatting and guffawing, descended upon the seats around Sunni and Blaise, crowding them as they leaned backward and forward to talk to each other. They were a motley assortment, from a young man who had the upright look of a soldier to a ruddy-faced one who talked continuously to another who was hawk-nosed and solemn.

"How do you do, Miss Featherstone? A good evening to you, Featherstone." The newcomers' confident voices rang out as they bowed their heads to the lady and then leaned over each other to shake hands with the man she called Henry.

"Monsieur Farlowe promises quite a spectacle," Henry said loudly. "Will this be the night we see real wonders and not the usual trickery? What do you think, Wheatley?"

The gaunt, solemn man next to Sunni said, "Judging by the ludicrousness of his program, I rather doubt this Monsieur Farlowe is the sorcerer he claims to be. I have met enough genuine magicians to know within five minutes whether he is one or not."

Sunni sat up straight and nudged Blaise.

"If he is not," said the ruddy-faced man, "I shall heckle him abominably."

"Oh, Mr. Trevelyan!" Miss Featherstone laughed and shook her head. "You will have us ejected."

A sweating, chubby man appeared in the aisle next to them.

"Good evening, gentlemen." He bowed to Miss Featherstone. "Madam."

"Mr. Smythe, isn't it?" asked Henry. "How do you do?"

"Very well, sir," he said, glancing at the pit, where the orchestra was still wheezing through its prelude to the spectacle. "The program begins in a moment. I hope very much that you gentlemen will refrain from shouting insults at my performers this evening. I ask this every time you attend, but you never oblige me."

"Why, Smythe," said Trevelyan, "if you gave us a quality program, we would be as quiet as church mice. But as you never do, and as we continue to buy tickets anyway, we shall express our opinions as we see fit."

Smythe puffed out his chest. "If you do not enjoy the program, gentlemen, why do you come?"

"We hope a diamond shall one day appear from amongst your lumps of coal," said Henry, smirking. The others laughed, and an animated argument followed between Trevelyan and Smythe.

Sunni leaned in close to Blaise. "Did you hear what the guy next to me said? He's met real magicians."

"Ask him who they are. Go on. What do we have to lose?"

Sunni steeled herself to face the solemn Mr. Wheatley. "Sir?"

Wheatley turned and scrutinized her. "Yes?"

She nearly faltered but forced herself to speak. "I didn't mean to listen, but . . . you've met genuine magicians?"

Wheatley peered even harder at her and then at Blaise. "What is it to you?"

"My friend and I need to find one," Sunni said. "It's a matter of life and death."

Miss Featherstone turned her ear toward them, listening discreetly.

"I see." Wheatley's eyes never left Sunni's. "What sort of life-and-death matter is it? A sick relative you wish to be cured, a treasure you wish to find, or someone you wish to lay a curse upon? Those are the usual problems for which ordinary persons seek magicians."

"N-no, sir, nothing like that."

Miss Featherstone turned all the way around, watching with curiosity.

"What then?" asked Wheatley.

Sunni's mind went blank. All she could see was doubt in the man's eyes.

Blaise leaned across her and said in a hushed tone, "If we don't find a real magician, we'll stay trapped here. Forever."

Wheatley did not flinch at this, nor did he laugh out loud. "Explain."

"We were kidnapped and brought here," said Blaise. "The man who lured us here will kill us if he finds us."

Wheatley exchanged an incredulous look with Miss Featherstone just as the orchestra finished playing.

"It's the truth," said Sunni, putting her hand on her heart.

The man squinted down at her. "You have my attention. We will speak further in the interval."

Sunni nodded, a flicker of hope rising inside her.

A weedy man in a tall wig and an ostentatious coat appeared from behind the curtain and bowed to sporadic applause. At the sight of him, Smythe hurried away and the gentlemen settled into their seats. Miss Featherstone reluctantly turned to face the stage.

"I am Monsieur *Farlowe*," the weedy man announced, his arms outspread and chin lifted as though he were about to burst into song. "I bid you welcome to the most astonishing spectacle seen in London for many a year. What you shall witness has thrilled the crown heads of Europe and enthralled men of learning. I, and I alone, have succeeded in convincing such elusive beings as mermaids and centaurs to travel the world with me and prove to you that they *exist*! By nature these beings are of a sensitive disposition, and I ask that audience members refrain from approaching them, shouting, or throwing objects to catch their attention. Thank you. And now, I present to you, dear ladies and gentlemen, *Neptune's Grotto*."

As Monsieur Farlowe vanished behind the curtain, the eerie music began again. Slowly the sea of red fabric parted to reveal a jeweled undersea grotto. The audience gasped at a fish-tailed woman reclining on a large scallop-shell seat, admiring herself in a mirror. A huge squidlike creature rolled past above her head, against a backdrop of billowing cloth meant to look like water.

Trevelyan laughed out loud, and his companions tittered.

"This is totally fake," Sunni whispered to Blaise. "You can see the wire holding up that squid—if that's what it's supposed to be."

"Wait, who's that?" Blaise pointed at a centaur strolling in and catching sight of the mermaid. "Hey, it's love at first sight between a mythical land creature and a mythical sea creature. Will it work out? Can he hold his breath long enough underwater?"

Henry and his companions suppressed laughter at the

centaur's rear legs dragging behind him as he walked — and so did Sunni. Their merriment made her feel lighter than she had in some time.

The centaur mimed a profession of true love to the mermaid, and dancing starfish dropped from above.

"This passes for magic?" Blaise sniggered as a jealous-looking merman was lowered to the stage on the back of Pegasus the flying horse, and the dancing starfish vanished back into the rafters. "Oh, this gets better and better."

"People are lapping it up," said Sunni, looking around them. "I can't believe they think any of this is for real. It's a farce."

"And Monsieur Farlowe is more like a ringmaster than a magician."

From the corner of her eye, Sunni caught sight of two thuggish men walking slowly around the far side of the theater, studying each row with grim expressions.

Onstage, the merman squared up to the centaur, jabbing his finger into his adversary's chest.

"Oh, wow, merman versus horse-man!" Blaise laughed out loud, not caring now, since no one else was quiet.

Suddenly someone threw a half-eaten pie at the merman, and Trevelyan shouted, "Let the centaur have her!"

A second gruff voice yelled, "No! Fight, fight!"

Another pie flew toward the mermaid. The centaur dragged himself and his lame hind legs to center stage, where he shouted, "Please desist! We centaurs are sensitive creatures!"

"You are no more a centaur than I!" called Trevelyan. A projectile hit the centaur square in the forehead.

Sunni couldn't take her eyes from the two men searching the benches. But when a third man appeared, strolling purposefully into the theater, and nodding toward one of the men, she froze. *Throgmorton.*

"Blaise." She clutched Blaise's arm. "Throgmorton! He's at the exit."

"Oh, man, no! Sneak toward the stage. Maybe there's another way out at the back!"

Sunni stumbled toward the aisle, getting tangled up in Wheatley's legs.

"What game is this?" he declared as she fell onto Trevelyan.

"Those men—that man—he'll kill us. We have to get out."

Trevelyan pulled her to standing, and Blaise pushed her into the aisle.

"He's seen us," he hissed into her ear. "They've split up. They're coming at us from all sides!"

As more pies and balled-up playbills sailed through the air, Sunni and Blaise scurried toward the orchestra pit, where the musicians were trying to play calming music. They had to climb over people and instruments, knocking off wigs and getting hit by missiles themselves. The music groaned to a halt as the crowd roared its approval.

Sunni scrambled onto the stage, with Blaise right behind her. She studied the audience, trying to locate their three adversaries, but all she could see were flying objects and a mass of bodies intending to join her stage invasion.

"Halt!" Monsieur Farlowe's voice boomed just before a laughing young man took him down. Someone else ripped off the centaur's false hind legs and threw them to the mob.

Blaise exclaimed, "Sunni, there!"

Throgmorton was about to pull himself onto the stage, his eyes riveted on them.

"You will not escape me again!" he seethed.

The mermaid tore off her own tail and ran backstage bare-legged, with the merman hobbling after her, his tail still wrapped around one leg. Hooting boys tore down the aqua backdrop and threw it over the musicians in the orchestra pit. Just as the fabric covered Throgmorton, Sunni scooped up a dancing starfish that had fallen down, its wire snapped.

Her heart thundering, she swung the plaster star backward. Then, with a mighty lunge forward, she brought it down on Throgmorton's head. The star shattered over him and he slumped under a wave of blue-green cloth, but it stunned him only briefly. He pushed out from under the cloth and elbowed his way after them, nodding at someone else onstage. Even when the giant squid crashed down onto Neptune's Grotto, crushing Pegasus and sending a hailstorm of plaster shards over the crowd, the man never blinked. His sights were locked onto Sunni and Blaise.

They bolted toward the other side of the stage.

"Jump off," Blaise panted. "Make for the exit."

Sunni sized up the sea of shouting people below the stage, but she had no chance to do anything. A rough sack came down over her, catching her like a butterfly in a net. Shrieking, she tried to twist and break away, but her captor's hands were too strong. Kicking didn't work. Her damp shoes flew off in seconds.

Throgmorton's voice hissed close to her ear. "You are finished, Jack Sunniver."

Her captor began dragging her but did not get far before something hit him hard. He grunted and fell away, releasing her. Feet kicked and tripped over her as Sunni lay on the ground amid a scuffle. She managed to roll away, her leather satchel digging into her side, and tore at the sack.

Just as she was finally about to extricate herself from it, a low voice commanded, "Keep this on. I promise you will be safe," and tugged it back down. Someone lifted her and hastily carried her away. Cool air on her legs told her she was moving out of the stifling theater, and the sounds of the human clash faded into the clatter of horses and carts.

Sunni was handed through a narrow door and onto a hard seat. Something else was dragged in and touched her feet. It was solid but soft at the same time — like flesh and blood.

A man slammed the door shut, shouting, "Away now, Rowley!"

They rolled forward to the sound of a whip on horses' backs. Hands began pulling the sack off her, and she strained away from them.

"You're all right, lad. You're safe," insisted a soothing voice. When the sack was removed, she saw it belonged to Henry Featherstone's friend, the one with the soldier-like bearing. He collapsed into the opposite seat, the sack across his knees like the captured flag of a vanquished enemy. His hair was a tangled mess and one sleeve was torn open at the shoulder, but he grinned at her. "I shall not make you wear this any longer."

"Thank heaven you are not seriously injured, Mr. Martingale." Miss Featherstone was next to him on the carriage seat, her face pinched with concern. "But what about this boy, Brother?"

A bruised Henry Featherstone crouched on the carriage floor. Blaise lay beside him, white as a bone and bloodied. "He took a heavy blow, but he is alive."

Sunni lowered herself to the floor and found a space to kneel next to her friend, her hands shaking. She took the sack from her rescuer and arranged it under Blaise's head, protecting him somewhat from the carriage's rattling lurches. Laying her hand on his chest, she waited for the reassuring thump of his heart and nearly broke down with relief when she felt it.

"Our doctor will see to your friend," Henry said. "We are taking you to safety in our home. There was no time to ask whether this was to your liking. Your pursuers were about to carry you off."

"W-who are you?" Sunni could not stop her voice from quaking.

"I am Henry Featherstone, and the lady is my sister, Miss Amelia Featherstone. That gentleman is Mr. Martingale. Rest easy—we mean you no harm."

"Why did you take us? We're nothing to you."

"I do not usually rescue runaways," said Henry. "There is often a good reason they are being chased. But my sister convinced me otherwise."

"I heard what you told Mr. Wheatley. He took you seriously, and he does not do that lightly," said Amelia. "Do not disappoint me by telling me it was a lie to gain his sympathy."

"It was no lie, miss."

"We shall determine that later," said Henry, heaving himself up onto a seat. The carriage jolted over uneven ground, and he let out a cry. Martingale laughed but had to press one hand to his own sore ribs.

"So you were not left unscathed either. I am disappointed, Martingale. You did not fight them all off with one hand," said Henry. He looked down at Sunni. "What is your name?"

"Sunniver, sir. My friend is Blaise."

"Well, Sunniver, you attracted much attention. A large brute attempted to carry you away. Another went at your friend, but there were enough of us to fight them off and spirit you both away. 'Twas far more entertaining than Neptune's ridiculous grotto."

"There was a third man after us, one who looked more like a gentlemen," Sunni said in a small voice. "I heard his voice in my ear."

Henry frowned as he tried to remember.

Sunni's heart sank. "He was there. I hit him with a star."

"I saw that," said Martingale. "He was briefly in the fray but disappeared."

"He's the leader. The others take orders from him."

"The man you called Throgmorton?" asked Amelia.

"Yes."

"He must want you badly if he attempts to snatch you under the public's nose. I hope we have done the right thing," said Henry, rubbing a smear of dried blood off his hand with a handkerchief. "If you do turn out to be criminals—"

"We aren't criminals. Throgmorton is." Sunni shivered. "He may only be one step behind us."

Henry leaned out of his window and shouted, "Anyone following, Rowley?"

The driver called no.

"You see? No one. You are safe with us. I expect you will sniff us out to see whether you can trust us. We shall do the same."

Sunni's head was reeling. *Say nothing more.* She held Blaise's arm tight and watched for a sign that he was waking.

The carriage bumped and rolled through dark country where few lights appeared. At last, they turned into a long drive, past an imposing gate of wrought iron and stone. Winding through groves of swaying trees, the carriage approached a large mansion. It was silhouetted ebony against a sky full of cloud and rain, with four imposing chimneys rising above the roof like sentinels. A few windows glowed with dim lights.

Sunni gazed down at Blaise's face, just visible in the darkness and as still as a marble statue.

Where are we, Blaise? What are they going to do with us? Sunni touched his chilly forehead with her fingertips. *Please, please, you've got to wake up.*

Chapter 15

A footman, holding a lantern aloft and squinting into the darkness outside, appeared at the mansion's front door.

Rain lashed the roof of the carriage as it came to a halt.

"Good heavens, Hodge," Henry shouted out the window. "Give us a hand here, man."

The footman gaped and rushed to the carriage door. "I am sorry, sir. I could not tell . . ."

"Who else would it be? Help carry this boy inside. And why are more candles not lit? The place is black as Hades."

"I am sorry, sir."

Henry handed the lantern to Sunni, and she led them as quickly as she could in her shoeless feet. The three men hauled Blaise up the front steps into a wide entrance hall flanked by two ornate stairways right and left. The lantern picked out a polished floor and a door in the back wall. It also highlighted alcoves high in the walls, where stark white busts of men stared out from the shadows.

Two younger footmen burst through the far door, half bowing to Henry and Amelia.

"Bring him to the Red Room," Amelia said, and the servants gingerly carried Blaise upstairs. "And get these boys clean nightshirts. Use Mr. Featherstone's if you can find no others."

As they laid Blaise down on the bed, Amelia bustled away, issuing instructions to a crowd of servants gathering in a gloomy corridor.

Blaise's face was pale against the crimson bedcover. Henry was attempting to revive him with a cold compress held to his forehead. One of the footmen lit candles on a stand, flooding the room with warm light, and a maid brought in a tray of tea.

"The boy has taken several good knocks," said Henry. "He's as chilly as a corpse. Hodge, light the fire, will you?"

The word *corpse* made Sunni feel sick. "Can't you get a doctor, sir?"

"My sister shall send for him forthwith, but it will take time for the man to arrive."

Sunni bathed the bloody graze on the side of Blaise's head and refused the hot tea offered to her. The maid whispered something to Amelia as she entered the Red Room with a clean nightshirt and a set of Henry's old breeches and shirt.

"That boy's wet clothes must be removed immediately. The bedding will be soaked, Brother. Did you not think of that?" she said fiercely.

"No, I admit I did not." Henry eased himself into a chair next to Martingale, who was massaging his ribs.

"You are no better, making those chairs filthy. Off with you both, and I'll send the footmen to help you presently. Mr. Martingale, you shall sleep in the Blue Room."

"Sister, after what we have been through tonight, a filthy

seat is the least of our concerns," said her brother. He and his friend limped into the corridor, asking a passing servant to bring them something stronger than tea.

The footmen pulled off Blaise's coat and threw it into a heap on the floor. Their money purse fell out with a faint clink.

"Your friend is in good hands now." Amelia turned to Sunni. "Go with Anne. They are drawing a bath for you."

But Sunni could not take her eyes from Blaise as his shirt was peeled off. The footman began to undo the boy's trousers, and Sunni felt herself go red. Part of her was tempted to look, and the other part wanted to run away.

"Your clothes will need laundering as well," said Amelia. "Anne will find a clean shirt and breeches while you are in the bath."

"I—I'm not a boy," Sunni whispered, finally averting her eyes. "I was forced to dress like this."

At first Amelia peered at her, then she glanced over her shoulder at Blaise. Pursing her lips, she steered Sunni toward the door. "Go," she said. "You will explain yourself, but not here."

Blaise was caught in a tempest of swirling lights and shadows. He tried to climb out of it and get to the surface, wherever that was, but the higher he climbed, the more frustrated he grew. There seemed to be no end to the fragments of color and snatches of conversation flowing around him, no matter how hard he tried to get away from them. It felt for some time as if the chaos would suck him in for good, when suddenly he began to fly upward, passing all the mayhem and leaving the murmuring voices behind.

He broke through the surface with a loud gasp. His eyes rolled around, trying to take in his surroundings, but nothing was familiar. Everything was red, like the color of the pounding pain in his head, but soft. He was lying in a bed fit for a king, hung with draperies from a canopy on four posts. A low fire glowed, and many candles threw shadows on the walls.

The last thing Blaise remembered was being dragged roughly over the stage floor, broken plaster spiking his cheek and scalp.

A strange man in a chair by the bed came awake with a snort. "Ah, you are with us then, are you?" He leaned over Blaise, pulling down his lower eyelids and prodding a bandage tied around his head. "Very well, my labors here are at an end. Do not exert yourself, and you will soon be fit again."

"Wait! Who are you?"

"Dr. Loftus. I shall alert your hosts that you are awake. Good evening to you."

The man packed an array of tiny vials and instruments into a bag and hurried off. A woman in a dark dress and shawl swept in and laid one hand on his brow. He vaguely recognized her from somewhere.

Blaise tried to talk, but only croaks came out. She shook her head with a smile.

"Do not speak." The lady propped him up and poured

some cold sweet tea into his mouth. Just lifting his head that much nearly did him in, and he dropped back to the pillow with relief. She pulled a chamber pot from under his bed and said, "Do you have need of this?"

He turned his head away in embarrassment and managed to say, "No, thank you."

"You are safe here." She snuffed out most of the candles and checked the state of the fire's embers before picking up the last lit candle and moving toward the door. "Sleep now."

He raised one arm and called, "Who are you?"

"Miss Featherstone. All will be explained."

"Where's my friend?"

"She is asleep. You will see her in the morning."

"M-my bag . . ."

Amelia pointed to a chair. The satchel Blaise had bought from Jenny was propped up against one leg. Their money pouch sat on a small table nearby.

"Sleep now," she said, and glided out the door, taking the light with her.

Where are we? Blaise lay in the blackness for some time, feeling his bandage and going over what had happened at Neptune's Grotto. He was okay, sort of. Sunni was okay, apparently. *That lady knows she's a girl.*

He knew he shouldn't get up, but he couldn't help it. He inched his way across the mattress and swung his legs over. Realizing he was wearing a nightshirt that made him look like Ebenezer Scrooge, he started to laugh, but it made his head hurt too much.

Blaise felt his way to the chair and picked up the

satchel, noting with a jolt of alarm that it was unbuckled. The earthy, smoky smell of it took him straight back to the Green Dragon. Anxiously, he fished around for the familiar shape of his own messenger bag and sandals mashed down to the bottom, and the soft jersey of his T-shirt and cut-off shorts. There was his phone, too, and a collection of London museum leaflets, pencil stubs, pens, and a pack of gum. At last he touched his sketchbook, flat against the back of the satchel, and heaved a sigh of relief.

He moved toward where he had seen the candles and stumbled into something, sending it and everything on it tumbling. A blinding pain shot through Blaise's ear, and he had to steady himself against what he guessed was an overturned table.

The Red Room's door creaked open and revealed Sunni in a white nightgown and shawl, holding a candle. "*What* are you doing?"

"Trying to get this." Blaise held up the sketchbook. "Bring that candle over so I can look at it."

"Are you crazy?" She quietly closed the door behind her and bustled to his side. "Your head . . ."

"Where are we?" he interrupted. "Who are these people?"

"We were sitting with them in the theater, remember? Two of them are a brother and sister, Henry and Amelia Featherstone, and this is their house, outside the city somewhere. The other guy's called Martingale. They got us away from Throgmorton and his thugs."

"The people in front of that guy we talked to? The one who said he'd met real magicians?"

"Yes," she answered. "You don't look too good."

"Thanks a lot. My head's splitting, but other than that, I'm okay. What about you?"

"Fine. I got off lightly." She shone her candle over the mess of objects on the floor. "Just leave this till the morning. You've got to rest and get better."

He held the satchel to his chest and nodded.

"I like your nightgown." Sunni smirked.

Blaise dived back into bed. It seemed like the least embarrassing option.

She grinned and padded to the bed, setting her candle down on the bedside table. "Is your sketchbook okay?"

He hastily leafed through it. "Seems to be. Throgmorton didn't get hold of it, anyway."

"Wouldn't it be useless to him without you there to explain your sketches? After all, he could have taken it from you before." Sunni perched near him on the edge of the bed.

"I suppose. But just in case," Blaise answered slowly. He dropped back against the pillows. "So these Featherstones rescued us. Why? They don't know us."

"I think it was because of the guy we talked to. Amelia told me he'd taken our story seriously."

"But can we trust them?"

"I don't know. My instinct says they're honest," said Sunni.

"My instinct was to follow Throgmorton through the painted door, and look where it got us."

"Stop beating yourself up," Sunni chided him. "I went into the labyrinth after Dean, and look where *that* got us."

"We got ourselves out of that situation. I don't know about this one," he said.

"Stop it, Blaise."

A stabbing ache made him cringe. "S-so they know you're a girl."

"Yeah, I told Amelia. They were about to throw me in the bath, so it would have been hard to keep under wraps."

"Any reaction?"

"Shocked. And I think she was intrigued, too. I gave her only the basics about why I was dressed as a boy, but we'll have a lot more explaining to do in the morning."

"We've got to keep Fausto Corvo out of this," said Blaise.

"I know. It's complicated enough without him."

He pulled himself up higher against the pillow. "Did you see what happened to me in the theater?"

"No, I spent almost the whole time with my head in a sack," Sunni answered.

"The sack-'em-up men," Blaise whispered.

"What?"

"That's how they took Will away—in a sack."

Sunni shuddered. "The last thing I saw was Throgmorton coming for us. Just as I was about to jump off the stage, one of his cronies caught me."

"Me, too. I wonder if they'll figure out we're here."

"No idea."

They sat quiet for a moment, and then she asked, "You're going to be all right, aren't you?"

"Some doctor looked me over. He said I'll live."

"He didn't want to put leeches on you, did he?" She grimaced. "Isn't that what they did in this century?"

"Yup, he's coming back with a giant jar of them in the morning."

"What?"

Blaise snorted. "I'm only kidding. I'll be fine once this headache goes away."

She shook her head and smiled.

"You look nice," he said sheepishly.

"Thanks, I scrub up all right. And it's nice to have my boy corset off. It was starting to itch something wicked."

"Your boy corset?"

"Material wrapped around my chest to make me look flatter."

Blaise raised his eyebrows. "Oh. Right."

"Oops, too much information." Sunni stood up. "Look, you'd better get some sleep. We have to be ready for questions tomorrow."

"Yeah."

"See you in the morning." She took the candle and quickly tiptoed from the room.

Late the next morning, Sunni followed the maidservant, Anne, along the corridor, half wishing she'd kept her mouth shut and let everyone think she was a boy. Her torso was laced into a corset Amelia called "stays," and the hoops under her skirt made her feel as if she were wearing a balloon she had to steer around furniture and people. Her leather satchel was slung across her chest, and she held it close; she knew it looked odd with the flouncy dress, but she was determined to keep her belongings with her at all times, no matter where she went.

"Where is my friend?" Sunni asked.

"The footmen have carried him down already. The master and mistress are waiting for you. This way."

The maidservant led her down staircases and across halls, winding through the enormous house with its seemingly countless doors and elaborately decorated ceilings.

At last Anne stopped before a tall door and knocked. She showed Sunni into a gloomy library crammed with books, urns, and statues that looked as if they could have come from Rome or Egypt. Henry Featherstone sat solemnly in an imposing wingback chair with several stone heads on plinths behind him. The group of gentlemen they had sat beside at the theater, and Amelia, were seated in high-backed chairs next to small tables bearing floral teacups, saucers, and a large teapot.

None of the gentlemen showed any of the boisterous camaraderie from the night before. They sat like a panel of judges, silent, with inquisitive eyes.

Blaise was among them, looking pale, his leather satchel by his feet. He gave her a wary nod, and Sunni's stomach clenched with nerves.

"That will be all, Anne." Henry Featherstone dismissed the servant and directed Sunni toward an empty chair beside Blaise. "Good morning, Sunniver—I should say, rather, *Miss* Sunniver. We trust you slept well."

"Yes, thank you." But Sunni remained standing, just out of reach, her mouth suddenly dry. "What are you going to do with us?"

"What shall we do with you?" Henry folded his hands together and looked at the other gentlemen. "We shall listen to your tale with open minds, though I must say you are off to a questionable start. You might have a good reason for disguising yourself as a boy, and I would like to know it. But if you turn out to be lying scallywags, we will thrust you so quickly into the arms of the Law that it will make your heads spin."

Chapter 16

"I—I was forced to dress as a boy so I would not stand out," said Sunni, holding the strap of her satchel tight.

"Stand out from whom?" asked Martingale.

Blaise hated seeing her squirm, so he spoke up. "From the other boys. In the place where we were kept."

"I cannot abide guessing games," said another man. "Explain properly."

"If we're going to explain everything, we'd like to know who you all are first," said Blaise.

Henry stood up and tugged his waistcoat down. "A fair request, I suppose. I am a man of business, and I run this estate. These gentlemen and I call ourselves the Pell Mell Supper Club. We meet for conversation and amusement over dinner, as we have done since our university days. With the exception of my sister, of course, who only happened to accompany me to Smythe's theater yesterday evening." He gestured toward each man in turn. "That gentleman is Mr. Trevelyan, a poet; Mr. Martingale, whom you have already met, is an architect; Mr. Wheatley is a natural philosopher."

He introduced the remaining gentlemen, but Blaise only half listened after Wheatley's introduction. *Is he going to help us find a magician who can get us home?*

Martingale spoke up. "Featherstone, I believe you have neglected to introduce one person."

"But I have introduced all the members of the club." Henry caught sight of his sister's irritated face. "Ah, yes. I could not run the estate without my dear sister, whom you have already met. She manages the house admirably, does very well at music, watercolor painting, and stitchery. And she reads a lot." He turned to his friends with a wink. "But, gentlemen, do not hold that against her!"

"Indeed we do not. Miss Featherstone is a lady of great intelligence," said Martingale.

Blushing furiously, Amelia said, "Sunniva, please sit down."

Sunni slid into the seat beside her friend, trying to smooth down her skirts.

"Are you all right?" she whispered to Blaise.

"Sort of," he murmured, holding his sore head.

"So, Miss Sunniva, formerly known as Master Sunniver," said Trevelyan. "I place your speech as Scots, but I cannot place your companion's."

"Colonial," said Blaise, girding himself for questions. "Massachusetts."

"Oh ho, how came you to be—?"

"Sir, it's a long story and has nothing to do with why we're here."

"Pah!" exclaimed Trevelyan. "I do not see how . . ."

"Gentlemen, let us call the Pell Mell Supper Club to order." Henry pressed his hands together. "We should question these two in a logical fashion. But first, I must say I am glad to see you all survived last night's fracas."

Blaise noticed that each of the gentlemen bore scratches and bruises.

A man the others called Catterwall, with piercing eyes, said, "Perhaps we should commend ourselves to the king. He may have use of us in his next campaign against the French. We saved these two urchins—bravo. But who is to say those men were not pursuing them for a good reason?"

"Hear, hear. We deserve an explanation as to why we were obliged to rescue them," said Trevelyan. He glared at Blaise, who shrank back into his chair.

"You seemed to enjoy the melee, Trevelyan," said Martingale. "I certainly did."

Trevelyan shrugged. "I admit it was the best entertainment I have ever experienced at Smythe's theater. But that is beside the point. I still want a justification for our involvement."

Wheatley leaned forward. "You may blame me if this escapade turns out to be a foolhardy venture," he said in a solemn voice.

"And I begged my brother to intervene," Amelia added, looking a bit nervous. "I will also take the blame if they fabricated their story."

"Well, let us have the answers from their own lips," said Henry.

Blaise blurted out, "Are we on trial here?"

"In a way," said Wheatley. "You made an extraordinary request of me last evening—to help you find a magician as a matter of life and death. Now one of you has turned from a boy to a girl overnight and things grow more murky than clear. I want an explanation."

The gentlemen of the Pell Mell Supper Club murmured agreement.

"What I told you last night was true," said Blaise, sitting taller, though it made his head ache more.

"That you were kidnapped," Amelia prompted him.

"Yes, ma'am, by a man called Throgmorton."

Sunni added, "He had trapped us, but we escaped."

"Why did he kidnap you?" asked Martingale.

"To make us slaves in his Academy," said Blaise.

Catterwall and Trevelyan shook their heads.

"This man kidnapped a Colonial lad and a Scottish girl to enslave them?" asked Henry, puffing out his cheeks. "Where did this supposed abduction take place?"

"We'll tell you everything if you promise to help us find a true magician," Sunni said stoutly. "Because if you can't, we need to move on and keep searching."

Trevelyan harrumphed. "Are you giving us an ultimatum?"

"Yes, sir," said Blaise. "We have no choice."

"You speak plainly," said Henry.

"We're in a hard situation, sir, with nowhere to turn."

"And how in the world would a magician assist you?"

Sunni stole a glance at Wheatley. "We hope a magician will know how to open up the way back to our home."

"Open up the way?" Henry repeated. "You make no sense."

Blaise took a deep breath. "Throgmorton came to our century and lured us into this time. We don't belong in 1752."

A grumble of disbelief erupted from around the library.

"Pah!" Trevelyan scoffed. "Slaves brought from another century? Very far-fetched, I say."

"Agreed," said Wheatley. "And how did a mortal man cross centuries, pray tell?"

"That's what we need a magician to work out," said Blaise.

Sunni added carefully, "Throgmorton told us that this moment in time is separated from the past and the future only by a kind of invisible barrier. We don't know how, but Throgmorton opened a hole in the barrier and we walked through it."

Trevelyan's expression softened as he thought about this, while Wheatley's grew more intense.

"Ether," he said. "When you say you came through a 'barrier,' do you mean ether?"

"I—I don't know what ether is," Sunni stammered.

Wheatley frowned.

"All we know," said Blaise, "is that we are in the wrong time, and we need to go back where we belong."

"And the only way back is shut," added Sunni. "Because Throgmorton closed it."

The Pell Mells shifted in their seats and muttered. Amelia hurriedly poured more tea into their cups.

"You think Throgmorton is a magician?" she asked.

"We don't know who or what he is, ma'am," said Blaise. "Just that he trapped us here and we have to find help."

"Wheatley, what do you think?" asked one of the men.

"Aye," said another. "Are any of your conjurors up to such a task, if this story is true?"

Wheatley did not move a muscle as he scrutinized

Sunni and Blaise. "Possibly. But this may need more than a magician."

The Pell Mells exhaled a collective breath, and Blaise's heart began to pound with hopeful excitement.

"Will you help us, please, Mr. Wheatley?" Sunni pleaded. "We don't know where else to turn."

"Yes, I think I may be of assistance," he answered. "Now, from what century did this man supposedly bring you?"

"The twenty-first century."

A roar erupted among the gentlemen. Several laughed and others snorted, while Wheatley pulled out a small notebook and began scribbling into it, his eyebrows knitted together.

Amelia was the only one who looked kindly on them. "How, precisely, did he do this?"

Blaise's head was throbbing from the din of the gentlemen's voices. "He brought us through a painting of a door—"

"A painting of a door?" Henry cut him off, incredulity on his face.

"Yes," said Blaise. "But it materializes into a real door so you can walk through."

Henry threw back his head and laughed.

His sister scowled. "Brother, let the boy finish speaking. You say you will hear their story with an open mind, then you do not allow them to explain!"

"But this is ludicrous."

"After two sentences, you have already made up your mind?" Amelia sniffed.

Sunni unbuckled her satchel, rifled through her things,

and slapped a handful of coins down on the nearest table. "Here's proof. Look at the dates stamped on these coins. Go on, see for yourselves."

The Pell Mells passed the coins around and turned them over and over, examining the coats of arms and crests, the Latin inscriptions, and the monarch's profile.

Sunni leaned close to Blaise's ear and whispered, "What else can we show them? All I've got with dates on are old Underground tickets. And my phone."

"Tickets, yes, but don't let them see your phone. It might be too distracting," Blaise whispered back, wondering what he could show them that had a date on it.

Sunni laid out several bent tickets. "And these are tickets from, er, transport in the twenty-first century. See the dates?"

"What sort of transport?" asked one of the men.

"A type that hasn't been invented yet," said Blaise. "It has a lot of wheels and an engine."

"An atmospheric steam engine?" asked Wheatley.

"I don't know about atmospheric. We don't use steam engines much anymore."

"Ah!" exclaimed several gentlemen, and Blaise put up his hands to ward off any more questions.

"I'm no engineer," he said. "All I can say is that the engines in our time do things you can't even imagine."

The Pell Mells went on examining the coins and tickets, but Blaise couldn't tell if they had been won over at all. He discreetly went through his own satchel and extracted a leaflet printed with photos, maps, and diagrams.

Gingerly, he got up and smoothed it flat on an empty table near Henry. "Here is more proof. There is a London museum in the twenty-first century called the National Gallery. Each room has paintings from the past. See, they're collected together by time period and country all the way to 1900."

Amelia and the Pell Mells clamored around, practically knocking over one of the stone heads on a plinth.

"This is printed in color—with exact images of artworks in miniature! What superb quality paper and ink." Martingale devoured the information on the leaflet. "How is this made?"

"There's going to be an invention that can copy things more exactly than a painting," said Blaise. "And printers can print those copies in any size, just like this."

Henry exclaimed, "Our own eighteenth century is included here, collected in several rooms." The others leaned in to look where he pointed. "The painter Mr. Hogarth seems to have his own room!"

"In a National Gallery," Trevelyan mused, his eyes wide. "Wait until Hogarth hears of this."

"You can't tell him!" Blaise prized the leaflet away and stuffed it back where it came from. "Maybe we shouldn't have shown you these things, if you can't be trusted."

Humbled, Trevelyan said, "I shall not utter a word. None of us shall." The other gentlemen nodded.

Blaise lowered himself back onto his chair. "Now do you believe we're telling the truth?"

"Have we seen enough to be convinced, gentlemen?"

asked Henry, gathering all the coins and Underground tickets into a pile and pushing them toward Sunni. She packed away her evidence and sat down again.

"Aye," the Pell Mells murmured.

"Is this why Throgmorton captured you?" asked Amelia. "To learn the secrets of the future?"

We can't tell them about Fausto Corvo, thought Blaise. "I guess so."

"Blaise," said Henry politely. "You were going to tell us about this painted door."

"It's in the Academy," Blaise said.

"The Academy that enslaves its pupils," Trevelyan said. "Enslaves them at what?"

"Drawing and painting."

The poet raised an eyebrow. "That is a soft sort of slavery. We are all slaves to our art, whether we are painters or poets."

"Working day and night?" Blaise tensed. "Never allowed to leave the Academy?"

None of the gentlemen looked surprised at this description.

"Sounds to me like disciplined instruction," Catterwall said.

"And pupils being sold to anatomists if they don't obey—is that part of disciplined instruction?" Blaise's head was ringing.

A gasp came from the Pell Mells.

"Throgmorton has dealings with anatomists?" Martingale asked, incredulous.

"Yes," Sunni said. "He'll sell me to them if he catches us."

Her words hung in the air. No one made a move to speak until Amelia leaned over and touched Blaise's shoulder in an encouraging way.

"Tell us what the painted door is like," she said.

He composed himself. "It's brown, painted to look exactly like a wood-paneled door on a white wall. The handle looks like brass. It was painted to match the real door in the room."

"Is the paint even, or does it have cracks?" asked Wheatley, pausing in his scribbling. "Are there any imperfections?"

Blaise closed his eyes for a moment. "Yes, there are some shapes scratched in the paint." He drew a curve in the air. "Like spirals, overlapping each other."

"What color are the spirals?"

"Darker brown, I think, with specks of red." As he described the door, Jacob's story came back to him. "Someone told me Throgmorton opened the door by drawing a shape on it with a sharpened shard of reddish stone that he dipped in a dark red liquid."

"I saw him with a red stone knife," said Sunni. "It's sharp as a sword."

"Describe it," ordered Wheatley.

She gestured with her thumb and forefinger. "About this long. Flat and narrow. It fits in the palm of his hand with the pointed end sticking out."

"Thank you." Wheatley stood up and thrust his notebook into Blaise's lap. "Draw the spiral on this page."

Blaise took his rough graphite pencil and drew a delicate arc next to the man's indecipherable scribbles.

Wheatley glanced at it and held up the book for the others to see. "I perceive that to be a nine rather than a spiral. Would you all agree?"

"A loosely drawn one," said Trevelyan. "But yes, it could be."

"You describe the shapes as having a sort of pattern," said Wheatley.

Blaise nodded. "They were all roughly in the same place and overlapped."

"Like writing?" suggested Trevelyan.

"Maybe. But it looked more like someone had drawn them on top of each other," said Blaise.

"They could be demonic symbols." Catterwall's face lit up. "Magical handbooks called *The Grand Grimoire* and *The Blue Sphinx* are easily found on the streets of London, brought in by French peddlers. They are full of diabolical marks and symbols."

Trevelyan rolled his eyes. "Have you ever seen a magical handbook? I have. They are full of recipes for potions to cure wind or baldness. Yes, there were also strange drawings and numbers in sequence, and supposed names of demons. But I question whether anyone would manage to cross time by merely copying them on a wall."

"Perhaps this Throgmorton has!" said Catterwall.

"And what, if anything, has he revealed about this door?" Wheatley returned to his seat, not even looking at them.

"He only said he has the ability to open and close the

door, but it was too complex for us to understand," said Blaise. "Nothing else."

"The more I hear of this man, the more I suspect he has diabolical powers to go with his diabolical heart," said Catterwall.

Wheatley had a coughing fit and wrote even more furiously in his notebook.

"Something interesting, Wheatley?" asked Trevelyan.

"In a moment," he replied without looking up.

Martingale asked, "Can you tell us anything else?"

Blaise looked at Sunni, and she shook her head. "That's all we know, sir."

"I would like a description of Throgmorton," said Henry. "I did not see him properly at the theater. Who is he?"

"Good question, sir. We don't know either," said Sunni. "We've been told he just turned up here one day, from who knows where. He has a broken nose and light-blue eyes. I've seen him in a white wig and a brown one, dressed like he has a lot of money: fancy pocket watch, embroidered waistcoats, and lots of buttons all over his coat. But last night he wore plain, dark clothes."

Martingale and several other men nodded. "A good description, Miss Sunniva."

"Oh, he has a daughter, too, and she is just as slippery as he is." Sunni turned to Blaise, her eyes narrowing. "Maybe *you'd* like to describe Livia."

"Livia is about sixteen and has light-blond hair and blue-green eyes," said Blaise, hoping that was bland enough.

Anything more complimentary might be a bit hard for Sunni to take.

"And wears expensive dresses," said Sunni, looking like she wanted to say something far more rude.

"A well-dressed man with a lovely well-dressed daughter," Henry summed up. "A useful disguise for a rogue."

"Yes, yes," said Catterwall impatiently. "But back to the possibility of diabolical powers. . . ."

"Quite!" called another gentleman. "Symbols that conjure up evil forces."

"We can rule nothing out," said Catterwall. "Magical names, magical drawings, magical numbers—all must be considered."

"We shall be happy for you to investigate the demonic possibilities," said Trevelyan. "Just beware of anyone with horns and a forked tail."

Wheatley snapped his notebook shut and stood up, announcing, "I must away. I cannot waste any more time over idle conversation."

"Idle conversation!" Catterwall spluttered.

"We need a plan before anyone leaves, gentlemen," said Henry, shaking his head at his friends. "My sister and I shall guard our two young friends here. Wheatley, will you seek out the magicians?"

The natural philosopher grunted a kind of yes.

"And, Catterwall, you will look into the whereabouts of magical handbooks."

The man nodded enthusiastically.

"We are already fixed to meet for a Club Supper

tomorrow night at the Jubilee Masquerade," said Henry. "Eight o'clock, in our usual box or in that vicinity. We shall look forward to your reports."

Wheatley bowed to Amelia and nodded to the Pell Mells. "Until tomorrow." He hurried toward the library door, glanced over his shoulder, and said, "Guard those two well, Featherstone. Trouble is at their heels."

"Wheatley!" Henry called, but he was already gone.

Chapter 17

Sunni hurried down the broad steps into the grounds behind the mansion and took a huge breath in. The distant sky threatened rain, but for now the sun shone and she reveled in the fresh air.

Blaise descended the steps behind her, and they strolled along the interlocking paths in the large ornamental garden.

"I thought I was going to keel over in there," he said. "My head was killing me."

"Is it better now?" she asked, noticing how pale he was.

Blaise stared down at his shoes as he walked. "Yeah, a little."

"We've got some hope now, haven't we? These people are willing to help us."

"Do you really think they bought everything we told them?"

"It seemed like it, after they saw our evidence." Sunni grinned. "None of the Pell Mells wants to be left out of the action now."

"What do you make of Wheatley?"

"It's hard to tell," she said. "Whatever he thinks, it's all down in that notebook of his."

They found a marble bench behind some shrubs and sat down. When Blaise began doodling in his sketchbook, Sunni almost cried at the comforting normality of it. They might have been sitting on a bench in Braeside, just being together, not even having to talk.

As Sunni watched him from the corner of her eye, she wondered what—or who—he thought about as he drew. Livia's self-satisfied face appeared in her head. Was she inside Blaise's head, too?

After some time, the sun disappeared under a cloud and Sunni murmured, "We were supposed to be back at school yesterday."

"I know," he said, putting his sketchbook away. "What I wouldn't give to be there right now."

"Me, too. And that's saying a lot."

Blaise touched his bandage. "I'm going to head back inside. Looks like rain and I don't want this thing to get wet."

"Oh," said Sunni, disappointed. "Okay."

He got up quickly, staggered, and sat down again.

"You want me to help you?" She touched his arm.

"No, I'm fine." He stood up carefully this time. "Just need to take it easy." At the edge of the shrubs, he turned. "Aren't you coming?"

Sunni bit her lip. "In a minute."

She was alone, feeling the first raindrops on her upturned face, when a gentle voice called, "Sunniva. There you are."

Amelia hurried to her side. "Where is Blaise?"

"On his way inside."

"You must come indoors also. There is a storm gathering."

"I will, miss," said Sunni, looking out at the darkening sky. "In a few minutes, if that's all right. I don't mind a little rain."

Amelia furrowed her brow. "I have disturbed you."

"No," said Sunni. "I was just . . . sitting."

Amelia seated herself on the edge of the bench. "I often sit here, thinking of nothing in particular."

Sunni gave her a tight smile.

"Is everything well, Sunniva? With you and Blaise?"

"Yes, miss," she answered, more sharply than she meant to. "Why?"

"Forgive me for asking, but I was wondering—and so was Mr. Martingale—did you and Blaise run away together before you fell victim to Throgmorton?" Amelia hesitated. "A young girl and boy such as yourselves . . ."

"No," Sunni answered, a pang shooting through her chest. "Blaise and I are only friends."

Amelia looked rueful. "Not sweethearts, then?"

Sunni shook her head and wiped a raindrop off her cheek.

"I must say something else," Amelia said, her eyes shining. "Your arrival has changed my life. Because of it, I feel part of something important. The Pell Mell gentlemen allowed me to attend their meeting. They seemed to take me seriously! Not my brother, for he never takes me seriously unless his dinner is delayed, but I could sense the others do. It has inspired their ideas—and mine. We are on a quest to help you, all together!"

"I don't know what to say, Miss Featherstone. I'm glad in one way, but in another, I'm not. Because Blaise and I have disrupted your lives."

"For the good," said Amelia firmly.

"How can we know that, miss?" asked Sunni. "We aren't meant to be in this time. I'm afraid we'll change things that aren't supposed to change. What if you are meant to live your life one way, but because you've met us, you decide to live it differently?"

Amelia smiled. "But that *is* life, Sunniva! Each day brings unforeseen events that move us in one direction or another."

"Y—yes. But what if you are meant to marry Mr. Martingale, and suddenly you fall for Mr. Catterwall instead, because you've been thrown together today. And what if that means the children you are *supposed* to have never exist in the future?"

Amelia's face blazed red. "Neither of those gentlemen would ever marry me."

Sunni wasn't so sure about that, given the way Martingale smiled at Amelia.

"I am not certain our lives are predestined, Sunniva. Though it is interesting to wonder about," she said. "And I am still happy, even if just for today."

Sunni smiled politely. A sudden breeze rushed in, sending the shrubbery wild and pelting them with rain.

"Oh!" Amelia covered her head with her shawl and began scurrying toward the mansion. "Come inside now."

With a sigh, Sunni followed. She rounded the shrubbery's natural screen and saw Amelia darting up the steps.

In that moment, she got the queasy feeling that she was being watched. She whirled around, checking all the lonely paths and squinting into the misty sheets of rain obscuring the far end of the garden. The fields beyond were deserted.

She sensed something lurking in the hedges and trees. Whoever it was — whatever it was — felt close by.

"Sunniva!"

Startled, Sunni ran, knocking her skirts into hedges and dragging the hem through puddles.

"Sunniva!" Amelia called again from the mansion door. "You must come in from the rain."

When Sunni rushed in, panting, Amelia stared at her. "What is it? What happened?"

"I thought I saw something," Sunni gasped, accepting the dry cloth Amelia handed her. "But it was nothing."

Amelia guided Sunni to the drawing room, where Blaise was quietly sketching a fireplace with twin carved lions on either side. When they entered, he smiled feebly. But seeing her wan face, he asked, "What's up?"

"I just got caught in the rain," she answered. "You all right?"

"Better than I was," he said.

Amelia looked over Blaise's shoulder at his sketch.

"You are gifted at drawing," she said. "Come, I will show you the picture gallery if you are interested."

She led them through stately rooms, which were stiff and formal and looked like no one ever spent time in them. Finally she threw open a door and said, "Our grandfather collected art and antiquities. He filled the library with his statues and urns, and this room with paintings. They come from Florence and Flanders and everywhere in between."

The huge room was covered from eye level to ceiling with paintings, large and small. They were hung so close to each other, it was almost hard to make out where one ended and the next began. Landscapes were next to saints, and portraits were stacked above still lifes.

The rain-soaked light from the tall windows barely lit many of the paintings, and some were completely in shadow.

"There are so many," said Sunni, turning in a circle, trying to take them all in.

"The light is too poor," said Amelia, moving to the door after a few minutes. "Come and look at them properly when there is sunshine."

She and Sunni stopped when Blaise did not follow.

"Come on, Blaise," called Sunni.

Reluctantly, he followed, but he kept looking back over one shoulder.

Blaise sat sketching by the cluster of candles in his room. It was late, and the house was utterly silent.

He and Sunni had stayed up after dinner, learning a card game from Amelia, while Henry attended to business with farmers on the estate.

"Amelia must be bored out of her skull," said Blaise to

Sunni as they climbed up to their bedrooms. "Knocking around this mausoleum all on her own."

"She told me how happy she is that we're here," said Sunni.

"That's good—" he started to say, but noticed her doleful expression. "Oh, right, maybe not."

"We're not supposed to be here. We have got to get home," she whispered as she entered her bedroom. "'Night, Blaise."

"'Night." Blaise hadn't told her what was bugging him about the picture gallery. He didn't want to say anything till he'd checked it out himself—and he must be wrong, anyway.

At some point he told himself he ought to go to bed, but once he was under the covers, his mind went over and over everything that had happened. When he finally dragged his thoughts away from the painful subject of being lost in the wrong century, they strayed to another place he couldn't avoid for much longer: the gallery.

He threw the covers off and, candlestick in hand, ventured into the corridor. Its oppressive blackness made him reconsider for a second, but the itch in his brain was too insistent. He set off for the grand double staircase, trying not to think of the portraits staring down at him in the dark.

On the third step, he heard something. A knock, a rattle, it was hard to tell where it came from. He waited for more, but nothing came, so he continued to the ground floor. Padding carefully in his stockinged feet, Blaise headed for the central door that led toward the picture gallery. With a click, it was open and another black corridor was ahead of him.

A sigh of air blew toward him and made the candle flicker.

He tiptoed to the second door on the right. It opened soundlessly, and he padded forward, relieved that he had found the right room.

As he moved around, the candle picked out details in the shadowy paintings: a saint's hand, a pomegranate bursting open, a hunting dog running in a forest.

The painting he needed to see was in a far corner, near the ceiling. He held the candle up as high as he could, but even standing on a chair, he could not make its light reach far enough.

He stepped down and sighed at his own stupidity for not waiting till morning.

Another breath of air came from behind him, sending his flame dancing wildly. Blaise turned around, but before he could see anything, the candle went out and a hand was clamped hard over his mouth.

Chapter 18

A tremendous explosion blasted through Sunni's head, and she jerked awake. Lights were flickering past her door, visible though the gaps, and one stopped outside.

"Sunniva?" Amelia knocked frantically, then pushed inside. "Are you there?"

"What's going on?"

"I do not know! Stay in here and lock your door." Amelia slammed the door shut and vanished down the corridor.

"Wait, where's Blaise? Is he all right?" Sunni felt in the dark for her shawl, wrapped it around her shoulders, and moved carefully to the door.

Slipping outside, she joined Anne, who was passing with a lantern, and they hurried downstairs together. Loud voices and lights emanated from the gallery, where a man's voice was yelling something about a "villainous snake."

Everyone in the household was gathered in a semi-circle, candles aloft, looking at something on the ground. Sunni pushed toward the front and gaped at the sight of Henry Featherstone, in a dressing gown, aiming a musket at Blaise and a strange man, who were crouched together against the wall like cornered spiders.

Blaise's nightshirt and awkward bare legs were bright against the man's dark clothing, but brighter still was the glint of the dagger at her friend's throat.

Sunni cowered behind the others, her heart in her mouth.

"Villainous snake!" Henry shouted again. "No house-breaker shall walk free from here!"

The man scraped the blade against Blaise's skin and rasped, "That is what I offer. I leaves with this boy in a carriage, or I gives him a bloody necklace."

Henry did not seem to be breathing. Only a fly sitting on the barrel of the musket would have noticed it lining up with the burglar's right shoulder. Three seconds later, it blasted a shilling's width of flesh off the man and the picture gallery had a crater in its wall. A dusting of plaster bits covered the floor where Henry had already fired into the ceiling.

The housebreaker dropped his dagger and groaned. Blaise broke away, and the assembled household descended upon them. Two footmen dragged the bleeding man into a corner, while Sunni and Amelia helped Blaise to his feet.

Slowly, Henry lowered the musket, but the fire didn't leave his eyes. "Where is the other snake?"

"He got away, sir," said one of the footmen. "Across the fields at the back."

The housebreaker let out a wheezing laugh that chilled Sunni to the bone.

Henry slung the musket over his shoulder and retrieved the dagger from the floor. With it, he set about digging the spent musket ball from the wall. "Get rope, Rowley, and secure this miscreant. Bind the wound and carry him to the library. I shall want him alive long enough to tell his tale." He curled his lip. "And to die on the gallows."

The maidservants drew in their breath. Henry spun around and said, "Enough gawking. Back to your beds and lock yourselves in. And not a word about this to another soul! If I hear of anyone talking, he or she shall be chased out of this house."

He nodded at wide-eyed Amelia. "Take yourself off to bed, Sister, and I shall check your door before I retire. Make certain you have locked it well. Sunniva, Blaise, you come with me."

A short time later, Henry sat in his wingback chair with the musket balanced across his knees, candles illuminating the statues around him. Hodge was stationed at the library door with a pistol in case the injured criminal made a run for it, but the man was tied to a wooden chair, a red bloom spreading over the cloth that bound his shoulder. His head lolled back as he stared at Blaise and Sunni with blood-shot eyes.

Sunni could barely stop shivering under his gaze.

"Nearly had you," the housebreaker croaked. "But others shall succeed."

"I gave you no permission to speak," Henry thundered.

"It matters not. I am as good as dead now."

"Do you recognize this man?" Henry asked Sunni and Blaise.

"No, sir," said Blaise. Sunni could only shake her head.

"I knows you both," the housebreaker said. "You was

pointed out at Smythe's theater. There's a reward on your heads."

"Offered by whom?" Henry demanded.

"The man that wants them."

"Throgmorton?"

"Aye." The burglar aimed a black-toothed grimace at Sunni and Blaise. "What has you told him? The truth?"

Henry glanced curiously at them, and Sunni's stomach lurched.

"Yes," she whispered.

The man went on, spittle gathering at the sides of his mouth. "That you run away from the Academy?" He leaned forward as much as the ropes would allow. "With them two nightsneaks? Where are they now, eh? Abandoned you, did they? They will be hunted down as well!"

Sunni couldn't breathe. She recoiled even though the man was several feet away from her.

"They ain't saying much," the housebreaker hissed at Henry.

"You have said enough—and none of it new to me. Rowley!" Henry shouted. The coachman hurried into the room. "You and Hodge take this scoundrel out to the stables and keep armed watch over him till morning, when I shall turn him in myself."

The housebreaker gasped in pain as the two men untied his restraints and marched him into the passageway.

"I shall see you out," said Henry, following them.

The housebreaker could be heard puffing, "I ain't alone. Others will take the boy and girl. Tonight. Or tomorrow." His voice faded down the corridor. "Who knows?"

When they were alone, Sunni put her head down between her knees and tried to breathe normally.

Blaise laid a quaking hand on her back. "Are you going to be sick?"

"I don't know," she whimpered. "H-he nearly cut your throat. I don't know what I would've done if—"

Blaise quickly withdrew his hand when Henry strode back in.

He shook the library shutters and said, "How did these culprits enter? The windows and doors were locked."

"Maybe they had a skeleton key," Blaise said.

"Perhaps." Henry checked the shutters again and said, "There is a weakness somewhere in this house, and I will root it out. This house will be fortified against their cunning."

"Did the thief say anything else to you, sir?" Blaise asked.

"Nothing you had not already told us."

He caught sight of Sunni's drawn face when she sat up and wiped her clammy brow. "Are you ill, Sunniva?"

"Just a bit dizzy," she said. "Must be the shock . . ."

"Yes, 'twas a shock." Henry glared at Blaise. "What, pray tell, possessed you to wander about in the small hours of the night?"

Blaise crossed his arms tight over his nightshirt. "I couldn't sleep. So I thought I would go downstairs and look at the paintings in the gallery."

"By the light of a single flame?"

"I didn't see much," Blaise admitted. "He jumped me as soon as I got there."

"You are extremely fortunate that I heard the commotion," Henry said. "Barton, Kelley, and I will take it in turns to watch for intruders. Return to your beds now and lock your chamber doors."

He escorted them upstairs, musket at his shoulder. Sunni locked her door and collapsed on her bed. As sleep took over, a fading image of the painted door floated above all the worries in her fuzzy brain, farther and farther from reach.

She was still dozing when someone began hammering on her door. She pulled on her shawl and tiptoed close to it. "Who is it?"

"It's me!" hissed Blaise.

As soon as she unlocked the door, he burst in.

"What time is it?" she asked.

"Morning."

"What's so urgent that you have to batter the door down?"

"Sorry. My head's all over the place." He looked around her room, agitated. "Are you all right? Did you get any sleep?"

"Some."

"Okay, good. Me, too." He scratched his head with a rapid movement. "Come downstairs. You've got to help me look at something."

"What?"

"Just come on, Sunni. It's doing my head in."

"What is? I'm not even dressed. . . ."

Blaise threw his hands up. "Then get dressed. Will you just come on?"

"Give me a few minutes then." She began pushing him out of the door. "Go on. Wait *outside*."

Sunni struggled into her stays and gown as best she could without Anne's help. She slipped her shoes on, locked the door behind her, and followed Blaise down the hall.

"Are you going to tell me what's up or just keep on commanding me?" she said with a sniff.

"You'll see what's up in a minute," he answered. "And you can tell me if I'm nuts or seeing things or what."

Morning light poured through the windows of the empty gallery. Yesterday's rain had given way to sun and the room was washed clean of the previous night's shadows.

The servants had finished sweeping up fragments of plaster from the floor and were nowhere in sight, but they had left a ladder propped against the wall.

"Help me move this ladder over there," said Blaise, tugging at it. "To that corner."

"Are you crazy?"

"Maybe." He began inching the ladder across the room. "Help me, will you? It's heavy!"

"You're out of your mind, Blaise. If this falls over, it'll bring those pictures crashing down!"

"It won't fall. Grab hold here!"

Somehow, in fits and starts, they pulled the ladder along and leaned it against the wall, nearly nicking the topmost painting's gilded frame.

"I am not moving that again," Sunni said. "So don't ask."

"You won't have to." Blaise began climbing. "Hold on tight."

He went as high as he could and leaned his whole torso toward a canvas hanging in the corner.

"You're going to fall if you lean any farther, Blaise!" she shrieked, throwing all her weight onto the ladder's bottom rung.

"I'll be all right," he gasped.

Carefully, he plucked the painting from the wall with both hands. He teetered with the unexpected weight of it, but managed to grab hold of the wire on the back with one hand, while the other grasped the ladder.

Slowly he began descending, clutching the painting to his side.

"You nearly dropped it!" She stood aside for him to jump down onto the floor. "What is it? What's the matter?"

Blaise's face was ashen.

"Talk to me. You're giving me a fright!"

"Look at the painting," he said shakily. "And tell me I've made a mistake. *Please* tell me I've made a mistake."

Chapter 19

Sunni was studying the painting when suddenly the door flew open. What are you doing?" Henry's booming voice startled Blaise, and he nearly lost his grip on the painting. Luckily, Sunni grabbed hold of the other end.

"So help me, if you two are stealing from us—"

"No, sir!" Blaise called. "We took this down to show you and Miss Featherstone. It's really important."

A letter dangled from Henry's fingers. "And I have news," he said, waving the sheet of paper at them. "Bring that painting to the library if you must."

Their host stalked out of the gallery. Sunni and Blaise hurried after him, gingerly carrying the painting through the halls. When they reached the library, Amelia was already waiting there. She managed a smile, but her brother's expression was stern.

Sunni and Blaise leaned the painting against a chair and sat down side by side.

"I have just handed the housebreaker over to the local magistrate," said Henry, sitting heavily into his chair. "But I do not think for a moment that our troubles are at an end. The criminal who escaped from my footmen last night will spread the word that you are here. Every scoundrel in London will be beating a path to this door." His jaw was set. "I cannot risk my household's safety, and I will not have my property attacked further."

Blaise half sensed what was coming next and held his breath.

"I had thought this house to be the safest place for you, but in light of last night's events, I think you will agree that you must move on."

"Brother," Amelia started, but he held up his hand.

"This has just come from Wheatley." Henry opened the letter. "I am to bring Blaise and Sunniva to him as soon as possible."

Hope began flowering out of Blaise's anxiety. "Does he say why, sir?"

"Wheatley seldom explains himself." Henry raised one eyebrow. "But he will have very good reasons."

"Maybe he's found a magician for us."

"Let us hope so," said Henry.

"But Throgmorton's spies may catch sight of Blaise and Sunniva on the journey there!" said Amelia.

"Not if they are dressed to go to the Jubilee Masquerade."

A smile spread over his sister's face. "Of course! Leave it to me, Brother."

"You will need to work quickly," said Henry, getting to his feet and nodding at Sunni and Blaise. "Gather your belongings. We leave as soon as my sister's work is done."

"Will you come with us, Miss Featherstone?" asked Blaise.

"I—I do not know."

"I think not." Henry frowned. "After we see Wheatley, I shall be in Ranelagh Gardens for supper with the Club."

"But Miss Featherstone is part of this, too, sir."

"Brother?" she appealed to Henry, who was stuffing Wheatley's letter into his coat pocket.

"It is not the usual thing," he said.

"Sunniva and I aren't 'the usual thing' either," said Blaise. "I think Miss Featherstone should be allowed to come."

Sunni nodded vigorously at this.

"Do you wish to, Sister?" Henry asked.

"Oh, yes!"

"It is not ideal. But as we are in extraordinary circumstances, I suppose you may come," Henry said. "But this time only."

Sunni had been silent throughout, listening to everything, but now she could barely contain herself. She whispered to Blaise, "We have to show it to them!"

"Mr. Featherstone," he said, touching the gold frame leaning against his seat. "Miss Featherstone. Does this belong to you? I found it in the picture gallery."

He and Sunni shifted the painting around to face the Featherstones. It was a portrait of a young woman against a dark background, holding a jeweled silver hand mirror. A high, short ruff framed her chin and set off a blue dress with an impossibly slim bodice and puffed shoulders joined to stiff white sleeves.

Blaise caught his breath again when he examined the

face. At first glance she was beautiful, but after a few moments he had seen something beyond that. The painter had made a likeness, but he had also brutally exposed her character. The eyes were hard and knowing, and the lips were tightened into an almost imperceptible sneer.

"Of course it is ours," said Amelia, puzzled.

Blaise's head began throbbing again. "It's a portrait of Livia, Throgmorton's daughter."

"The same Throgmorton who is pursuing you? How can that be?" Henry examined the portrait. "And in *our* picture gallery? I have never noticed it before."

"Never?" Blaise murmured. "It was there, hanging in the top row."

Henry turned to his sister. "You are certain you know this painting?"

"Yes," Amelia said. "It has always been there. I have watched the servants dusting it."

"You were seeking this last night." Henry peered at Blaise. "The housebreaker caught you there."

"Yes, sir." Blaise hung his aching head. "I had to have a closer look at the painting."

Sunni spoke up. "You don't know why there is a portrait of Livia in your house, sir?"

"Our grandfather collected the paintings before we were born. They have nothing to do with us." Henry shrugged. "Besides, how can one be expected to remember them all?"

"Maybe this girl only looks like Throgmorton's daughter," Amelia said. "I often see resemblances in paintings."

"It *is* her, miss," Sunni said. "If you look carefully, the name *Livia* is painted into the background. There, to the left."

Amelia blinked. "So it is."

To Blaise's relief, she didn't notice the other name he and Sunni had found on the hand mirror, painted to look as though it was engraved in the silver. It made him shudder every time he read the tiny letters.

"But we don't know who painted it." Blaise pointed at the bottom right of the painting. "The artist only signed his initials: *M.B.*"

"Do you have any idea who M.B. is, miss?" asked Sunni. "Sir?"

"I know very little about painters," Henry said unapologetically.

"Neither do I," Amelia said.

Blaise's wound was aching, and he had to sit down.

Sunni turned to him. "Are you all right?"

"Still a bit sore," he said. "Go on. Show them the date."

Sunni moved her finger below the artist's initials, and the Featherstones crowded close to see.

The four numbers were small, so she read them aloud: "This portrait of Livia was made in 1583."

Amelia put one hand to her cheek, looking perplexed.

"Are you sure you don't know anything about this?" Blaise asked.

Henry glared at them. "I am telling you, my sister and I know nothing of this person Throgmorton, and even less of his daughter! I have never seen either of them in my life."

"Sorry, sir, but I had to ask," said Blaise. "We thought

Throgmorton and Livia were from your time, but after seeing this portrait, we don't know which time they come from."

"But," said Sunni, "this painting proves Livia has been in 1583. And she was there long enough to have her portrait done."

"They move freely into the future *and* the past," said Amelia, eyes wide.

"I do not know what to make of all this. It is the most puzzling thing I have ever encountered," Henry said. "But what I do know is this: Throgmorton has put a price on your head, and his blackguards could be waiting on our threshold at this very moment. Go with my sister now and let her do what needs to be done."

Sunni and Blaise went to remove Livia's portrait, but Henry waved them away. "Leave that here. I will return it to the gallery myself. Perhaps it is time I learned what else is there."

Amelia ushered them upstairs. "Sunniva, you come with me. Blaise, gather your belongings and wait in your chamber until I summon you."

It felt as if hours passed. Blaise lay on his bed, fully clothed, his satchel carefully packed. His head was no longer throbbing, but it was spinning with questions.

When Amelia finally knocked, he had already counted all the carved leaves and birds on the bed's headboard twice, trying to keep his mind off the name on the mirror in Livia's portrait.

Amelia led him by the elbow to her sitting room, a

comfortable hideaway filled with her books, watercolor sketches, and sewing materials. But he nearly jumped out of his skin at the sight of a black-caped figure at the window, gazing out over the garden.

Amelia laughed and the figure whirled around, revealing a white mask covering the face from forehead to nose. Black fabric hung like a hood from under its three-cornered hat, covering the hair and neck. A long gown poked out from under the floor-length cape.

The figure snapped open a red lacquered fan and twirled around.

"Do you know me?" a voice purred.

"Sunni?"

"What do you think?"

"You look amazing," said Blaise. "And creepy. All that's showing is your mouth and hands."

"And the bottom of a gown," said Amelia. "Unless they know better, Throgmorton's men may still be searching for two boys, so dressing as a girl will be a further layer of protection."

"You're not getting me to wear a dress, miss." Blaise shrank back. "There's no way."

"Relax," said Sunni. "You're getting a cape and a mask like mine."

"It is simplest and most anonymous. My brother brought these masks from Venice, and they are very effective." Amelia steered him toward a table piled with fabric and a sewing box. "There is a grand Jubilee Masquerade at Ranelagh Gardens tonight, and both men and women will be wearing costumes exactly like this. No one will look twice at us. We shall be able to move freely to Mr. Wheatley's."

"But I'll wear breeches under the cloak, right?"

"Yeah, with these shoes." Sunni held up a pair of black shoes with gigantic bows on each buckle. "Have fun."

"Now, to construct your cloak. It will hide you and your satchel from prying eyes." Amelia pulled a midnight-blue cape from the jumble on the table. "This was mine, but we shall adapt it for you." She draped it across Blaise's shoulders, and he groaned inwardly that he was going to have to wear a woman's clothes. "I shall add some trim at the bottom to lengthen it for your height."

She measured and pinned and snipped. An old hat of Henry's was called into service. Amelia tacked a black drape inside it that would hang down to cover Blaise's head and chest.

"I shall have to line this hat with stuffing," she announced. "Even with your bandage, my brother's head is still fatter than yours."

When Sunni and Blaise were dressed up to her satisfaction, Amelia made them remove their masks long enough to eat a three-course lunch. It was mid-afternoon by the time she let her brother know that everything was ready. At his orders, the footmen streamed out of the mansion, combing the gardens, stables, and fields for spies. The maidservants peered from the upper and lower windows, then scoured every passageway and room till they were certain no one was secreted in the house.

One of the footmen brought the carriage around and held its door open for the strange parade of cloaked figures that floated toward it. Once they were inside, all that could be seen through the carriage windows were two rows of stiff white masks. The carriage rolled away toward London like a spectral hearse.

Chapter 20

They made their way through villages on the outskirts of London.

"We are not far from Wheatley's home in Chelsea," said Henry. "The footman shall drop us there and take the carriage to a nearby inn. Keep your masks on at all times."

"Yes, sir," said Blaise. "And thank you. I don't know what we'd have done without you and Miss Featherstone."

"Do not thank us yet," Henry said. "There is still the small matter of transferring you into the hands of your next protector."

At last the carriage came to a halt in a quiet street. Sunni and Blaise struggled out of the narrow door in their long capes and special-occasion shoes and gazed through their mask holes at Wheatley's house. Unlike the others in the street, all its shutters were closed. Sunni had never seen a house that said "go away" more than this one.

"Oh, dear," said Amelia. "Has Mr. Wheatley left? His house looks abandoned."

"No," said Henry, sighing. "His house always looks this way." He waved to the footman, and the carriage tottered away.

When, after Henry's repeated knocking, a servant pulled open the door, he jumped back at the sight of the four cloaked, masked figures.

"Mr. Wheatley is expecting us," said Henry, his voice muffled.

"Who may I say is calling?"

"You are new to this establishment, are you not? I have not seen you before."

The servant frowned. "Yes, sir. May I have your name?"

"By heaven, is Wheatley expecting such a string of visitors that I must give my name?" Henry pushed past, pulling Sunni and Amelia with him. The surprised servant backed away when Blaise stepped in and shut the door behind him.

Sunni examined the dark hall, swiveling her head around to see through the mask's eyeholes. Books were stacked against the walls in crooked towers. A dusty mirror hung slanted on one wall, catching the light of the single candle illuminating the narrow space. But the thing that she noticed most was the smell: a faint odor of rotten eggs.

"Now," said Henry. "Will you let your employer know that Mr. Featherstone and his party have arrived?"

"If you had only said so, sir," the servant muttered sourly. "He is expecting you." He flung open the door to the shuttered front room, where a round table was set with a cold meal. He lit a few candles against the gloom. "He is occupied and begs you to take refreshment while you are waiting."

"Occupied!"

"Yes, Mr. Featherstone. Please wait in here. He will see you when he is able."

"Is able!" Henry raised his mask like a visor on a helmet, revealing his deep scowl.

The footman scurried away. "I will bring tea, sir."

They filed into the dingy dining parlor and hesitantly took seats around the table. Once Henry had taken off his hat and mask, the others followed. Sunni and Blaise swung their satchels into their laps.

"Why are all the shutters closed in daytime?" Blaise murmured to Sunni.

"And why does it smell so rotten?" she whispered back.

Amelia wrinkled her nose as she ran a finger through dust on the tabletop. "The edges of these meats are curling up, they have sat out so long. Is that what I smell?"

Henry said, "Knowing Wheatley, it is sulfur."

"Why has he got sulfur in his home?"

"The man is a natural philosopher, Sister, and takes an interest in chemistry. He investigates the workings of nature and the universe as a matter of course."

Sunni eyed a pot of cheese and wondered what chemical changes it was undergoing as it sat there. Blaise prodded a piece of ham with his knife, and a small army of ants scattered.

Sunni squeezed her eyes shut. Between the sight of the ants and the eggy smell, her big lunch was in danger of moving upward and out.

Amelia scanned the table with horror. "Mr. Wheatley does not seem used to providing hospitality."

"I cannot help that." Henry crossed his arms over his chest, looking slightly uncomfortable.

The servant backed into the parlor with a tray containing a tarnished teapot and stained cups, deposited it on the table, and disappeared without a word.

Amelia poured several cups out and wrinkled her nose again. "This tea is fishy."

"Leave it, then!" said Henry, getting up and pacing around the parlor.

No one spoke. Sunni fidgeted in her seat, trying to keep her stays from digging into her, while Blaise sat rigid in his chair, looking as if he were scarcely breathing.

Henry kept checking his pocket watch. "We have been here for over half an hour. What is occupying him?"

As if on cue, the servant put his nose around the door. "Follow me, if you please."

Late afternoon sun filtered in through the small windows in the stairwell, highlighting floating dust motes in the air as they climbed. The rotten-egg smell grew stronger and was tinged with other unidentified but equally unpleasant odors.

On the second floor, the servant opened a door and bowed, before ducking away with a strange look on his face.

"Come!" Wheatley growled from within.

The room was a darkened pit of heat and stench. Wheatley was slumped in a wooden chair, dressed in a loose dressing gown, with a striped cloth wound around his wigless, and seemingly hairless, head. His gaunt cheeks were shaded with dark stubble.

There was no furniture, other than a few tables covered in opened books, papers, skulls, broken clockworks, and a large hourglass. Stuffed reptiles and snakes were suspended from the ceiling on ropes, like prey waiting for a giant spider to consume them. Several small, glowing furnaces stood in and around the hearth, their outflow pipes hooked into the chimney to take smoke and fumes up and away. Fearsome iron hooks, tongs, and bellows were scattered about.

A number of graceful but oddly shaped glass vessels balanced on stands and tripods. Some were like the head of an elephant, with a long, tapering trunklike appendage on one side and a small spout on top. There was a dark substance smoldering at the base of one vessel.

"By heaven, Wheatley, do you intend to poison yourself and everyone else?" Henry cried, shaking his friend by the shoulder. "Is this why you cannot keep a servant for long?"

Wheatley's eyes were wide and bloodshot. "Good day, Featherstone . . . Miss Featherstone. And the two runaways . . . Ah, you are costumed for the masquerade." He got up, teetered slightly, and came to greet them. "Welcome to my laboratory."

"More like the Devil's inferno." Henry fanned the air with his mask. "Explain why you summoned us. Quickly, man, before we are overcome by fumes."

"I have been working since I last saw you," said Wheatley. "It is going well."

"Working at what?"

"You shall see."

Sunni thought she would vomit if they didn't get out

of there soon. "Mr. Wheatley, have you spoken to the magicians?"

"No." Wheatley shrugged. "The magicians I know of are not capable of solving this."

Blaise held his nose. "What do you mean, sir?"

Wheatley sidled over to one of the furnaces and checked inside. He slammed the doors shut and turned back to them. "A question. Does the painted door grow its handle out before one's eyes? Like a plant bursting from soil?"

"It's more instant than that," said Sunni. "The handle just appears."

"And then retracts when a person has passed through? Returning to its flat, painted state?"

Sunni and Blaise both nodded.

"That sounds to me like the work of astral magic. If we were in Venice during the 1580s, we could perhaps call upon certain artists there who were said to have mastered celestial forces to bring their paintings to life." Wheatley darted about, picking papers off the floor and peering at them. "But their magical abilities died with them. I know of no one who can work with such powers now."

Sunni gulped. *Fausto Corvo was a master of astral magic. He had to be one of the artists Wheatley meant.*

"Artists had magical abilities?" Blaise asked with a waver in his voice.

"None more than one named *il Corvo*—the Raven. But he vanished under mysterious circumstances, never to be seen again. There was one other I heard of, who might have learned some magical skills." Wheatley screwed up his face as he thought. "Bellini. Maffeo Bellini."

Sunni started coughing. She had never expected to hear *that* name again: the rival painter Soranzo had paid to ferret out Corvo's magical secrets using deception and bribery. Maffeo's treachery had forced Corvo and his three apprentices to flee Venice, thereby provoking Soranzo's obsessive hunt for him.

"That is all very well," said Henry. "But we are in the year 1752."

Amelia held a handkerchief to her nose. "Can anyone aid Sunniva and Blaise in *this* century, Mr. Wheatley?"

"Miss, I have been working all night toward this goal." Wheatley's bulging eyes gleamed. "I believe the painted door's magic is quite simple. Throgmorton knows how to awaken it and then put it back to sleep, as one lights and extinguishes a candle. But his power goes beyond this simple action."

"How?" Blaise burst out.

"He opens not only the door, but time itself."

"Using the symbol he writes on the door?" asked Amelia.

"I have not got to that yet," said Wheatley. "Though perhaps the number nine identifies him and allows him through." He suddenly weaved away toward his glass vessels and peered into the one containing the dark substance. "No, there is much more to this than a number."

"Come, man, explain — or I shall fall dead from this toxic air," said Henry.

"I am grappling with the question of the red elixir."

"The red elixir?"

"Alchemists who desire to make gold must seek the

red elixir," Wheatley muttered as if he were talking to himself.

Blaise breathed out. "Alchemists?"

"Throgmorton may have used a cunning version of the alchemical red elixir on the painted door. That is my conclusion."

"But we don't know what the red stuff was," Sunni pointed out.

"They said it was crimson," said Blaise. "But that's all."

Wheatley gave a low snort. "Not crimson. Crimson is extracted from scaly insects. That will hardly open the door of time." He gazed at the substance in the glass vessel and checked the hole at the top, which was tightly sealed. "It was more likely vermilion, and even then . . ."

"What has alchemy got to do with this?" asked Blaise.

"Alchemists believe that all matter is alive and can be transformed under the right conditions, hence their attempt to transmute base metals into gold. Everything in the universe contains an element called ether, a substance that fills all space, like an invisible glue holding everything together." Wheatley touched the glass. "I believe that an innovative red elixir, unlike any other, has been used on this painted door. One that can bend ether and dissolve the membranes separating the strands of time."

Henry raised his eyebrows. "You think Throgmorton makes alchemical pigments?"

"It would require a laboratory with the correct equipment, like mine," said Wheatley. "And the process is lethal in the wrong hands."

"There's no laboratory in the Academy," Blaise insisted.

"The only paint we ever saw was carried inside pigs' bladders."

"Then I do not know where he could have obtained such an elixir," said Wheatley. He pawed through a pile of books and papers and held up a crude manuscript. "There were a few men who openly sought to transmute ether. One was Peregrin, a London alchemist of the distant past. This is one of the only records of his recipe, and I paid dearly for it. Inside that vessel is my first attempt at creating the elixir, but Peregrin's directions are almost impossibly cryptic, and I may only guess at them." He nodded at the sealed glass container. "To begin, I have married quicksilver with sulfur. This will produce a vermilion-colored red pigment."

"Quicksilver is mercury," said Sunni, covering her nose in alarm. "It's poisonous."

Wheatley scrutinized her as closely as he had in the theater. "How do you know this?"

"We learned about it in my t-time," Sunni stammered.

He raised his eyebrows but said nothing.

Amelia sat down on the chair and, from behind her handkerchief, asked, "Mr. Wheatley, did this alchemist—Peregrin—succeed in making his red elixir?"

"I have found no proof that he did." Wheatley wobbled slightly on his feet. "And he died, poisoned by his own experiments, in 1583."

"1583!" Amelia blinked. "That is the second time today we have heard that date."

"How so?" asked Wheatley.

"A date on a painting in our gallery." Henry coughed

loudly. "Wheatley, I think you should beware or you will also poison yourself. Now the most important question: when will this red elixir of yours be ready?"

"According to Peregrin's recipe, in forty days. The work must incubate like an egg, and no one may interfere with it as it does so."

Forty days! He might as well have said forty years. Sunni nearly fell over with the heat, putrid air, and her own disappointment. And there was no guarantee that it would even work.

"Is that not hopeful news?" Amelia asked Sunni and Blaise.

"Very hopeful, ma'am," Blaise muttered, and Sunni knew that he was as crushed as she was.

With a determined look, Amelia whispered something into Henry's ear. He listened, poker-faced, and nodded.

"Excellent work, sir. We shall await your results," he said. "In the meantime, Sunniva and Blaise shall have to stay with other members of the Pell Mell Club. I will explain later, but it is too dangerous for them to reside with us. You are far too occupied with work, Wheatley, so we will ask Martingale to take them after our meeting at the masquerade tonight."

"I see," said Wheatley.

Henry smiled. "Come, now, sir, enough work for today. You must ready yourself for the masquerade. Time is flying."

Wheatley burst into wheezing laughter at the mention of time.

"Have you a costume, Mr. Wheatley?" asked Amelia.

"Yes, yes."

"We shall wait for you in the dining room." Henry offered his arm to his sister and they quickly made for the door.

Shielding their noses, Sunni and Blaise followed.

"Wait," Wheatley called to them in a hushed tone. "What do you make of my news?"

"Very good, sir," said Sunni, trying to keep moving out of the foul laboratory.

"Excellent," Blaise agreed. "If the elixir works."

"It shall work," said Wheatley. "I will see to it. No matter how long it takes."

The oddness of his voice made Sunni glance back at him again.

Wheatley's eyes were unnaturally round and glittery, riveted upon the sealed glass vessel. "And it will be a work of *genius*."

Chapter 21

When Wheatley finally appeared in the dining parlor, he wore a tattered cloak, a white wig, and a three-cornered hat above a startling mask with a long pointed bird's beak.

His mouth was set in a thin line. "I am ready."

Masks back on, they left the shuttered house, setting off in the direction of the river Thames. They had to pick their way around discarded animal bones, horse manure, and other unmentionables. For Sunni, this meant having to hold her dress and cloak up the whole time, while getting used to her high-heeled ladies' shoes. Blaise was not much better off, contending with the oversize bows on his shoes, which thwacked against his ankles.

"Look at that traffic jam," he whispered to Sunni as they turned into the main road leading toward the sprawling Royal Hospital. "I thought our traffic was bad."

There was a cacophony of clattering hooves, bellowing coachmen, and irate pedestrians all the way to Ranelagh Gardens, where the carriages stood three deep at the entrance. They had to thread their way through the chaos, even resorting to crawling under the bellies of horses and stepping over railings to join the costumed revelers streaming into the masquerade.

"We shall make for the Rotunda building and secure a private box in which to have supper. There is one we Pell Mells particularly like," said Henry. "From there we shall have a good view of the entertainment."

"Make sure you stay close to us," Amelia said to Sunni and Blaise. "It will be easy to become separated."

"Yes, I strongly suggest you do not become lost." Henry held up a finger in warning. "The Rotunda is surrounded by tree-lined paths. That is all well and good in daytime, but at night you must keep your wits about you, even though the paths will be well lit. Anyone may attend Ranelagh Gardens, including pickpockets, and all will be masked until midnight. Perfect conditions for anonymous mischief."

"But you will have no reason to be wandering about the gardens. And we shall be gone by midnight, I hope," said Amelia, shivering. "I wish to be well away from Chelsea before then."

Where will Sunni and I be at midnight? Blaise wondered as they arrived at the Gardens.

"Yes," Henry agreed. "I do not want to be away from home for long. Blaise and Sunniva, you should refrain from speaking. Keep your voices low at the very least."

By the time everyone had squeezed through the entrance, paying their few shillings for tickets, the sky was bloodred over the darkening lines of trees leading down toward the Thames. A thousand lanterns twinkled in the branches, and strains of music came from a huge round building with three levels of windows.

Blaise swung his head back and forth as they headed

toward it, trying to take in everything—and everyone—through his narrow eyeholes. Unsettled by the strangeness of people's costumes lit only by flickering candles, he concentrated on following Henry and Amelia and keeping Sunni by his side. Wheatley trailed behind them.

They filed through the Rotunda's high-arched entrance, where a costumed orchestra played under huge chandeliers. Blaise looked around at the strolling guests smiling under their eye masks and elaborate headwear, sweeping their wide gowns and capes behind them and causing little breezes in the stuffy air. Some wore no masks but were dressed as Turkish pashas, country shepherdesses, or other extravagant characters. Others were covered head to toe like he was, wearing similar Venetian masks that startled him every time he caught sight of one. *I look just as creepy as they do.* He let out a breath and tried to relax behind his camouflage.

Three floors of small candlelit rooms, like boxes in a theater, overlooked the round hall. Henry led them to the second floor, and they snaked along a corridor until they came to a particular box whose table was spread with a supper of sliced ham, bread and butter, and a pot of tea.

The lone man seated in the box turned his nightmarish masked face toward them. Blaise shrank back against the wall, disconcerted.

"I am sorry, this box is occupied," said the masked man, adjusting his giant red papier-mâché nose.

Henry ignored him and swept inside. "Good evening, Trevelyan. Your voice gives you away. Where are the others?"

Trevelyan got up and bowed. "Ah, good evening, Featherstone. The streets are a pretty tangle of carriages and revelers intent upon ale and mischief, so I am not surprised they are delayed." He stared at the two sets of ladies' shoes on the newcomers' feet, but said nothing. "I ordered supper in the hope you would all arrive soon. I see we have unusual company this evening."

They settled themselves, and Amelia began pouring tea and handing around platters of meat.

"Yes, the Club must welcome ladies for tonight only." Henry lowered his voice. "Throgmorton has put a price on our visitors' heads. Villains broke in during the night and nearly took one of them, but did not succeed."

"Good heavens," Trevelyan murmured. Wheatley flexed his hands on the table and mumbled something.

Henry went on. "Our visitors will travel incognito

tonight and find refuge elsewhere until a way is found to return them home."

"Yes, yes, I see."

"Since we met yesterday, Wheatley has begun concocting an elixir that may transform matter and ether. He believes it could open up the fabric of time."

Trevelyan turned his large nose toward Wheatley's beak. "Extraordinary work, sir! If it succeeds, it will bring you the recognition you well deserve." He paused. "Have you deduced anything concerning the mark of nine that Throgmorton scrawls on the door?"

"I cannot think of everything at once," Wheatley muttered. "The elixir itself has occupied every moment of my time. One must first possess the substance before one can make a mark with it."

"How long will your work take?"

Too long, Blaise thought. The warmth of his costume and the din of the orchestra were making his heartbeat quicken and his head throb.

"Where is Catterwall?" Henry peered down at the crowd on the Rotunda floor. "He is meant to be seeking out magical signs and ciphers."

"Perhaps Beelzebub has made away with him," Trevelyan scoffed.

"I shall be very annoyed if he has."

"Well," said the poet, "I myself have been pondering signs and symbols since yesterday. England's greatest poets and playwrights played with numbers. Words were made into numbers and numbers made into words using ancient Greek and Hebrew numerology. It is said that Mr. Shakespeare's and Mr. Marlowe's plays were rife with secret codes."

"To what end?" asked Henry.

" 'Twas the so-called art of mystical writing," Trevelyan whispered, "meant to rouse hidden powers."

Like the powers of the painted door? Blaise knew he was not supposed to speak, but he could not help whispering, "How did they make their codes?"

Trevelyan hunched over the table, and the others bent closer. "The simplest way is this: assign a number to each letter of the alphabet. Therefore, A is 1, B is 2, C is 3 — and so on," he said. "Using this method, the letters in TREVELYAN add up to 122. We add 1+2+2 and get 5. Therefore, 5 is my numerical name-symbol. Though I doubt it shall open any magical doors."

"Maybe it would if you used the red elixir," said Sunni in a small voice.

"Do you think Throgmorton has to write his personal number every time he goes through?" he whispered to Sunni. "Like a password. Maybe we'd have to do that, too."

A = 1	N = 14
B = 2	O = 15
C = 3	P = 16
D = 4	Q = 17
E = 5	R = 18
F = 6	S = 19
G = 7	T = 20
H = 8	U = 21
I = 9	V = 22
J = 10	W = 23
K = 11	X = 24
L = 12	Y = 25
M = 13	Z = 26

"Since Throgmorton isn't a nine, he must use another name," she replied under her breath.

In his head, Blaise began transforming the name THROGMORTON into a number. It added up to ten. But the other name painted onto the silver mirror in Livia's portrait was a nine. His own name, Doran, was a seven.

Wheatley stuffed a piece of bread into his mouth. "The nine must awaken the inert, and once it is active, it may be transmuted. But for this, one will need the elixir."

Blaise watched his thin lips move under the monumental beak. He knew this guy was helping them, but it didn't mean he had to like him or enjoy being around him.

"Explain, sir," said Trevelyan. "That is all Greek to me."

"I think he means that the painted door has magic embedded in it," said Blaise. "When Throgmorton draws a nine on it with his elixir, he makes the door materialize and open."

"Why could you not just say so, Wheatley? Inertia and transmutation, indeed." Trevelyan's outlandish red nose bobbed up and down, and Blaise had to look away. He watched the swirling cloaks and masked faces below on the Rotunda floor and imagined elbowing his way through them to get to the fresh air outside.

Henry slapped the table. "By heaven, where are the others? I am especially surprised at Martingale."

"If he does not hurry, he will miss this once-in-a-lifetime occasion," said Trevelyan with a slight sneer. "And he will welcome in midnight by fending off ignorant oafs in the street."

"I do hope not," said Amelia, alarmed.

"Not all Englishmen are celebrating tonight's event. Some feel cheated and they will be cross. Especially after they have had a drink," Trevelyan said, spreading butter on bread.

"But why should they feel cheated?" asked Amelia.

"They do not understand why the calendar must be altered and believe that Parliament is stealing time from them," said Wheatley.

Blaise shifted on his seat, wanting to ask what on earth they were talking about, but it was Sunni who said, "Calendar? Stealing time?"

Everyone looked at her.

"Of course, you would know nothing of this," Henry said. "It is September second today. The calendar will change at midnight."

"How?"

"At midnight, England will change to the Gregorian calendar, like other countries," Amelia explained. "Parliament has decreed it, and the king ordered Ranelagh Gardens to open for this public celebration."

"We have been told this new calendar must be synchronized with heaven's planetary cycles, so we must drop eleven days this month," added Henry. "At midnight, we shall jump past them, as if they never existed."

"Just like that? Eleven days will disappear?" Sunni asked, bewildered.

"Yes, just like that."

"No one told us anything in the Academy," Blaise said in a hushed voice.

"I suppose not," said Trevelyan, chewing. "No use in child-slaves concerning themselves with the calendar."

"Quite," said Henry.

"If I'd stayed there much longer, I wouldn't have known which day it was anymore, anyway," Blaise muttered.

Henry lowered his voice again. "You shall not be obliged to go back there, Blaise, unless it is to leave this century. Trevelyan, our visitors need protection in a safe house. I had expected Martingale or Catterwall would take them tonight, but neither is here and time is flying. May I rely upon you instead?"

The poet dropped his shoulders. "I cannot risk it. My children . . . It would be too much."

Wheatley leaned forward. "I shall take them."

Blaise could almost smell the stink of the man's house, and a wave of disgust rose in him.

Henry hesitated. "Thank you, Wheatley, but no. As I said before, you are far too occupied for guests."

"I shall take them," Wheatley insisted.

Amelia twisted her body toward her brother as if entreating him to refuse, but she could say nothing aloud. Through the holes in his mask, Blaise made eye contact with Sunni. He could see his worries reflected in her eyes, too.

"If you are certain," Henry murmured awkwardly. "Only for tonight. Tomorrow, they must go to Martingale. I will send him a message as soon as I am able."

Wheatley nodded and pushed away his plate. "I have no interest in remaining here. My work calls me." He nodded to Sunni and Blaise. "If you have eaten enough, we will go."

"I wish to leave, too, Brother," said Amelia, her mouth drooping under her white mask.

Trevelyan stuffed a hunk of ham into his mouth and stood up. "Then there is no point in my waiting here alone."

Blaise followed the others out of the box, moving like a robot and imagining how foul the beds at Wheatley's house would be. An aching tiredness came over him as he anticipated being shuffled from safe house to safe house, waiting for the elusive elixir to be ready.

On the ground floor, they joined the swarm of unwashed and perfumed revelers. Henry forged ahead with Amelia in tow. Being taller than most people, Blaise could keep them in sight, but chattering herds of people held him back, and he could only watch helplessly as the pair moved farther away. Sunni was right beside him, bracing against bodies bumping into her. He presumed Wheatley and Trevelyan were behind them, but he didn't bother to look back.

The multitude swirled around them, and Blaise's heart hammered. He thrust his hand out from under his cloak and whispered to Sunni, "Hold on."

He was straining forward, about to pull Sunni around a knot of stationary people, when there was a commotion ahead. Over several wigs, he could see a scruffy masked stranger pulling Amelia deeper into the masses, while another grappled with Henry to the shrieks of nearby ladies.

Blaise yanked Sunni close and hissed, "Someone's jumped Henry and Amelia. Come on!"

His manners disappeared, and he pushed people aside to get forward. The leather satchel slung across his chest made an excellent battering ram. Sunni used her elbows when she had to and even kicked a few ankles to get people moving. They scythed through the mob toward Henry, whose mask now hung around his neck and revealed his livid, shouting face.

"Sunni. Find Amelia," Blaise urged. "They've taken her that way."

He moved forward, his arms outstretched to grab Henry's attacker by the back of the neck, but someone came from behind and hauled him aside. Just as he was about to fight back, a familiar voice made him stop.

"Are you mad, boy?" asked the man. "This way."

A body was pushed hard against Blaise's side. He could not see who it was, but from the wide skirt brushing his leg, he guessed it was Sunni. The noisy mob parted as powerful hands steered them toward the exit. There they hit a tide of oncoming bodies streaming into the Rotunda and were maneuvered through, gasping and sweating.

Blaise tried to turn, but the voice said, "Face forward."

They squeezed through the exit and were guided around the curved side of the Rotunda to a place where fewer people milled.

"Stop here," said the voice, releasing the grip on his arm. Blaise whirled around and faced Wheatley. The man's other hand was still on Sunni's shoulder.

"Why did you make us leave, Mr. Wheatley?" he said hoarsely. "We were trying to help the Featherstones!"

"And call attention to yourselves? You would have been taken."

"Now what?"

The beak nodded up and down. "Trevelyan has gone after Miss Featherstone—who should never have been here in the first place—and no doubt Henry Featherstone is dealing his attacker blows he shall never forget."

"That's good news, I guess," said Sunni, trying to twist gracefully out of Wheatley's grip. But he would not let go.

"It is, indeed," Wheatley said. "But we must make haste. It is too dangerous to stay here now."

"Your hand is hurting—" whispered Sunni.

"Can you let go of her shoulder, please, sir?" Blaise asked as politely as he could.

Several passersby looked curiously at them, and Wheatley said under his breath, "I apologize," as he dropped his hand to his side.

Sunni sprang away, panting under her mask.

"I do not mean to harm you," Wheatley said breathily. "Far from it. You know so many things I wish to know. Things I *must* know!"

Blaise took Sunni's arm, saying nothing.

"I will help you, but you must also help me." Wheatley held out one hand. "Come, we should leave this place now."

"How are we to help you?" Sunni asked. Blaise held her arm fast, and they made no move to go anywhere.

"You need my red elixir, but it has a price."

Blaise's blood rose. "A *price*?"

"It is little to ask," said Wheatley, his open hand curling into a fist. "In exchange for my elixir, I demand to go with you to the future."

Chapter 22

"Y ou can't come with us!" said Sunni, incredulous. "You belong in our time as much as we belong in this one—not at all!"

"You have nothing without me," said Wheatley between gritted teeth. "I am taking the trouble to make the elixir, at no small risk to myself."

"That doesn't mean you should use it yourself," said Blaise. "And you won't be able to if we don't tell you where the painted door is."

"Tell me where it is, or I shall not give you my elixir!"

"You said you'd help us, not hold us to ransom," Sunni said, indignant. "We're not bargaining."

"You deny me so much as a glimpse of your world," Wheatley croaked. "You would keep me chained to this time, when I, more than any man in this century, deserve to go to yours!"

A cool breeze swirled up, catching cloaks and causing a loud rustling in the trees. Sunni's skin prickled at the sight of a dark shape darting behind a trunk in the distance.

"Blaise," she mumbled, "we can't stay here."

"My home is safe." Wheatley's tattered cloak billowed. "Come with me now!"

"No. I want to make sure the Featherstones are all right," said Blaise. "Let's go, Sunni."

Wheatley's mouth hung open. "You would throw my assistance and hospitality back in my face?"

"Your price is too high."

Wheatley lunged. "How dare you!"

Another gust rattled the leaves as Sunni and Blaise bolted away toward the network of paths around the Rotunda. Wheatley pursued them briefly, then staggered to a halt and stared after them.

"You shall return!" His voice followed them on the wind. "You have nowhere else to go. And I am the only one who can help you!"

Sunni held her mask tight with one hand and her leather satchel with the other. Her shoulder was rubbed raw from the strap, but she kept pace with Blaise. "What are we going to do now?"

"I think we should head back to the Rotunda," said Blaise, constantly checking over his shoulder as he slowed down to a rapid walk.

"Then why are we going this way?"

"It's the long way around. More chance of shaking off Wheatley."

"What if we can't find the others?"

Blaise's voice was gruff. "Don't worry about that now!"

He and Sunni wove in among strolling guests parading up and down the walkways, watchful that Wheatley had not caught up. Blaise turned into a quieter path leading down toward the river.

"This isn't taking us back to the Rotunda," Sunni protested.

"It will eventually. There'll be a turn."

"I don't like it."

"It's just for a little bit longer," he said.

The farther they walked, the more the crowds thinned out, as did the number of twinkling lanterns. The path grew darker and darker. The Thames was a horizontal black stripe ahead of them, bordered above by a starry indigo sky.

"This is creepy," said Sunni, looking all around her as they came to a junction with another path. "Let's get out of here."

"Okay, okay. We want to be heading in that direction," said Blaise, turning left. "This should take us toward the Rotunda."

"It looks like a dead end."

"No — I bet there's another turn but we can't see it from here."

"I don't know." Sunni stopped and peered at the solitary path. They were completely alone. "Remember what Henry said."

"There's no one here." Blaise offered his hand. "Come on."

She followed him, unconvinced, and they walked farther up the new path, chilled by the wind off the river. With every step, the buzzing sounds of the crowds grew fainter and silence surrounded them. She wanted to rip the mask from her face so she could see properly, but she didn't dare.

"This is a lonely place to find oneself," said a languid voice behind them.

Sunni gasped as she and Blaise whirled around. Some distance away, farther up the path, stood Throgmorton. He was dressed completely in black except for a gold-embroidered waistcoat that glinted in the light of a nearby lantern.

"You are well disguised," he said, standing completely still. "But when I noticed two young figures talking with a man-bird about going to the future, the costumes became pointless."

Blaise took Sunni's arm and began to move away.

"Corvo's three magical paintings!" Throgmorton said. "You know where they are, and you will tell me now."

"We are *not* telling you anything!" Blaise replied angrily.

"Then you have had your last chance. Livia and I are leaving before Starling's house is destroyed, and with it, the painted door. It is the only way back to your time."

Destroyed! The word shot through Sunni's head. Why should it be destroyed? Once again, she envisioned the blue plaque on the front of Starling House, its words and numbers fuzzy and hard to remember. Had *destroyed* been one of them?

"What are you talking about?" Blaise shouted.

"Even I cannot change destiny, Blaise, much as I would wish to. The Academy was always destined to end in September 1752. I have made the most of it while I could."

"You're making this up, like everything else you've told us!"

Destroyed. Sunni's memory of the blue plaque snapped into focus as if a lens had been adjusted. *Destroyed on 14th September 1752.*

"The house will be destroyed at some point in the next few hours. It will be impossible to pass through the painted door, for it will not exist anymore."

"No, you're wrong! It won't be destroyed until September fourteenth," shouted Sunni, clutching at Blaise's cloak. "I read it on the blue plaque at Starling House."

Throgmorton's laugh rang out. "But the calendar changes at midnight!"

"He's right," Blaise whispered. "Today is September second, and we're about to lose eleven days."

Henry's words came back to Sunni: *At midnight we shall jump past them, as if they never existed.* She frantically counted on her fingers: 3, 4, 5, 6, 7, 8, 9, 10, 11, 12, 13. "Oh no—tomorrow is September fourteenth!"

Sunni almost staggered and fell as this sank in. Her head began to spin, trying to cope with the enormity of it.

"Correct!" came Throgmorton's voice. "And it will soon be midnight." He cupped his hand around his chin. "I am certain your stepbrother, Dean, will help me find the paintings instead. I shall see him very soon."

"Dean! Stay away from him," Sunni gasped. "He doesn't know anything!"

"You shall pay the price for defying me." Throgmorton's embroidered waistcoat glinted as he raised one arm high. "Stay in this world and see how you fare."

He brought his arm down, and several nearby tree

trunks seemed to come alive as hunched figures emerged from behind them.

Blaise and Sunni took off in the opposite direction, their satchels flying.

"Run away!" Throgmorton's laugh faded. "Run away for the last time."

"Come on!" Blaise pulled Sunni off the path and out of the lantern light. Her feet moved jerkily in her high-heeled shoes, as if some outside force were operating her legs. They cut through brush and round statues, interrupting kissing couples and pick-pocketings in progress, outrunning Throgmorton's henchmen. At last, they burst onto a brightly lit path full of laughing revelers and merged with a crowd moving like a lazy river. They pushed into its center, camouflaged by people's tall wigs and outlandish costumes.

"Can you see any of them?" Blaise panted, peering around through his eyeholes.

"No . . ." Sunni tried to catch her breath. "We've lost them . . . I think."

Blaise unbuckled his satchel and squinted at his watch hidden there. "If this is right, we have only a little more than an hour before midnight."

"No!" Hot tears started down Sunni's face. "What do we do?"

"We get transport—fast. If we can outrun Throgmorton and get back to the house first . . ."

"Then what?"

"I don't know, but it's our last chance. We've just got

to get back there!" He yanked the mask from his face and tossed it into the bushes.

"Okay." She cast her mask aside and rubbed the tears from her face. Blaise put his arm around her shoulders and they moved with the crowd toward a long rectangular pool, glittering with reflected light. In the pool's center was an ornate pavilion, with a pagoda-like roof, connected to land by a short footbridge. People milled around the pavilion, leaning out from its angular corners and waving to others on shore.

When they got to within a few yards of the footbridge, Blaise slowed down and scanned the people inside.

"What?" whispered Sunni.

"We need to find Henry and the others. He's got a carriage." His lip drooped in disappointment. "I don't think they're here."

"How are we ever going to find them?" She gestured at the brightly lit Rotunda in the distance. "That place is packed, and they might not even be there anymore."

"Then we'll find another way to Jeremiah's."

They dodged in and out of the hordes, careful not to be followed, then sneaked through the exit, where a jumble of horse-drawn vehicles vied for space. Once again they had to push past hawkers, porters, and angry drivers; dodge more manure; and slip through gaps between coaches that might shift at any moment.

When they came to the edge of the jam, Blaise began asking drivers to take them to Phoenix Square, but the carriages were either reserved or were asking exorbitant fees. "Let's find Henry and Amelia's coach. Maybe the driver will take us if we explain. And if that doesn't work, there might be cheaper carriages farther away from here."

As they turned into the back streets of Chelsea, the lights of Ranelagh Gardens and the Royal Hospital disappeared. Nearing Wheatley's house, Sunni half expected him to leap out at them, but she kept telling herself that he was still at the masquerade. She wrenched her foot on some rubble and cursed under her breath, wishing they were as clever as Sleek at weaving through the dark. Soon, Blaise bent down and tore the fussy ribbons off his shoes.

"I think the Featherstones' carriage turned here after it let us out," he said, taking them down a side road just before Wheatley's dark house.

"Are you sure?"

"Look," said Blaise, pointing at three silhouettes walking ahead of them. Two men were escorting a woman between them. "Hurry!"

They caught up, getting so close that they could hear one of the men.

"I am delighted I arrived when I did, Miss Featherstone," the voice said. "For once I was pleased to be delayed, for it meant I could fight that villain off."

"You have your uses at times, Martingale," said the other man.

"It's Henry!" Blaise squeezed Sunni's arm. "Mr. Featherstone! Miss Featherstone!"

The trio spun around. Even in the dark, Sunni could see that the Featherstones' masks were gone. Martingale was also barefaced.

"Blaise and Sunniva?" Henry's mouth hung open. "By

heaven, we lost you in the fray! We hoped you were with Wheatley but saw no sign of you."

"He's still at the masquerade. Please, sir, we need to go to Phoenix Square immediately!" said Sunni.

Henry hesitated, as though he might demand some explanation on the spot, but Amelia put her arm firmly on his and he relented.

"Come, then," he said, and they hurried to the inn, where the footman was snoring on the backseat of the carriage.

"Wake now, man," Henry barked. The man was out and up in his seat like a shot, allowing the party to squeeze inside. "Take us to Phoenix Square immediately."

The startled footman stuttered, "Y-yes, sir, but I am not certain where Phoenix Square is."

"By heaven, we should have brought Rowley instead."

"He might have been recognized from last night. You said so yourself," said Amelia.

Sunni put her head in her hands. "Now what?"

"Fear not. I know the way," said Martingale. "Jeremiah Starling lives in Phoenix Square." He shouted directions from the window, and the carriage clattered out of Chelsea's village streets.

"You know Jeremiah Starling?" asked Sunni, astonished.

Martingale looked at her curiously. "Featherstone and I are acquainted with Starling from Old Slaughter's coffee-house, though we have not seen him in months. But how would you know him?"

"The Academy is in Jeremiah Starling's house. He made

the painted door—and if we don't get there by midnight, we can never go through it again!"

"The painted door is in *Starling*'s house, made by his own hand?" asked Martingale, aghast.

"Yes, and it's going to be destroyed on September fourteenth!" said Sunni. "Throgmorton is going to escape before that happens, and we have only one more chance to get through."

"Destroyed on September fourteenth!" said Henry, pulling out his pocket watch and squinting at it in the gloom. "Are you certain?"

"Yes," said Sunni. "It's part of history. That's why we have to get back through the door before it happens."

"If I am seeing my watch correctly, it is just after eleven o'clock," Henry said. "You have little time—and no red elixir."

"My brother is right," said Amelia worriedly. "What will you do without the elixir?"

"We don't even know if it works," said Blaise. "All we can do is get to the painted door and see if we can find a way through somehow."

"If you do not succeed tonight, perhaps Wheatley can discover another way when his elixir is ready," said Martingale.

"We have to go through that door," said Sunni mournfully. "It connects to one in our time."

"Besides, Wheatley put too high a price on his elixir," Blaise said. "He demanded to come with us to the future in return for it."

241

"What? Wheatley set a condition upon his assistance?" Martingale was astonished.

"I cannot believe he would do such a thing," said Henry, outraged.

"He won't get anywhere without the painted door," said Sunni.

"That is some comfort," said Henry. "But I am appalled that Starling let such evil-doing happen under his own roof."

"I don't think he had any choice. Throgmorton controls everything," Blaise said quickly. "He has a hold over Jeremiah. We think it's about money."

Martingale shook his head. "This does not surprise me. Starling is a talented painter, but poor as a church mouse and in debt."

The carriage made a turn into the heart of Covent Garden and stopped abruptly.

"Sir, there is a problem ahead," shouted the footman from his seat in front. "A blockage of carriages, and something burning in the road."

"As we feared, there is mischief afoot. I shall have a look." Henry jumped out of the door. When he returned, less than a minute later, he was breathless. "We can go no farther east through Covent Garden. It is nearing midnight, and a mob has gathered, angry at losing their eleven days. They are moving south apparently, in packs like wolves, intent upon making trouble."

Sunni reached forward and squeezed Amelia's hand. "We can't wait."

"You must," Amelia objected. "It is not safe—"

Before anyone could say or do anything, Sunni pushed herself through the narrow door. Blaise jumped out after her, mumbling, "Thanks for everything."

"You must help Jeremiah Starling after his house is destroyed," Sunni called over her shoulder, and Blaise added, "Please buy his paintings, or something, so he can rebuild it. None of this is his fault!"

By the time Henry and Martingale leaped from the carriage, shouting for them to wait, Sunni and Blaise had already melted into the nearest dark lane.

Chapter 23

Sunni and Blaise moved steadily eastward toward Phoenix Square. Blaise's homing instinct, and his memory of escape with Fleet and Sleek, said this was the right way. They evaded link-boys wandering about with their glims, offering to show the way for a few pence. They spoke to no one and kept their three-cornered hats low over their faces, ready to lash out at anyone who attempted to divert their attention with a view to snatching their goods.

"We didn't say proper good-byes back at the carriage," murmured Sunni. "I feel bad about that."

"It doesn't matter," said Blaise, even though it did matter to him, too.

The sound of high yelping voices and low growling ones floated over the rooftops from somewhere. Sunni and Blaise skirted the edge of the buildings and peered around the next corner.

A motley assortment of men half marched, half staggered along the street, some bearing flaming rushes that had been dipped in fat to make them burn. One or two rabble-rousers called for everyone to go and speak to the king about the problem of their stolen eleven days. Others followed, some smashing windows and others brandishing knives in their teeth, like pirates. Several turned into the lane where Sunni and Blaise were and reeled straight into them.

Just as one of the drunks was about to connect his fist to Blaise's chin, Sunni yanked her friend away. They had to run clear across the main road, dodging men waving their torches before them like scythes, and urchins who followed at their heels, taunting them. Several men lurched as if to give chase but wobbled to a halt, shouting a stream of abuse at them, as if Sunni and Blaise were responsible for midnight coming and stealing time.

The pair did not stop running till they were four or five streets away, and when they finally stopped, Blaise panted, "Look over there!"

Phoenix Square was within view. Other houses in the street leading into the square half hid it, but Blaise knew this was the right place. A shudder of trepidation ran through him.

"Are you ready?" he asked, and took her hand in his.

"Yes."

They set off with the unsettling knowledge that they had walked this same way only a few days before, but in the twenty-first century. The square was mostly in gloom, the elm trees planted in its center garden looming like dark giants. Each entrance was lit with a twinkling lantern hung over the top of the door, and Blaise no longer had to guess which one they wanted. He had been here before, with only a map on a paper napkin to guide him.

"Wait," Sunni breathed. "Maybe we should go in the back way." She pointed at the candles burning in the front windows of number 36, including the workshop. "People are up."

They hastened back to the mouth of Phoenix Square and hunted for the alley Fleet and Sleek had taken them through. It was there, like a black tunnel.

When they reached the courtyard door, Blaise felt around under his cloak and fished something out.

"Fleet's skeleton key," he whispered, and fumbled to fit it into the lock. The door swung open with a high squeak.

To their relief, Throgmorton's study window was dark, so they moved past freely and Blaise went at the back door lock. Once inside the dim ground-floor hall, they undid their cloaks and threw them into a corner.

They tiptoed up the stairs, carrying their damp shoes and praying that no boards would groan under their feet. They climbed from murkiness to the dim light of the second-floor landing. A single guiding candle flickered, but no one seemed to be about. The front and back rooms were empty, though well lit. *Had they managed to get there before Throgmorton?*

Sunni and Blaise moved up to the third floor, where more candles burned in wall sconces. Livia's door was slightly ajar, and a candelabrum glowed, but there was no sound.

One more floor. Blaise could hardly breathe as they inched their way up the last set of stairs. The Academy boys' bedroom door was opened slightly, but it was dark within. The workshop blazed with light, and there was the sound of movement inside, but no voices.

Blaise caught a ghostlike shape out of the corner of his

left eye. Toby peeped from the boys' sleeping room, his face as white as his nightshirt and his eyes wide at the sight of the returning pair.

Sunni quickly held a finger to her lips, and Toby nodded, while at the same time gesturing wildly for them not to go into the workshop. Blaise gestured back at him to wait there, that it was all okay, and moved to the workshop door with Sunni.

There were so many lanterns and candles alight, every nook and cranny was illuminated. At the center of the room, Throgmorton loomed over a table in his black overcoat and gold-embroidered waistcoat, folding a painting up in a cloth.

Blaise's heart sank. They had no choice but to confront their enemy, even if it was the last thing they did.

Livia was examining wrapped paintings leaning against the wall. Her satisfied smile seemed almost painted on, Blaise thought.

"Do not forget anything, miss. Shall I also give you the shirt off my back?" Jeremiah leaned against a wall, a dusting of snuff grouts covering his front like dead gnats.

"I should not want that putrid thing," Livia said, the smile unwavering.

The painter lurched toward Throgmorton. "You leave me with nothing, sir!"

"On the contrary," said Throgmorton, one arm out to hold him off. "I leave you with your home. That is ample payment for your services. And I am taking the stolen artworks away so that you will not be caught with them."

"How thoughtful. I am sure they will bring a pretty penny in whichever place you sell them," Jeremiah said with a sneer. "And the boys? What of them? You brought them here, and now you drop them."

"It is not my choice. Our travels must end, and destiny says tonight is our last journey through the door," Throgmorton said. "The Academy is yours. Do with it what you will."

Jeremiah gave an angry laugh. "With what funds? It costs money to feed and house the boys."

"You will have to find money yourself from now on." Throgmorton frowned as he finished wrapping the painting of the musketeer. He glanced at Livia. "Soon, my dear."

"I cannot wait, Father," said Livia, smoothing her curls.

Blaise peered at her, trying to see what he had found so irresistible only a few days earlier. His heart was beating hard, but not because of Livia. She no longer raised as much as one butterfly in his stomach.

Sunni took hold of Blaise's forearm and squeezed hard. He nodded and she waved her arm to Toby. The boys appeared, one by one, and pressed up behind them. Sunni and Blaise put their damp shoes on and slid into the workshop with the boys in tow.

"Throgmorton's not telling you everything, Mr. Starling," Blaise announced, trembling with nervous energy. "They're running off, like rats, because they know this house is about to be destroyed!"

"Liars!" Throgmorton snarled. "You are the rats— trying to save your own skins. But it's too late."

"Blaise, Sunniva!" Jeremiah exclaimed, his eyes out on stalks. "What is this news?"

"Throgmorton told us himself. This house will be destroyed on September 14, 1752, and that's today!" shouted Sunni. "It's just past midnight!"

"What will you and the boys do then, Mr. Starling?" Blaise darted through the tables and easels, closer to Throgmorton. "He's lying when he says you can continue with the Academy!"

Livia rushed to her father's side and shrieked with indignation. "My father is not a liar!" Her eyes could have cut through stone.

"Yes, he is," Sunni yelled. "And so are you, Livia! Your name isn't Throgmorton at all. Why does your father have to hide who he really is?"

"By heaven," Jeremiah shouted at Throgmorton. "Who are you, man?"

"He's the greedy slimeball who chased Fausto Corvo out of Venice in 1582 because he wouldn't sell him three of his special paintings. He got so angry, he hired spies to dig out Corvo's secrets. When Corvo got wind of it and ran, this creep put a bounty on his head!" Blaise shook as he looked their enemy straight in the eye. "Your name's not Throgmorton. It's Soranzo!"

Chapter 24

W hat?" Jeremiah moved forward, and the boys spread out behind him.

Blaise pointed at Soranzo. "He lured Sunni and me here to force us to give him information about Fausto Corvo."

"Fausto Corvo!" Jeremiah gasped. "But he vanished two centuries ago."

"Soranzo's still hunting for him and his three paintings," said Blaise.

Jeremiah's brow furrowed. "But Corvo must be dead."

"I think not. And I *shall* find his lost paintings, even if he is dead. At long last, their powerful secrets will belong to me," growled Soranzo. "Thanks to Sunni and Blaise's discovery, I have the magic word, *chiaroscuro*, and I shall pass through the labyrinth at Blackhope Tower myself." He gave Blaise a hard look. "It may be closed in your century, but in my time, it is still open!"

"Blackhope Tower?" Jeremiah repeated. "*Your* time?"

"Soranzo and Livia belong in the past, Mr. Starling," said Sunni. "Not here in the eighteenth century."

"Someone with the initials M.B. painted a portrait of Livia in *1583*," Blaise said. "Maffeo Bellini maybe?"

Livia's face fell. "Where did you see *that* thing?"

"It doesn't matter," muttered Sunni.

"The name *Soranzo* was painted into the silver hand mirror," Blaise said.

"That portrait was the last thing Bellini ever made." Soranzo narrowed his eyes. "He made a mockery of my daughter's beauty. I saw to it that he never painted again."

"Not even to make you a door that could come alive and be opened?" Sunni demanded. "Someone in 1583 had to know enough magic to do that. How would you have gotten here otherwise?"

"Maffeo's sorcery skills were a poor substitute for Corvo's, but he managed to materialize a simple painted door before his career ended so abruptly. It sufficed for my aim of crossing time."

"You walked through a door in Venice and arrived in this house."

"No," said Soranzo. "Not in Venice. Here, in this place."

"You were in London in 1583?"

"My spies said Corvo escaped to Britain, so I came here with Livia to take charge of the hunt. I brought the best artisans from Venice and built a magnificent house on this land—a house with a painted door!"

"On my land, beneath our very feet?" Jeremiah's eyes grew round.

"*My* land, Starling. I owned it before your father was even born."

"What became of this grand house of yours?"

"In 1666 the Great Fire burned it to the ground," said Soranzo, clenching his fist. "And years later, your father built his house on its ashes. Then, Starling, you painted a door in the workshop and a miracle happened. I could pass through my own painted door into yours—and into the future."

"I am no magician!" Jeremiah exclaimed, appalled. "How could my painted door be possessed in such a way?"

"The sorcery passes like a ghost into any painted door on this land." Soranzo guided his daughter away from their interrogators.

"Go ahead, Soranzo! Go back and try finding Corvo in 1583!" Blaise shouted. "You can get in through the labyrinth, but you won't get out alive. There are plenty of skeletons in Blackhope Tower to prove it!"

"I shall not become a skeleton." Soranzo waved him away. "But you soon will."

Blaise pushed past the worktables and propelled himself at them, but Soranzo turned and shoved him to the ground.

Livia hissed, "You stupid boy. For that is all you are—a boy."

"Miss, you know nothing! Toby, all of you, fall in!" Jeremiah shouted as he leaped in and began grappling with Soranzo. The boys joined the fray, shouting and jumping on their enemy.

Sunni squeezed her gown between the tables and hurried around them to the painted door, but it was as flat and inert as ever. "Take us home, Soranzo! You can't leave us here!"

Livia came straight for her, one arm raised, her sleeve dripping with lace. She swept over a candle, knocking it sideways onto a drawing. Blaise could have sworn she'd done it on purpose. He heaved away from the melee and caught the girl's arm. She cried out in such pain that he nearly let go, he but managed to hold her back from Sunni.

"I owe you nothing. You will never get out!" Soranzo let out a huge belly roar and rose like a colossus, white wig ripped away, revealing his close-cropped hair. His iceberg eyes were fixed on Blaise.

With a stinging kick, Soranzo lunged and took Blaise's legs out from under him. Blaise fell to the ground, groaning and holding his head. Sunni ran to him, trying to help him and beat out the burning paper at the same time.

"Fire!" she screamed, hauling Blaise to his feet.

"Boys, beat it back!" Jeremiah bawled as he took a running punch at Soranzo and brought him down. "Take the original works and run to safety! Let the copies burn!"

"Yes," Blaise shouted. "Or else he'll take them and sell them in the twenty-first century!"

"Do you think I am a fool? They would be unmasked immediately," Soranzo gasped. "I have far better centuries to take them to!"

Livia leaped upon Jeremiah, clawing his face as she tried to tear him away from her father. In a frenzy, the Academy boys ripped the wrappings off the paintings leaning against the wall, arguing over which were the copies. When Toby took charge and handed them those he thought were originals, they bolted from the workshop, armed with paintings and drawings, while he threw the copies into the fire.

"Toby!" Jeremiah bellowed in pain, from somewhere on the floor. "Leave now!"

"Yes, boy, go into the streets with the other beggars!" Soranzo rolled on top of Jeremiah. Livia got to her feet, triumphant.

"Better than being sold to the anatomists like Will!" Sunni shouted, as she and Blaise tried to smother the flames with filthy work shirts. "The other boys didn't go to the country, did they, Soranzo? They went to the anatomists!"

Toby's face twisted in pain at hearing this. He wrapped several paintings together in a large cloth and dragged it along the floor, shielding it from the fire's sparks with his back. With one last look at the workshop, he vanished down the stairs.

Soranzo dealt Jeremiah a heavy blow, lumbered to his feet, and steered Livia toward the painted door. Blaise crawled over to Jeremiah, who had gotten to his knees and was gazing around in horror. The fire had started to consume his books and stuffed animal specimens.

"This is your destiny," sneered Livia, her hair loose and tangled. She leaned back against her father's shoulder, and he took her hand in his.

Soranzo undid his cravat and yanked his shirt open at the neck. With one swift movement, he pulled out a vial of red liquid suspended on a silver chain. It dangled there, shining. Then he reached into his waistcoat and slid out the stone shard with its curved tip.

"My precious firestone," he said, holding it up. "It was carved centuries ago by a wild Norseman and 'found' its way into my possession. This blade has spilled the blood of many animals—and men." He whispered something in Italian to his daughter, and she nodded. Her face crumpled, and to everyone's horror, Soranzo sliced the shard across her palm.

A streak of crimson bubbled up, and he gently scraped the shard over it, gathering the blood.

"You cut your own daughter," Jeremiah croaked. "You are the Devil!" He began pushing unsteadily toward the pair.

Soranzo pointed the bloodied shard at him. "This can slice your throat, Starling. Stay back."

Jeremiah froze as Soranzo released Livia. She licked her bleeding palm and laughed.

Soranzo drew the shard across his own palm and collected his blood on its tip. He opened the vial and dipped the shard in, mixing and stirring. When he withdrew it, the shard gleamed crimson.

"Red elixir," said Blaise, his eyes wide.

"You know far more than you ought, but it does not matter anymore," said Soranzo. "This is the last of the elixir, and now our blood has activated it. A great pity that Peregrin died while making more for me."

"You knew Peregrin?" Blaise's mouth hung open.

Soranzo smiled and drew Livia to the painted door. The fire threw great shadows behind them as he drew a looping number nine on the door with the wet tip of the crimson shard.

Livia opened the door and stepped through it without a backward glance.

Sunni knew it was now or never. She moved to Blaise's side and whispered, "Steal the shard. I'll distract him."

He nodded once.

"Why did you draw a nine?" Sunni called, her voice shaking as she moved closer to the painted door.

"My number-name is nine." Soranzo wrapped the crimson shard loosely in a white handkerchief and put it in his pocket.

"So my number-name is seven!" Blaise said, inching along after Sunni.

Soranzo laughed out loud and patted his pocket as he turned to follow Livia. "Little good it will do you without the elixir."

Before he stepped over the threshold, Sunni launched herself at Soranzo and threw her arms around him in a desperate embrace. "You must take us with you! Please!"

She clung on, knocking Soranzo slightly off balance, and locked eyes with Blaise. He moved in close and wrapped one arm around them, while the other hand felt for Soranzo's coat pocket.

"Get off! I am finished with you!" Soranzo pushed Sunni so hard, she fell to the ground and Blaise jumped away.

Before she could gather her wits, Soranzo had disappeared through the open door. It shut and began to return to its flat, painted form.

Instantly, Blaise was at Sunni's side, with Jeremiah hovering above them.

"Did you get it?" she whispered.

Blaise nodded and unfolded Soranzo's handkerchief.

The crimson shard was slick with red elixir. "The night-sneaks would be proud."

"Yeah, but we need a knife," said Sunni. "I'm not letting that thing touch us."

Jeremiah took one of his tiny pocketknives from his waistcoat. "Use this one."

Sunni held out her palm. Blaise cleaned Jeremiah's blade on his breeches and gently cradled her hand.

"You want to do it instead?" he asked.

"No, you." She closed her eyes and felt the pressure of the knife's edge sweeping over her skin.

Blaise collected Sunni's welled-up blood and wiped it onto the shard's tip, mingling it with the elixir. After quickly swabbing the knife clean on his jacket, he handed it to her. "Go for it."

If it were not for the rising heat and sparks coming ever nearer, Sunni might have hesitated. She had had to use a blade in Arcadia, and it still filled her with revulsion. Before the idea of cutting her friend could get too terrible, she pressed the metal through the fleshy bit at the base of Blaise's thumb. He winced and the blood sprang up.

Sunni drew the knife over his wound as lightly as she could and added Blaise's blood to the shard's mix, whispering, "Sorry."

Their blood was now mingled not only with Peregrin's red elixir, but with Soranzo's and Livia's blood. She had no time to dwell on how revolting this was.

"Let's go," said Blaise, wiping his cut on his breeches.

Jeremiah pulled them both up to standing and pointed at his painted door. "Draw, boy, draw!"

"Draw what?" Blaise pleaded. "A nine? We're not named Soranzo, like they are."

"You said you are a seven," said Jeremiah. "And you, Sunniva?"

"I don't know . . ." she replied faintly.

"Try the seven, boy!" Jeremiah exclaimed. "Maybe you can go through together!"

Blaise's hand juddered as he drew over the scratches Soranzo had made, and a shaky number seven emerged, glistening crimson. The handle and wooden panels took shape. He pressed on the door and it gave. "Come on—now, Sunni! Grab my hand!"

She looked back into the blazing workshop.

"Go, Mr. Starling!" she shouted. "You can't die in this fire! You're supposed to live and build a new house full of your murals here."

"Sunni!" Blaise said sharply. "We can't tell him any-thing!"

"But we've got to tell him *this*!" Sunni shrieked. "Mr. Starling, you've got to paint another door in your new house. If you don't, we won't be able to get back through it now—because it won't be there!"

"What?" Jeremiah reeled backward, holding his head. "Paint another infernal door. . . . I do not understand. . . ."

"Please just do it. Don't worry, Soranzo will never be able to come through painted doors again. Not without the elixir!" She pointed at a cloth-covered package. "That's the musketeer painting. Toby missed it. You must take it and get out of here!"

The sweat from Jeremiah's forehead mixed with tears rolling down his cheeks. "It is all I have left—and it is not even mine."

Blaise thrust his hand in his pocket and pulled out their pouch of coins. "Take this. It's hardly anything, but take it."

Jeremiah bowed and took one anguished look around him as he snatched up the painting and ran from his burning workshop.

Sunni grabbed Blaise's hand and left the painted door slightly open, and the fire's radiance lit their brief journey across time. But there was something odd about the way back into Starling House. A crack of light silhouetted the door.

It's the middle of the night, Sunni thought. *No one should be there.*

Blaise pushed the door open, and they stepped in. This was not Starling House, but an unfamiliar room lined with bookshelves; there was a large oak table in the middle, piled with books, papers, and old instruments. A single candle burned on the table, and the place was utterly silent. Sunni looked at the door they had just come through and noticed two carved faces in the frame overhead.

"This isn't right," she whispered, holding Blaise back from going any farther. Every hair on the back of her neck was standing up straight.

"I'm just—" Blaise suddenly whirled around and pushed her back through the door, yanking it shut. "Soranzo! Go back, Sunni!"

She fell backward into Jeremiah's fiery workshop and Blaise toppled onto her, dropping the shard on the floor. The door slammed behind them.

"What do we do now? If we end up behind the wrong door, we're doomed." Blaise scrambled to his feet and banged his fist against the door, returned again to its painted state. "How can we control what time we end up in?"

"I don't know!" The crimson shard lay close to Sunni. She picked it up and handed it up to him. "Try again! We can't stay here!"

Choking, she got to her feet and pressed one hand against the door as Blaise traced the number seven again. There was so little elixir, all he could do was drag and scrape the shard's tip against the wall, hoping it would work.

A huge section of flaming ceiling beams crashed to the workshop floor, and they both shrank against the door. Suddenly it gave way and they stumbled into cool blackness. Sunni shoved the door closed with her foot, and the pair lay there for a moment, neither in one time nor the other.

Blaise crawled forward and felt for the door they sought. He pushed through to a room that was almost pitch-black, but not quite. The windows glowed with the radiance of streetlights and London's all-night illuminated skies.

"This is the right place . . . I think. Hang on." He bumbled around tables in the dark and ran his hand along the far wall until he found a switch. A cluster of electric candles burst into life in the chandelier above. The Cabinet of Curiosities was intact, exactly the same as when they had left it, with Jeremiah's murals of animal specimens and cases of insects.

They ran to the windows. More electric lights brightened the doorways in Phoenix Square, and a lone pedestrian walked below them, staring at the illuminated face of his phone.

Overwhelmed with joy, Sunni and Blaise turned and buried their heads in each other's shoulders. After a few moments, they went back to the painted door, which was as flat and inert as when they had first seen it. Their oversize felt slippers were on the floor nearby.

Sunni touched the door, half expecting it to feel hot from the inferno they had just left. But it was wonderfully cool.

"Where were we?" she asked. "That place where Soranzo was?"

"I don't know. It looked older than Jeremiah's." Blaise shuddered. "He was just standing there, staring at me."

"Was it 1583?"

"I couldn't tell you! Listen, wherever they are, they can't travel anywhere else because the elixir is gone." He uncurled his hand from around the crimson-stained shard. "And we've got this."

"Unless Soranzo goes to Blackhope Tower in 1583 and gets into Arcadia."

"We were just there a few months ago, Sunni. Did anyone even mention seeing him? They were all worried about him and his spies, but I don't remember hearing about anyone who looked like him."

"I don't know," said Sunni slowly.

"Or maybe he did get in and has already come out as a skeleton? Yeah, he could be one of the skeletons they described in that Blackhope Enigma leaflet I have at home."

"I hope you're right." She swallowed hard. "Jeremiah got out of the fire and lived to build this house. But he's long dead now, and so are Amelia and Henry. They're all dead."

They were silent for a few moments. Blaise had a funny look on his face, the kind he hadn't directed at her since before he met Livia. He reached out for her hand.

"Ouch!" Sunni pulled her cut hand away.

He sighed. "Sorry."

"We've got to call your dad!" she said, embarrassed.

"Yeah, let's get out of here." Blaise dug around in his bag and found his watch. "One a.m. People will think we're coming back from a costume party."

"We are." Sunni wished he'd take her hand again. Why did she always blow it?

Blaise adjusted his satchel on his shoulder and pulled open the door to the landing. "Come on."

Sunni extinguished the light in the Cabinet of Curiosities and flicked the stairwell light on before they scurried downstairs. On each landing, they had to turn one light off and turn on another. Anyone watching from outdoors would have wondered what poltergeist was busy in Starling House.

When they reached the main entrance hall, Sunni glanced up at the painted blue sky and clouds above the English country landscape. The electric lights were harsh and showed the paint strokes, but it didn't matter to her as long as the murals were all there, unchanged by their trip to Jeremiah's time.

As she neared the front door, she crouched down and pressed one finger to the painted ladybug. Blaise knelt beside her.

"Do you think Jeremiah was happy in the end?" she asked. "After everything he went through?"

"I don't know. But I don't think an unhappy guy would paint ladybugs in his hallway."

Sunni's eyes were soft. "Maybe not."

"We've got a lot of explaining to do," said Blaise. "Just like when we came out of Arcadia."

"Your dad will believe us, and so will mine. Rhona will go mad, and Dean won't want to know, but they're all going to have to accept it."

"You think it's finally all over now?"

"I don't know," Sunni answered. "It wasn't over before. Look what happened at school—and all the publicity. Then we go on vacation, thinking we can be anonymous in a big city, and this happens."

"We've always got each other," said Blaise.

"Really?"

He cocked his head at her. "Yeah, *really*. Why do you even have to ask?"

"I dunno. I've felt kind of, you know, w-weird lately," she stammered. "Like we weren't such good friends any-more. Or something."

"You're my best friend. Honest."

"But you really liked Livia. Didn't you?" It all came out in one big, breathy, embarrassing spew.

Silence.

"I did like her," he said. "At first but not for long."

Something in the way he said it made her feel the subject was closed.

"Okay," she said, smiling to herself.

"Hey. What do you look so pleased about?"

"None of your business."

"Oh, really? Even if it's about me."

"It's nothing to do with you," Sunni said with a toss of her head.

"Liar," said Blaise, taking off his hat. He slipped his arm around her back and slowly moved his face toward hers.

Just as she could feel his breath on her lips, she heard a metallic clicking noise and the front door burst open with an explosive bang. Two grim-faced London Metropolitan Police constables pushed into the hall amid the squawk of voices from their two-way radios.

"Stay where you are!" barked one of them.

"We're in," said the other into his radio, as they closed around Sunni and Blaise like huge black-and-fluorescent-clad aliens. "And we've got two trespassers. Over."

Chapter 25

By the time Sunni and Blaise stumbled out of the police station, propped up by their haggard, unshaven fathers, the sky was pink and the pigeons were already hunting for breakfast. The silent taxi ride to their hotel was a blur. Sunni could not keep her eyes open, but every time she dozed off, the memory of the two constables' stern faces woke her with a start. Their eyes had been hard as granite, as if they'd seen and heard every bad thing in the city, and they hadn't given her and Blaise any ground when they'd questioned them at the police station.

"A tour guide kidnapped you?" they had scoffed. "And took you through a door that doesn't exist? You expect us to believe that?"

Sunni had tried to tell them who Throgmorton really was.

"Time-traveler, kidnapper, conman? Right," one of the officers had said, shaking his head. "Enough of this malarkey."

Even the arrival of their fathers hadn't done much good. Mr. Doran waved around the missing person report he'd made, but the police said he should have taken more responsibility for her and Blaise. He'd looked terribly stunned for a few minutes, and it had fallen to her dad to stand up for them all. In the end, the police remained unconvinced by anything she and Blaise had said, but they had finally been let go. Mr. Forrest and Mr. Doran had to give in their contact details and agree to bring the pair back to London if their presence was required for further inquiries.

Sunni lay in her bed all day, curtains closed against the sun, drifting in and out of sleep. Now Blaise's face kept appearing in her head, closer and closer, then reeling backward as the police barged in. She caught her breath every time. *Will he ever try to kiss me again?*

When her dad knocked on the door at four o'clock, she croaked, "Come in."

"Time to get up, sweetheart. We managed to get two cabins on the sleeper train for tonight," said Mr. Forrest. "You'd better get those packed up, if you're taking them." He nodded at Sunni's battered eighteenth-century dress, hat, and shoes lying on the floor.

"I'm taking them." Sunni's face was half-hidden under the quilt. "You believe my story, don't you, Dad?"

"Of course I do." He sat in a chair and rubbed a hand over his tired face. "I believed you last winter, and I believe you now."

"We didn't go looking for trouble," said Sunni. "And it's not Mr. Doran's fault, either."

"I know that," said Mr. Forrest. "He and I talked. I don't blame him — or you. But we'll be keeping an extra-sharp eye on you for a while, Sunni. Until we're sure the dramas around Blackhope Tower and Fausto Corvo are over, once and for all."

"If they ever will be," Sunni mumbled into her pillow.

"What, sweetheart?"

"Nothing. Sorry you had to come down here to look for me." She poked her head up. "What are we doing after we're packed?"

"We'll need to get a decent dinner," said Mr. Forrest. "It's a long train ride back home."

"I'm starving. Where are we going?"

"Don't know yet."

"Can I choose?" She sat up, fully energized now.

"If Blaise and his dad agree . . ."

"Okay! Give me half an hour to take a shower and pack my stuff," said Sunni, patting down her unruly hair.

"Deal." Mr. Forrest winked and left the room.

With one leap, Sunni was out of bed and rummaging about for her London map. She laid it out flat on the bed and ran her finger over its central streets and squares.

"Where would you be?" she murmured. "You must be somewhere still."

An hour later, Sunni was leading Blaise and their dads along High Holborn. It was warm enough for a summer dress and sandals, and she was reveling in having air on her arms and legs again.

"Don't we want to turn here for Covent Garden, Sunni?" asked Mr. Doran.

"No, it's up this way," she answered.

"Where is this place then? Near the British Museum?"

Sunni stopped at a junction and looked around for street signs. "Not quite. It's kind of . . . hidden away."

"As long as the food is good and we're almost there, it's fine with me," said Sunni's dad.

Blaise nudged her shoulder with his as they crossed the road. "We should have turned off at the last block."

"Huh?"

"If we're going where I think we're going." His eyes twinkled.

"Really. Then why don't you take over, Marco Polo?"

"Okey-doke." He turned in the opposite direction and said, "This way, dads."

"Lead on, buddy," said Mr. Doran. "Just don't take us someplace where you vanish again."

"No worries, Dad."

They left the main road and wound through smaller, quieter streets. Blaise stopped a few times to look around, and made them backtrack once, but eventually he stopped at the entrance to a narrow lane.

"This isn't it," said Sunni. These weren't the houses they had passed with the nightsneaks, all crooked and neglected. This lane was lined with a tidy, scrubbed row of houses. She pointed at the street sign on the wall: GREENGAGE LANE.

Blaise shook his head, grinning. "Look higher up."

An old, very faded plaque read BANDY LANE.

"What's the story?" asked his father. "I don't see any restaurants here."

"Down at the end," said Blaise, setting off toward a

building decorated with hanging baskets full of brightly colored flowers.

Sunni hastened after him, her heart jumping as she noticed a small wooden sign above the door. It looked freshly painted, but the design hadn't altered in over 250 years. The green dragon still reared up on its hind legs.

Apart from clean windowpanes and the profusion of flowers sprouting from boxes and baskets, nothing else about the front of the Green Dragon had changed. Blaise opened the door and breathed in.

"No smoke and some new furniture," he said to Sunni. "But the rest is the same."

The Green Dragon's fireplace was cold and there were no raucous pickpockets slurping ale, but it didn't matter because Sunni could still hear, see, and smell all of that in her head. She went straight to their "usual table" at the back, where they had eaten with Fleet and Sleek.

"These are the same benches we sat on—I'm sure they are," she whispered to Blaise as he slid in next to her.

"Have you been here before, kids?" Mr. Doran had to bend down under the low ceiling beams.

"Yeah," said Blaise. "While we were . . . away."

Mr. Doran got a funny look on his face. "Why did you come here? This must have been a pretty rough and ready joint in those days."

"It was," said Blaise. "These two guys brought us here for safety. We learned how to get around from them."

A waitress brought menus laminated in plastic. There was no pea soup, but there was roast chicken, which Sunni and Blaise ordered eagerly.

"What happened to them?" asked Mr. Forrest. "Do you know?"

"No." Blaise stared at the table. "They're dead now."

"Only in *our* time." Sunni moved close to him and made an empty space next to her on the bench. "In *their* time, they're probably sitting at this table right now."

"Sunni, they were on the run," said Blaise. "They couldn't come back here."

The two fathers raised their eyebrows.

"They were thieves, but they helped us." She patted the empty bench. "Maybe they sneaked back here for one more meal. Or maybe they came back after everyone gave up hunting for them."

"That would be cool," said Blaise.

"What were their names, these two guys who helped you?" asked Blaise's dad.

"Fleet and Sleek. And we wouldn't be here if it weren't for them."

Mr. Doran took a long breath in. "Let's drink a toast to them." He called over the waitress and ordered drinks for everyone. "Oh, and two half pints of ale, too, please."

When the drinks came, Mr. Doran pushed the mugs of ale to the end of the table, where Sunni had made space. "Here's to you, Fleet and Sleek. Didn't know you and never will, but you helped save our kids, and, for that, we thank you."

They all clinked glasses and laughed. The two mugs sat untouched all evening.

Later, as they got up to leave, the waitress asked, "Didn't

you want those ales, sir? Was there something wrong with them?"

"No," said Mr. Doran. "They're for absent friends."

"Or for the ghosts of the Green Dragon?" said the waitress. "We do have some, you know."

"I bet we know a couple of them," said Sunni.

"Like the lady who sold me this." Blaise tapped the side of his leather satchel as he followed the others out. "And let us sleep up in the Nook."

"The Nook?" The waitress's mouth hung open. "How do you know about that?"

Blaise grinned and raised one finger up to the brim of his imaginary three-cornered hat.

GREEN DRAGON

Epilogue

"D on't throw that away, Dad." Sunni folded her father's crumpled newspaper into a neat rectangle and stuffed it into the outside pocket of her backpack. "Thanks. I want to find out what I've missed."

"Not much, compared to what you've been through." Mr. Forrest stretched out on the upper bunk bed.

Sunni wedged her bag against the wall of the bunk and curled up under the covers. The top of the newspaper was sticking out, and she was half tempted to read it now, but her eyes were swimming. As she drifted off, her eyelids fluttered open once more, and two words stood out: *National Gallery.*

It's probably nothing, she thought. *Then again, what if it's not?* She went back and forth like this for a few minutes before snatching the paper out of her pack and reading the article.

September 3
Real or Fake?
The National Gallery to investigate claims
    A prominent art expert claims that one of the National Gallery's most popular paintings, *The Angel* (commonly known as "The Flemish Angel") by

Marius van Hoost, is a forgery. The expert, Bertrand Rose, says he has evidence that the painting was not made in 1625 but in 1752.

The Whiting family, who gave *The Angel* to the National Gallery in 1996, deny his claim, stating that the painting was in their ownership from 1668 until it was donated. They admit that *The Angel* did disappear briefly when it was stolen from the Whiting home in 1752, but claim that it was returned there a few days later, albeit under unusual circumstances. An urchin boy allegedly handed it in, telling the housemaid he had rescued it from a fire.

Mr. Rose believes the boy gave the Whitings a forgery of *The Angel,* though the family disputes this.

"This is not the only case of a boy supposedly returning a stolen painting in September 1752," he said. "It was reported that boys returned a number of other artworks that month. How many of them are also forgeries?"

Other experts have laughed off Mr. Rose's theory. "Bertrand enjoys setting the cat among the pigeons," said one art historian, who asked not to be named. "Next he'll be claiming these mysterious boys made the forgeries themselves in some dingy attic hideaway."

Mr. Rose thinks he will have the last word on the subject. "Examine the angel's wings yourself. If you look carefully, you'll find 'William 1752' painted into the feathers. There's your forger's name."

Sunni stopped reading and let out a low cry.

"Sweetheart, what's up?" Mr. Forrest's voice came from the bunk above.

"Nothing, just something I read in the paper." She threw a hoodie over her pajamas and slipped her sandals on. "I've got to tell Blaise something."

Before her dad could object, she was out in the corridor, tapping on the Dorans' cabin door and murmuring Blaise's name until he stuck his head out.

"Read this." She thrust the newspaper into his hand. "It's about Will."

Blaise frowned. "What? You mean Will from the Academy?"

"Yes. Some art expert says the Flemish angel in the National Gallery is a forgery. That means Toby saved the wrong painting from the fire."

"But Will didn't get to finish his copy of it," Blaise said.

"Well, he hid his name and the year 1752 in the angel's wings."

"Will signed the copy before it was done?" he asked, unconvinced.

"Guess so." Sunni blinked. "Yeah, why not?"

"It just seems weird. Unless . . ." Blaise said slowly, "Jeremiah put Will's name there. To make sure a trace of him was left behind."

Sunni stared out the window into the black countryside, her eyes stinging. The carriage swayed, and Blaise steadied her.

"He'll stay with me," Sunni whispered. "Just like the others."

"Me, too."

"Why us, Blaise?" she asked. "Why did we get pulled into all this?"

"Well." He screwed his face up. "I seem to remember something about a weird bearded guy. And a map on a—"

"Paper napkin!" She poked him gently in the ribs. "That's right, this is all your fault."

"Okay, maybe it is. But at least there weren't any sheep-like tourists where we went."

Sunni smiled. "Or any china shepherdesses. Or Roman mosaics."

"Exactly," Blaise said. "If it wasn't for me, we'd just have spent the day lounging in some park instead."

"Oh, so you did me a favor then?"

Instead of responding, Blaise wrapped his arms around her.

"I think I did us both a favor!" he said.

"You know," Sunni answered, hugging him back, "I think I might just agree with you."

ACKNOWLEDGMENTS

Writing *The Crimson Shard* was an enjoyable and challenging creative journey. I had great help from friends and colleagues along the way. Painter, art conservator, and restorer Brian McLaughlin, who advised me on Renaissance painting techniques for *The Blackhope Enigma,* also helped in my research on *trompe l'oeil* and the history of paint pigments. Jo Logan recommended valuable resources on the history of art forgery. My thanks to them and to everyone else who shared their knowledge with me.

My editors, Anne Finnis and Emily Hawkins, were, as ever, a joy to work with. I am grateful to them and to everyone at Templar Publishing, as well as editor Kate Fletcher and the team at Candlewick Press, who published the U.S. edition. I also count myself extremely lucky to have Kathryn Ross as my agent. Her sound judgment and encouragement are deeply appreciated.

I am most thankful for the support of my family and friends, especially my husband, Pablo, who has cheerfully accompanied me on this writing journey. I treasure their enthusiasm and their contribution to my work.

Whatever you face in the chamber,
you must never let the flame go out . . .

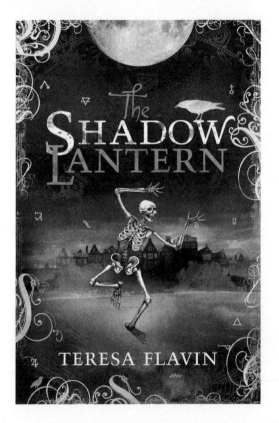

Sunni and Blaise face their most dangerous
challenge yet in their third and final adventure.

Available in hardcover and as an e-book